Mother from Lott

THE

WOOD-CARVER OF 'LYMPUS

" O Lord, by these things men live,
and in all these things is the life of my spirit :
so thou wilt recover me and make me to live."

" *The stranger, looking back, saw the child still standing motionless beneath the butternut tree.*"

THE WOOD-CARVER OF 'LYMPUS

BY

M. E. WALLER

Author of "A Daughter of the Rich,"
"The Little Citizen," etc.

*With a Frontispiece from a Drawing
by C. C. Emerson*

BOSTON
LITTLE, BROWN, AND COMPANY
1908

The University Press, Cambridge, Mass., U. S. A.

CONTENTS

I

THE OLD CHURCH SETTLEMENT

The
Wood-carver of 'Lympus

I

THE OLD CHURCH SETTLEMENT

THE yellow glory of the stage-coach still illumines some of the valley roads in rural New England, and still by means of it, if one bestir himself betimes, he may overtake that Past which is fleeing from us with accelerated speed.

This is specially true of the larger river valleys of our North Country. Here the four-horse coach still swings cumbersomely on its antiquated leathers and, rolling and pitching like a lumberman's lugger in the La Chine rapids, lunges along the post-roads of Northern and Central Vermont.

At regular intervals the horses stop to water at some roadside trough of hollowed log, or stone, or iron in the shape of a huge sap-kettle. At noon there is always the hour's halt at some wayside tavern — two thirds horse-sheds and one third dilapidated dwelling, of which the greater part on the ground floor is given over to the barn-like office, the colorless monotony of its sanded floor relieved here and there by the accidence of reds and browns in wooden chairs and earthen spittoons, in a pot or two of hardy blossoming geranium, and the leaping flame in the depths of a cavernous fireplace.

Here and there during the thirty miles of posting the stage stops at a farmhouse, and mystifying packages are left at the gate or door. Here and there in a woods'-road or on a hilltop the driver draws rein and winds a blast on his tin horn that wakens a sevenfold echo among the green heights, and summons the dwellers on the "back farms" to the rough box nailed to guide-post, cross-roads' tree, or fence that still serves for the rural post.

On an afternoon in mid-September, in the year of our Lord eighteen hundred and ninety—, the stage from Alderbury was slowly climbing from terrace to terrace of the overlapping foot-hills of the Green Mountains, with now and then a galloping spurt on the short levels. The Hornet, yellow-bodied, banded with black, was empty save for a heterogeneous collection of bags, boxes, and packages piled higgledy-piggledy on the floor and seats. Several plethoric sacks of burlap leaned their top-heavy weight against the old-fashioned back-strap of the middle seat, and lurched and lunged with the chop-sea motion of the lumbering vehicle, but always righted themselves at the critical moment of unstable equilibrium.

It was so late in the season, and the passengers so rare, that the outside seats — that vantage ground for travellers — had been removed and the space filled with freight, among which were two crates of Rhode Island Red pullets, a woven-wire cot of peculiar construction, and a newly weaned pig in a grocery box.

There was but one passenger, who sat on the seat by the driver.

They had been several hours on the road, following the White Branch of the Connecticut upwards to its source in the still uninvaded forest belt. The hill-slopes behind the valley farms, through which they passed, were gay with hundreds of hop-pickers in their red and white head-kerchiefs, their plaid shoulder-shawls or blue-jean blouses. To the traveller, looking upward to the slopes from the road, the poles with their largess of rioting vine and delicate green blossoms seemed to lean from out the clear, sun-filled sky of deep blue. Shout, and laughter, and waving of kerchiefs and sunbonnets greeted the passing of the Hornet.

Farther on, the entire population of the small factory village of Scawsville swarmed at the noon hour before the one store in the place — " department " on a small scale, and post-office and barber's shop to boot — to await the arrival of the Alderbury stage.

Five miles beyond, on the slope that rises behind the Bend, — that sharp turn of the mighty White Branch at right angles to the north, where it rushes downwards through the straight five miles of mountain gorge, — lay the deserted hamlet of the Old Church Settlement: a half dozen of dilapidated houses clustered about the abandoned House of God and its well-filled graveyard. The white walls and white headstones dominated the valley below, east and west, for miles.

At sight of it the driver, whose loquacity was spasmodic, grew reminiscent. He shifted the quid of tobacco from his right cheek to his left and, turning to the passenger, pointed with his whipstock upwards to the church.

"Ther ain't ben er weddin' thar sence I was knee high t' er grasshopper, 'n' the las' bur'al but one wuz er double one." He slowly gathered up the slack of the reins to give the man a chance to put a question. He had not miscalculated.

"When was that?" said the stranger, but indifferently.

"Twenty-two year ago come Chris'mus — two on 'em ter onct! Beat all how Si Prindle's fam'ly petered out! Jest ez nice er set er boys 'n' gals ez er man could raise, 'n' all on 'em, 'cept one, layin' five foot under ground. Ain't but two young uns left, 'n' they're kinder collat'rals; one's er grandson, 'n' t' other's his youngest gal's niece-in-law, or, I guess, out-er-the-law."

Again he jerked his whipstock, but backwards to the slope below them, for the horses were pulling up a steep rise to an upper mountain terrace.

"Jule was Si's oldest gal, smarter'n er steel trap, 'n' harnsome too. She married er feller over 'n York state — city chap I heerd, 'n' lived in Troy; wuz studyin' ter be er minister, 'n' went inter er decline arter they'd ben married nigh onter two year. Jule hed ter do the supportin' — likely 'nough she wuz willin'; fer I heerd 'em tell down ter Scawsville, thet she said she warn't goin' ter marry nobody but er perfessional ef she hed ter work fer her livin' ter do it." He paused for another question, but it was not forthcoming.

" Guess likely she done it fast 'nough; 'coz 't warn't more 'n two months arter he died thet they brought 'em both up here ter bury, him 'n' her. He 'd ben in er tomb t'll then. We hain't got no receivin' tomb up here," he added as an afterthought. Then suddenly seizing the post-horn from its leathern socket, he sent forth so powerful a note that the green heights rang with prolonged echoes, and the leader on the off side showed his heels above the traces and pulled bravely up on the bits.

" This is the fourth time since we left Scawsville that this instrument of yours has rivalled the Last Trump in sound, and yet I have n't seen a living soul nor a living thing but that old crow on the fence that those swallows are tormenting. Where is everybody?" said the stranger.

The man chuckled. "Thet's my special fer Somebody — ye 'll see in er minute." He handed the reins to the stranger. — " Jest hold onter them ribbons, will yer? It 'll take me quite er spell ter git the truck off; 't ain't more 'n twice er year ther 's anything ter be hauled up the Pent Road; but she 's allus on han' — Look er thar! What 'd I tell ye?"

The stage had drawn up beneath a butternut tree that stood in the angle formed by the highway and the Pent Road that trailed its grass-grown, rocky length over the undulating pasture slopes, through acres of sweet fern and ground-hemlock, around dense growths of spruce-bush, but up, ever up, to the dark forest belt on the mountain top, where it was lost to sight in a narrow clearing. Between the turnpike and these woodlands the Pent Road, where it intersected fences or stone walls, was crossed by four sets of bars.

As the passenger's eyes followed the direction indicated by the driver's whipstock, he was aware of a little figure that lightly leaped the bars nearest the road, and came racing down the long, steep slope to the butternut tree with the unshod security of a fawn.

" Jest in time, Twiddie," said the driver, as the child, stemming herself against her own impetus and extending both hands to break the force of the impact, brought up rather suddenly against the tree. " Here 's the truck ye 've been lookin' fer more 'n er month — who 's comin' down fer it? "

" Uncle Shim ; — be them all ourn? "

She passed her lean, freckled hands rapidly along the invalid's adjustable cot the driver of the Hornet had just placed against the tree, and of which the stranger took note for the first time ; she tugged impotently at the piece of sheep-twine that tied the mouth of one of the bulging bags deposited near it ; then suddenly hoppety-skipping to the opposite side of the trunk she sprang with outstretched arms at the sturdy bole, and, clasping it close, with the agility of a monkey shinned up to a limb that, at the reach of a man's arm, projected at a right angle to it.

Thereon she balanced herself, swinging her bare, brown sticks of legs, and laughing gleefully in a clear, high voice at finding herself so nearly on a level with the astonished passenger on the box.   He responded to her mirth with an encouraging smile and by lifting his hat.

" ' N' thet ain't all," said the stage-driver, as he climbed to the top of the yellow-bodied Hornet, — " ye fergot ter look inter yer post-office — "

Hardly had he spoken the words before the child hung by her hands from the limb and dropped to the ground. The swift grace of the movement would have claimed the stranger's admiration, even if his attention had not been arrested by the sudden transfiguration of the peaked, yet healthily tinted face that, seen from above, looked like a vast freckle beneath a thatch of dark red hair, faded and sunburned.

Thrusting her arm into the opening of a narrow squirrel-hole in the trunk just above her head, she drew forth one yellow envelope.

" 'Tain't fer us?" she exclaimed in an awed, questioning voice, half-breathless in her sudden excitement.

" Don't ye b'lieve it, Twiddie; ef 't ain't fer your folks 't ain't fer nobody on 'Lympus." He took the reins from the stranger, and swung the whiplash at arm's length with such professional skill that the one sharp crack sounded like the report of a pistol and, at the same moment, the leader on the off side felt the stinging clip of the cracker on the tip of his right ear. The horses strained to the steep hill before them, and the stranger, looking back, saw the child still standing motionless beneath the butternut tree, gazing, as if fascinated, at the envelope in her hand.

" Where does she live?" he queried, as the horses rested on the first water-bar, whence, looking back

again, he could see that she had not stirred from
the spot.

"Couple er miles back on the Mountin'."

"What did you call the place?"

"'Lympus — O-lympus, I s'pose city folks 'd say.
Thet's what 't is on the county map, but thet's only
the Mountin'; they're good five mile from 'Lympus-
Gilead, thet's the nearest settlement, 'cept the one
jest erhead. See? 't ain't much of er settlement —
no stores, no mill, no nothin' but er pass'l er log-
skinners 'n' Canucks, 'n' er dozen er more houses."

"Who is she?"

"Twiddie? — She's one er them collat'rals I told
ye 'bout. Si's youngest gal married er poor shote
of er feller, Shim Lewis. They hain't no children,
but Shim's sister died four years arter thet little gal
wuz born — out er wedlock, too, — 'n' Shim took her
hum. Folks say he sets er sight by her, 'n' so does
Lize."

"Is any one of the family an invalid? I noticed
that cot was an adjustable one, such as they use in
hospitals —"

"Ye did, did ye? Wal, ye know er thing er two.
Ye're right — thet's fer Hugh, t' other collat'ral I
told ye 'bout. Thet's Jule's son. Si took him when
he warn't but er year old, 'n' willed him ter Lize.
I see the will — read kinder queer, but Si was sound
'nough when he drawed it up. Ye see, he willed the
old place, thet was his father's, 'n' the furniture —
what ther' wuz on 't — ter Hugh, thet wuz his oldest
gal's; 'n' then he willed Hugh ter Lize; 'n' ter Shim
he willed Lize 'n' all the live-stock.

"Ye see, Shim was his hired man — sort of er scape-goat fer all the old man's crotchety doin's — 'n' he'd ben courtin' Lize fer nigh onter fifteen year. Si wuz so dead set agin it, 'count er Shim's shif'less-ness, that Shim dassen't pop, 'n' Lize dassen't en-courage him er mite; 'n' so 't went on t'll jest 'fore the old man died, then I guess he kinder wanted ter make his peace all roun', so he gin 'em his blessin', 'n' told 'em not ter lay it up agin him, 'coz he'd fixed it all right in the will.

"Lize wuz some disapp'inted 'coz the place warn't hers; *but*, she thinks 'bout ez much er Hugh ez ef he wuz her own, so I guess she don't lay awake nights over it — 'n' it'll be hers, anyway, 'fore long."

"How's that?"

"Hugh hed bad luck. He come hum er year ago las' spring ter help Shim with the cuttin', 'n' jest over thar, by thet clearin' the Pent Road leads up ter, in thet very spot, er shoe give way on the traverse 'n' er log pitched right off onter Hugh — he hain't so much ez moved er leg sence, never will; dyin' by inches, so folks say, jest like er blasted tree — only t' other end to.

"Gosh! — I feel bad fer the feller; he wuz er smart un, jest like his mother. He'd worked out his free-dom with Shim 'n' Lize, 'n' laid by er leetle suthin' ter start in ter the 'Cademy down ter Alderbury, — wuz tryin' ter be er preacher like his father, — 'n' hed ben thar er full year 'n' some on ter the next. He wuz ter hum arter the winter term helpin' Shim cut 'n' haul logs, 'n', all of er suddin, he wuz felled jest like er straight, thirty-year maple, full er sap, 'n' hez laid thar ter hum goin' on two year wuss 'n useless. I feel bad fer Shim, 'n' Lize too. Ther wuz er morgige on the place when Si left it big 'nough ter mildew every crop they 've raised. Hugh 'n' Lize hed worked off some on 't, but sence Hugh wuz laid up, they 've hed er tough time on 't, no mistake — "

The flow of his discursive reminiscence had, thus far, suffered no check from the stranger's unresponsiveness, but a sudden flank movement of the leader on the off side served to deflect the current of his speech into other channels and more forcible expression. While he was busy with the horses — putting on the check-rein, testing the traces, adjusting the drag — the passenger rose, stretched his legs, and looked about him.

They had halted on the height of land that forms the watershed between the White Branch and the eastern tributaries of the Otter Creek. The warm, golden peace of a mid-September afternoon lay upon the softly swelling sea of rounded, overlapping hills and mountains wooded to their summits. Here and there mere shining ribbons of water glinted in the valleys far below. The forest belts, from which they had just emerged, lay on the mountain's flank like the tarnished bosses of a huge shield, the yellow of birch, the brown of beech, subdued and enhanced by the massed shadows of hemlock, spruce, and fir. Here and there a weather-blackened farmhouse with adjoining barns and sheds found shelter from the north at the edge of the heavy timber line, and viewed from that height closely resembled, both in appearance and size, the swallows' mud-nests beneath overhanging eaves.

The stranger breathed long and deep. The sun-filled air at that height, two thousand feet above the sea, was life-giving. As he took his seat again by the driver, who had made all fast for the rapid descent before them, he said, pointing to a scattering dozen of houses just below on the next level:

"I take it that is Farnsfield. Is there an inn there?"

"Sech ez 't iz; — wuz ye cal'latin' ter put up thar?"

"I thought I'd stay over a day here — I like this region — and return with you on your next trip to Alderbury, that's — ?"

"Thet's ter-morrer," interrupted the other; "I'll be 'long 'bout noon. Guess ye can't stan' it longer 'n thet; — fodder's dirt cheap, but 't ain't A 1 — Whoa-ah!"

With a deft turn of his wrist and a crack of his whip, he drew rein before the open door of an old, red, two-story-and-a-half inn which, as it stretched its ramshackle length along the dusty highway, presented a full front view of its fallen estate in the gradual deterioration of its architectural members — ell, wood-shed, horse-sheds, barn, pig-sty, cow-house, hennery, cart-shed, and outhouse.

As the stranger swung himself down from the top of the stage, a hen, roosting on the threshold of the main entrance, flew, squawking, into the passage. The driver chuckled.

"Thet's more 'n most folks git fer er welcome in this God-fersaken hole; — guess ye'll git all ye want er the *region* 'fore twelve ter-morrer noon. Lay ye ten ter one, I 'll meet ye on the road 'stid er here ! " He shook his head dubiously, whereat the stranger smiled.

"You 're safe, for you 'll pick me up at the butter-nut tree by the Pent Road over the Mountain. I 've stayed over to make the acquaintance of Twiddie."

"Wal — I vum ! " Uncle Jo Cheatle, the driver of the Alderbury stage for a quarter of a century, slowly removed his straw hat, and drawing forth from its crown a new bandanna, wiped and polished the bald, pink dome of his skull till it shone like a billiard ball ; then he carefully folded and replaced it, put on his hat, and, gathering up the slack of the reins, gave vent to a series of sputtering wheezes which were accompanied by varied and curious contortions of his rotund body. They might have continued indefinitely, had not the leader on the off side chosen that inopportune moment to make known his equine displeasure at the preten-sions of a mammoth turkey that, appearing around the corner of the house, suddenly claimed the whole road, and displayed the full circle of his tail and the entire register of his powerful gobble.

Amid imprecations full and free, the frenetic crack-ings of the whip, the all-pervasive gobble of the terri-fied turkey, and the gymnastics of the leader on the off side, the yellow-bodied Hornet disappeared in a whirl of dust down the road, leaving the stranger laughing heartily on the doorstep.

II

THE MOUNTAIN AND THE MAN

II

THE MOUNTAIN AND THE MAN

September 10th, 189–.

TWENTY–THREE to-day, and I have lain here just one year and seven months — as useless as the log that fell upon me. Where is that log? I've wondered time and again where the thing lay, how it lay, how it looks after the year and seven months. I've wanted to ask Uncle Shim about it, but have been too cowardly.

I'd like to have it snaked down here before it turns to punk and get at it, just once, to hew and hack it into dead half-inch pieces — the damned, senseless, half-cord hulk that has taken the life of me as a man, and cheated me of my birthright.

Birthright? Birthday! What do I *know* about it? I'm thinking a man has to take a good deal on trust in that direction. How do I *know?* I don't; and this impotent ignorance gives the lie to Life in the beginning of things; — beginning? God! I'd rather the log had struck higher up and left me mad as a March hare with legs to run, and jump, and leap, and get away from it all, than to chain me here to a bed, just as I've read they chain the convicts in the galleys, with all my thinking apparatus intact.

The brain reels at times, and a terrible rage possesses me: a mood of destruction if I could get at some living thing, or even if —

I try not to show this. I know I must not; I've still will enough left for that; for day before yesterday Twiddie happened in with a big bunch of hooded gentians for me. She came skipping in joyfully enough, but stopped short before she reached the bed, dropped the flowers, and ran from the room. I heard her sobbing out in the woodshed after that. My hearing has grown strangely acute.

I used the shepherd's crook, that Uncle Shim made for me when I was a six-year-old and ran wild in the Old Pasture with the sheep and the lambs, to hook up the bunch of gentians from the floor; she had tied them with a bit of striped grass. I have put them on the bed, and I hope the child will see them from the kitchen, as she passes the door.

I hate to see that terrified look in her eyes at sight of me! I've seen it there before — but only when that horrible mood of destruction is upon me.

This morning I caught Twiddie looking in at the crack of the bedroom door — I hope she saw the gentians in the pitcher on the table — and I called to her to fetch me a needle — a coarse one. Instead of answering me, she ran out to the barn, and I heard her call Aunt Lize, but under her breath. Then I heard Aunt Lize hurry in through the shed; in a moment more she stood by my bed with such a strained, anxious look on her face that I could but wonder.

"What d' ye want, Hughie?" she said; and I noticed her voice trembled.

"Nothing but a needle, Aunt Lize; I asked Twiddie to get me one — no harm in that, is there?" I know I spoke sharply, but I hate this eternal questioning as to why I want this or that, and I hate to have her call me "Hughie" — I'm enough of a baby in my helplessness without that reminder.

"What d' ye want on 't? Men don't take ter needles — not nat'rally; let me do it fer ye, Hughie."

Then I blazed away; I could n't help it. It maddens me so to be thwarted in such little things when I can't stir a foot to get it for myself — tied to a woman's apron-string and a child's little finger —

"I'd like to know why you won't give me what I ask for? it's little enough. You would n't give me my jackknife yesterday, and last week you stood out about the shears — what on earth ails you? Can't you see it's taking the meanest kind of an advantage of a man — a man! O my God! —"

I stopped short, for I felt the rage coming upon me, and the window space looked black against the light outside. I put out my hands to shove her away.

"Go away, Aunt Lize — go, go!" I cried. But she stemmed herself against my little strength, and, flinging her apron over her head, broke into dreadful sobs, crying out:

"Oh, Hughie, Hughie! don't ye know why? I'm 'feared — I'm 'feared — "

At the sound and the words my sight cleared; I have never known Aunt Lize to give way so, — and to see a woman cry like that! I myself have never shed a tear; the hot rage has scorched my eyeballs till whatever moisture there was dried before it fell; I have seen red and black during all these nineteen months, — and I drew her hands down from her face, and with them the apron. I lifted her bowed head on my palm — I had strength enough for that — and said:

"Aunt Lize, look at me." And therewith she raised her reddened lids and looked at me through the streaming tears — such a look! Then I knew the thing she had feared — knew *why* they had kept every harmful utensil from me, or watched me when I was using one. I knew why they had let my beard grow, and I had never seen a razor — knew why I was watched and spied upon even by the child, Twiddie. The thought I had dwelt with so long had left its imprint on my face, and they could but see and read!

It was a shock. I thought I had hidden it. It belonged to myself, what there is left of me; but I never meant *they* should see, never meant to terrify them so — a woman and a little child.

But the shock did something to me. It seemed as if some tendon gave a little somewhere about my heart, and I could take a longer breath than I had done in all these past months; and, suddenly, I spoke as I felt, and my voice sounded more like the voice of the man I used to be. I spoke slowly, looking straight into her eyes:

"You need n't fear, Aunt Lize; there 'll be nothing to make you afraid after this."

And hearing my voice, such, I suppose, as it once

was, she quivered like a popple in a south wind; her knees gave beneath her, and she fell upon them by the side of my bed, and spoke brokenly, to herself, or to me, or to —

At any rate, I laid my hand on her head, and felt better — more eased — than for a whole year and seven months past. Then Uncle Shim called from the shed:

"Lize, where be ye?"

I have never known him to be absent about his work for an hour even, but that, on entering the house again, those were his first words. Hearing them, Aunt Lize rose quickly, found the door half-blindly through her tears, and, going out, shut it to — softly.

September 16th.

This morning, after a sleep such as I have not had for months, I found a good, sharp darning-needle run through a slip of paper and again through the hem of the sheet. I seized it so quickly that it pricked me — a right smart jab; the sensation it gave me is a thing to remember. The needle and the prick have both done me good. She trusted me.

Afternoon.

About three o'clock, when Aunt Lize was out with Uncle Shim cutting fodder, and Twiddie had gone down the Pent Road to see the stage pass, I experimented with the needle.

I tried both legs — thighs and calves; ran it a half inch into each — and felt nothing. But the blood spurted — good red blood, too.   Somehow the sight of it has given me courage, for what, I can't say.

September 17th.

I wish I could see farther from my one window. I think every sense must have been benumbed during these nineteen months, for I don't remember to have been conscious of seeing anything from the window until yesterday afternoon.

But there could n't be a worse prospect for me.   I can look for five hundred feet straight up the slope of the Mountain, across the stony corn-fodder patch where Aunt Lize and Uncle Shim are at work, into the black gloom of the heavy timber, and the narrow clearing, where —

No, by God! I 'll fight it down like a man so long as there is a drop of red blood left in me ; to frighten a woman and little child so!   And to lie all through that summer and fall and winter and spring, and now a second summer, like a dead nightmare weight upon those I 'm dependent on for everything except breath —

There 's Twiddie in the clearing, running for dear life!   She has something in her hand — is waving it to attract Aunt Lize's attention, and hoo-hooing like a looney.   It 's a letter!   And now all three, loaded down with shocks of green fodder, are hurrying to the barn.

I can hear Prince backing out of the stall, and the collie has gone daft. — Has it anything to do with the letter, I wonder?   Twiddie has shunned me since that day she brought me the gentians ; I wish she would n't, but I can't blame her.

I hear the wheels of the light farm-wagon strike the two big rocks in the Pent Road just above the house; I know it is that, because the last time I used it, the king-bolt chinked just as I heard it a minute ago, and Uncle Shim said he'd put on some axle-grease. — How long ago was that? Just two years; I don't suppose he has thought of it since. That's just like Uncle Shim.

September 18th, 5 A.M.

I am glad it is light enough to see to write, or rather to talk with myself. I have n't slept well, and the nights are growing longer.

I could n't sleep for thinking of the change that is coming into my life to-day. Yesterday, after dark, Uncle Shim came home with the light farm-wagon, bringing a cot-bed : an adjustable one, made for such as I; and, in time, I may be strong enough to raise myself to a sitting position — and lower myself, when tired — by means of the ingeniously rigged pulleys and ratchets.

The small possibilities of, at least, the fag end of a life like mine filled all my thoughts; — well, perhaps that's better than —

I'm *bound* to live, as a matter of gratitude to Aunt Lize and Uncle Shim for this. They've scrimped along on next to nothing to procure it for me — have been planning and saving and scraping a year for this one thing. It was intended for my birthday. What have n't they gone without to pay for it!

I tried to thank them — but it was too much for me; the tears came — at last — with no hot rage, no

scorching eyeballs to dry them before they fell. I
cried like a child, and Aunt Lize comforted me like a
child. I fell asleep, exhausted, and, as it was early —
just after supper — I was awake again at eleven, and
have had but one hour's sleep since.

What a day that was! Uncle Shim came in after
breakfast and got me on to the new cot; that is, one
end of me. Aunt Lize managed the other, for my
six foot one of hulk has to be moved on the instal-
ment plan.

Then they adjusted the pulleys and raised me to a
half-sitting position. Oh, the relief of body and mind!
A man's position on this earth, I take it, is intended
to be upright; only horizontal in the final sleep, and,
transiently, when imitating it once in twenty-four
hours.

Later on I asked for a looking-glass. Aunt Lize
brought me a cracked three-cornered piece I remember she kept on the shelf over the kitchen dry-sink.
I should not have known myself.

I remember that, during that last week at the
Academy, I shaved off my mustache because I over-
heard one of the Scawsville girls, Linnie Lane, laughing at it. I was the oldest in the class, and the girls
made me feel it. What a pretty minx she was! She
wrote me a note congratulating me and begging for
one hair! I vowed then I'd make her smart for it.
I came home with the smooth face of a boy, but that
which looked back at me from the three-cornered
piece of fly-specked glass was a man's face, full-
bearded, sunken-eyed, the cheeks furrowed, and a

stripe of white hair, silver white, running from the left temple to an inch behind the ear.

I called to Uncle Shim in the kitchen:

"Let's make a clearing, Uncle Shim; hone your razor and strap it well, and, Aunt Lize, give me your sharpest shears till I do some tall cutting into this underbrush."

And when I was lathered, and razed, and shaved, and clipped, and washed, and dressed in a clean blue flannel shirt, and I felt as if I had, at last, an inch or two more of backbone in me, I heard the sheep-dog — not old Tag, Uncle Shim tells me, but her pup — bark in the woods, and in a minute Twiddie rushed in, half breathless, as she always is when excited.

"Come quick, Aunt Lize! Ther's er strange man comin' out er the clearin' down the Pent Road! He's the one I told ye 'bout — wuz on the stage, 'n' smiled 'n' bowed ter me when I was sittin' in the butt'nut yesterday, 'n' when the stage drove off, he took off his hat jes' ez he did jes' now when he see me feedin' the hens out back. Come, come!" She tugged at Aunt Lize's dress, and Aunt Lize was so flustered — for a stranger finds his way about once in two years to our place over the Mountain — that she smoothed out her apron, forgetful of the recent barbering, and all the length and fulness of my brown beard and extra long locks of hair fell to the floor; then hurried out, shears in hand, to the kitchen door, exclaiming:

"Land sakes' alive! Who on earth —" then caught up her words, for the man stood on the step.

I could not catch what he said, he spoke in so low

a voice; but I heard Aunt Lize ask him in, and say she would call her husband; I heard Twiddie set a chair for him, and then run to the water-butt in the shed and bring him a dipper of water.

By good luck I had the three-cornered piece of looking-glass in my hand, and turned it at such an angle that I could see the man without his seeing me, although he was in direct range of the beard and the hair lying just on the threshold. He must have thought there was some Samson and Delilah business going on just before his arrival, for Aunt Lize met him with the shears in hand. She was back from the barn before the stranger had finished drinking, and, knowing that I had steadily refused to see any one save the doctor for nearly two years, quickly shut my bedroom door; but not before I had taken in his appearance and sized him up.

A city man, — I knew by the cut of his clothes; I have seen such in Alderbury and on the Hornet, — an eye that saw everything in the room without apparently noticing it; dark hair, parted in the middle like the dudes I've read about, but nothing namby-pamby about *him* for all that — I'd hate to run up against him in the dark.

I was wishing I could catch his voice, and hear what he was saying, when, without warning, the bedroom door flew open, and Aunt Lize came in with more boldness of manner than I've ever noticed before in her, saying:

"Here's a gentleman wants ter see ye, Hughie; he's come for the view."

View! — How dared he! I'm afraid I said, "Damn

him," under my breath; for what was he to come before me with his health?

And I — I was a fool, and answered without looking up:

"I hope the prospect is a pleasing one, sir; " and pointed to my useless legs under the old patch-work quilt Aunt Lize had thrown over them when they got me on the cot.

Then, for decency's sake (for I know what is due to a stranger beneath my roof), and for very shame at the manner of my greeting, I put out my hand, and felt the firm, warm clasp of the man's — the palm tingling with health.   It held mine close ; I looked up, and the eyes that met mine compelled me to keep on looking, — and so I continued to stare like a fool, and knew not when to withdraw my hand.   Before I knew how it happened, the stranger was sitting beside my cot, Aunt Lize had disappeared, and only Twiddie stood with her finger in her mouth at the foot of the cot, staring as I had stared — so how could I blame her?— and we were talking together like old acquaintances, and I telling him of the year and seven months at the Academy, and how I had hated the farmer's life and wanted to study for a profession — I didn't tell him what; and when he rose to go, and said "Good-by," I bethought me he had not expressed sympathy for me by so much as a word or look, and I was grateful to him — if he had, I think I must have struck him.

Uncle Shim offered to take him down to meet the stage, but the stranger — no, he is no longer that — the man said, no, with thanks, that Twiddie was going down with him ; and from the window I saw them going up the Pent Road together, the child skipping along, holding by his hand. When they reached the clearing, I heard her laugh, and the man's, hearty and ringing, answering it. She never does that with me. She is so young I suppose what I am at present means to her what I have always been. I wish she would, though.

I paid the penalty for that day with ten days on my back again.

When I began to learn the multiplication-table, I used to wonder why two times two always made four, and concluded, in my small way, that the saw-horse in the middle had something to do with it. I'm not much wiser now.

Curious! I was so taken up with the man, that I never thought to ask his name. Uncle Shim says he told him he came from below in York State, and Aunt Lize said there was that about him she dared not ask him — I can understand that; but Twiddie tells me that, as she sat up in the butternut tree, she could look onto the top of the stage into the space where my cot came from, and there was only one valise up there, a light one, with two black letters on it, P. V. During these last days, I have caught myself saying over and over again, " P. V.," and have tried all sorts of names to fit the initials.

Aunt Lize says, when she was a little girl she knew of a man who lived over the Mountain, and moved to York State years ago; his name was Peleg Ven- ables — and maybe, " P. V." is his son. Peleg Venables — I don't like the sound, and it does n't fit the man. Peleg Venables! — Oh, no; no Peleg Venables of Olympus ever fathered the cut of those trousers.

Tuesday.

Aunt Lize has been helping Uncle Shim load on the ripened corn — doing *my* work! I have been watching her. Time was, I should have pitied her, but now I envy her, so lean and scrawny, but agile and wiry —

Oh, to hoist and lift and heave, to pitch and toss! To race, and run, and corner the colts! To roll over and over down the pasture slope, till sun and sky and earth whirled around *me* as centre of the universe! — I can't help it; I 've struck twice — hard — with my shepherd's crook at the log-end of me; if I could but feel the tingle of the blood again — clod — clod — clod that I am!

Even a clod can nourish a kernel, and I 've had the germ of an idea, — at last.

There 's Aunt Lize this very minute doing the work I, and not she, was cut out to do. I know her back ached yesterday, by the way she sat down after supper while Twiddie was wiping the dishes. See her now, trying to hoist that shock! —

"Don't, don't, Aunt Lize; drop it!"

I 've hollered for all I am worth, but she can't hear me; if she but knew it, the way she lifted that would strain even a man about his middle. I feel guilty. —

My idea came out of the hole of one of Uncle Shim's stockings. I heard them talking in the kitchen

before they went to bed. Just as soon as cold
weather comes, Uncle Shim always goes about in his
stocking-feet after supper when the chores are all
done, and Aunt Lize can't break him of the habit.
To-night I heard her, as I have heard her a hundred
times before.

"Shim Lewis, put on yer down-ter-the-heels."

"No, no, Lize; my feet air tired; it rests 'em."

"I tell ye, Shim Lewis, I can't grow wool 'n' spin
'n' knit it fast 'nough ter keep ye in stockin'-feet —
let erlone yer legs; ye wear 'em out so fast ker-
hewing eround regardless er black frost sech ez
we're goin' ter hev ter-night."

"Wal, wal, Lize, I'll stretch out here on the
settle 'n' save my woollen shoe-leather, ef ye say so.
I'm glad the corn's in."

"So be I; — what ye haulin' up yer right foot fer
thet way?"

"Sho, Lize! Can't a man git er cramp 'thout er
woman's axin' him how he got it?"

"No, he can't, not ef thet woman's his lawful
wife; — see here, Shim, stretch out that foot, now
do."

When Aunt Lize pleads there is no resisting her.
I heard Uncle Shim stretch out his leg; there
followed a shrill outcry:

"Oh, my soul! Shim Lewis, when'd ye change
yer stockin's last? — sech er hole! big toe 'n' middle
toe clean through. 'Cramps!' I'll hev ter knit
from now t'll sugarin'-off to keep ye clear er sech
cramps ez thet."

I heard Uncle Shim chuckle.

I've proposed to Aunt Lize to swap work: I'll knit the stockings for the family if she'll show me how. The look on her face! But we're agreed. I heard her singing afterwards, for the first time since I've lain here — an old verse of Watts's. I've heard her sing it ever since I can remember anything; but I've had to put my fingers in my ears — it irritates me; still I can hear it, for the mind hears as well as sees.

> " 'Change me, O God! my flesh shall be
> An instrument of song to thee,
> And thou the notes inspire.' "

October 5th.

I heard them say they were going to gather the apples next week. I wish I were where I could see the orchard, but it's on the other side of the house.

It's my own house, and I don't see why I can't have any room in it I choose.

I told Aunt Lize this morning, when she brought in my breakfast, that I'd like to move over into the best room. I saw by her face she was taken aback, but I wasn't quite prepared for her reply.

"Ther ain't no reason why ye can't, Hughie — only, what be we goin' ter do fer the fun'rals 'n' weddin's, ef we give up the best room? Ther's ben more 'n er dozen of each in 't already."

"I'll be the one to move out for the next funeral, Aunt Lize — don't you fret about that; and as for the weddings — "

But she interrupted me, speaking sharply, — and I know I hurt her; I suppose I meant to, —

"Don't, Hughie, oh, don't!" and flung out of the room. Afterwards I heard her moving and sweeping and re-settling, and the Sunday passed in confusion. At night they moved me in on the cot. Upon my suggestion, Uncle Shim took down the air-tight stove and the fire-board, and cleaned up the fire-place. Twiddie brought in an armful of dry pine boughs full of rosin, and in five minutes the room was light enough to knit by. Aunt Lize gave me my first lesson Saturday afternoon. I'm on plain "backwards and forwards," she tells me.

I snarl up so dreadfully — I can't get the hang of the kink of yarn around my little finger joint. Even cursing does n't help it.

I find Aunt Lize has removed the coffin-plates from the mantel-shelf — there were fifteen of them — and taken down the family hair-wreath. She left the Bible, but I asked her to put it away, as well as some theological books of my father's; — I don't want to see a book around; it puts me too much on the defensive.

I like this room. I don't get every smell from the kitchen as I did in the other. When Aunt Lize was washing and getting dinner, whew! — I could n't breathe, and had to ask Twiddie to open the windows wide. And yet I've known the time when the smell of a boiled onion and the crisping sizzle of the salt pork in its own fat was a thing to say my prayers for, by reason of the keen hunger gnawing at my stomach.

I don't think my friend P. V. — I like to call him so — could find many outs about the views from this room. He said I did not have much from the other; only the corn-patch and the woods and the cursed clearing to help me not to forget — that I could see Twiddie coming down the Pent Road just after stage-time, if I chose to look.

I vowed I would speak out all my thoughts in this one-sided written talk of mine; but I find it is best for a man not to look too closely at himself sometimes, nor to hear his own voice too often.

My cot is in the south-east angle of the room, between the one east window and the two southern ones. I can look both ways. This afternoon they have been harvesting the apples, young Tag and Twiddie helping. I used to be proud of our orchard; twenty of the young trees I set out thirteen years ago on the slope south of the big hemlock "bush," that comes down over the ledge from the timber line, wedge-shaped — its entering point a rod or two from the end of the house.

The slope is so steep that I can look over the orchard to the valley of the White Branch, and the great peaks of Killington and Pico a little east of south. The Pent Road runs between the house and the orchard; to the south, I can see it trailing along down the pastures to the highroad from Gilead.

To-day, looking from the window, I found myself a stranger in thought on every foot of my land in sight; — yet there is not a square rod I have not been over as a boy.

Twiddie is driving the light-weight truck up the road from the orchard; it is loaded with a dozen barrels of apples — she is driving it well, too! Even at this distance, I can see their complexions, for I am looking down upon them; the tanned russets, the noble pound-sweets — forty-five to a bushel! — the darker winter-greenings, the red Northern Spies. How wholesome and thrifty and pleasant and sound they look — sound to the core, I'll warrant. They're too young for a scab or worm; too young and sound — and I!

Last night, as I lay awake, I tried to count up the things Aunt Lize and Uncle Shim must have gone without to buy me this cot.

I have noticed lately that everything is sweetened with maple sugar, and am convinced that I am the only one who has had white sugar for a year past.

Then there's the semi-weekly county paper that Uncle Shim used to take; — I haven't seen Twiddie bring it in once since I began to take notice of things, back in September. Neither have I been conscious of the strength of Uncle Shim's cut-plug since — I don't know when; and as they dragged the cot through the kitchen the other day, I missed an old-fashioned bureau, that Aunt Lize told me was a part of my grandmother's first housekeeping outfit. Her mother gave it to Aunt Lize; I know she set great store by it. It had brass knobs and little fluted columns, and a queer inlaid vine-pattern of curled maple. The piece was cherry. — What more? Oh, how long is this to last!

This morning, when I heard them at breakfast, I called to Aunt Lize:

"Aunt Lize, bring me in a cup of your coffee; something is the matter with mine."

She came in looking distressed and anxious.

"I made it jest ez usual, Hughie: cream 'n' sugar, 'n' beat up an egg, 'n' all.—P'r'aps I b'iled it too long; le' me taste." She was about to take the cup, but I caught her two hands.

"Aunt Lize, you know you can't tell a lie; you have n't got any coffee for yourself or Uncle Shim — now confess!"

She brightened up a bit at that, and, looking me straight in the eyes, lied just like a Christian woman — so eagerly and convincingly!

"Why, no, Hughie; we hain't drunk er drop fer more 'n er year. The doctor said 't wuz the wust kinder thing fer liver-complaint, 'n' yer uncle 'n' I both hed er tech on 't jest 'bout er year ago this time —" I drew her down beside me — resisting, — but I find I'm much stronger in my arms; perhaps, after all, I sha'n't belie my name, Hugh Armstrong.

"Aunt Lize, there is n't a sounder liver in this township than yours; but if you tell such whoppers about it, you 'll have a bad conscience, and that, and worry, the doctors say, are the root of every liver trouble in the world since the days of Job and bad blood."

But she stuck to her point. "The doctor *did* say so — I ain't er-goin' back on what I said —"

"Well, if he did," I interrupted her, "you got him to say it to fool me — now did n't you?"

For answer, she changed the subject, picking up my first stocking from the table by the cot. — " I see ye 're heelin' neat ez er pin; ther ain't nothin' more ter learn but ' toein' off '; ye 've learned awful quick, — now le' me go — thar 's Shim er-callin' ! "

Yes, Aunt Lize, I 'm " healing " in another sense; I know by the change in Twiddie. To-day she came to the door while I was knitting, and stood on the threshold, the hollow of one bare, brown foot curving over the instep of the other, and all ten toes wriggling like cut-worms beneath a hobnail shoe; both hands behind her; silent, but watchfully observant. Tag, however, the six months collie, who had followed her into the house, suddenly brushed past her with a switch of his tail that sent her over the threshold, and, stemming his paws on the cot, nosed my hand until I caressed him.

I have n't wanted him around before — and even a dog knows when he is n't welcome. To-day neither child nor dog fought shy of me. The dog leaped joyfully to my face, and the rough tongue gave the return caress in its own way; the child drew near, and held out to me a bunch of late violets, blue and white, which she had found in a warm, sun-beshone angle of the sheep-pasture, beneath some fallen leaves.

I put my arm around her, and drew her down upon the cot. I said nothing, but I held her two feet in the clasp of my warm hand, for they were half-numb with cold — I shall knit her some stockings at once. I waited, for she is always shy with me; and when I saw she was ready, I met her more than half way; —

she nestled into the hollow of my arm, threw back her head on my shoulder, and when I smiled down at her, she smiled up at me — and I knew I was forgiven.

So late in October, yet the warm wind draws in through my open south windows, and I can hear the rush of the brook and the plunge of the waterfall into the rocky basin of the pool down in the Hollow — what a hillside that is that rises almost perpendicularly three hundred feet just across it! The bare poles of white and yellow birch are set as thick on the face of it as a hedge-hog's quills. The delicate tops catch the sunlight in a curious way, and the result, as seen from my window, is a luminous vertical perspective. There used to be a vulture's nest just under the rock that overhangs the cliff at the top; I climbed to it when a boy. There's an outcrop of quartz that marks — the spot from here.

Just then, I heard the whir of a partridge rising from cover somewhere near the hemlock-bush, — I wonder where they've put my gun? I always kept it in the rack at the head of my bed. I never knew when I might need it — for a fox sneaking into the open, or a deer ranging the clearing, for a hen-hawk or an eagle.

Many a fifty-cent bounty on a fox, as well as the price of the pelt, went into my French and Latin text-books and the two dictionaries — useless lumber now.

It is the interest on the mortgage, and the taxes, and *I*, as I am, that will ruin this place in the end.

I am on my second pair of stockings — for Twiddie.
Uncle Shim was good enough to say I beat Aunt
Lize "all holler." I should be ashamed if I could n't,
for the strength is coming back into my fingers and
wrists and arms. Night and day I think, think, think
— what *can* I do? till the blood pounds against my
ear-drums, and prevents sleep.

I am beginning to understand something of what
a woman may feel when she knits, or sews " to ease
her mind." I 've heard Aunt Lize say that many a
time. I 'm knitting "ribbed" stockings, and have to
attend to my business of counting fairly closely, or
the " three plain and three heel " interfere with one
another.

Then, too, the mere rapid motion of the fingers is
easing, and the steady click of the needles means
progress towards a definite toe — something, in fact,
made.

If it is such a pleasure simply to make, to manu-
facture — what must it be to create?

I startled myself to-day by laughing — out loud,
too, and gave Aunt Lize a fright into the bargain.
She came in on the run — hands all dough, a big dust
of flour on her nose, her eyes like green gooseberries,
and insisted upon putting the camphor bottle to my
nose. At which I laughed immoderately, and that
did n't improve matters; but in the end she laughed
as heartily as did I.

Aunt Lize was making bread on the kitchen table,
and I was knitting, when a man came along the Pent

Road by the east window and around the house to the kitchen door. Just then I heard Twiddie rush in from the shed and herald his approach.

" What 's he look like? " said Aunt Lize.

" Like the man at camp-meetin' las' summer, the one with the queer nose 'n' — "

" I know all 'bout *him*," said Aunt Lize, grimly. — " Go out to the barn, Twiddie, 'n' hender Uncle Shim from comin' in fer er spell; Shim can't abide 'em — 'n' don't ye come back t'll I call ye, both on ye ! "

As Twiddie scudded away, the man knocked and entered without waiting for an invitation from Aunt Lize.

" Sister Lewis, hope ter see ye well."

" Thank ye," said Aunt Lize, still kneading; I could hear the thumps. " Ye 'll never see me any better."

" The fear of the Lord is the health of the righteous, Sister Lewis; but from all I hear roundabouts, the law is wiped out fer sech ez yew." (Thumpity-thump-thump.) " I have called ter-day — " here he cleared his throat admonishingly, but Aunt Lize gave no sign, — " to confer consarnin' the state of yer soul, fer 'now is the accepted time and now is the day of salvation ' — even fer backsliders."

" Ye must n't take it ermiss ef I keep right on with the bread," said Aunt Lize, cheerfully; " I 'm kinder behindhand this mornin'."

" Do ye know Who said, ' I am the bread of life '? "

" Wal, I ain't er fool ef I do live on 'Lympus," retorted Aunt Lize, sharply.

"Sister Lewis, I perceive we air at variance on this subjec' — may I ask ye a simple question ? "

"I hain't no objection." The thumps were increasing in vigor.

"Is yer soul saved, my sister ? "

" Oh, yes, 't is," said Aunt Lize with cheerful assurance, "but I don't like ter brag much on 't — 't ain't my way."

" An' hez it ben scourged ter the glory of God, my sister, ez is meet fer them that aspires ter the everlastin' crown of the martyrs ? "

" Guess ye 'd think so ef ye wuz ter go down ter Old Church Settlement ; — ye 'd find fifteen headstones all in er row — nine on 'em 's marble, but the rest is slate — all mine, too. I guess them signposts don't lie when it comes ter ' scourgin'.' — "

I thought I heard a break in Aunt Lize's voice, but I was n't sure ; she was still thumping so unmercifully that I could n't catch the man's next words, but in a lull I heard him say : " Let us pray, my sister." By the aid of the three-cornered piece of looking-glass I had begged of Aunt Lize, I saw him kneel before the settle. Then I heard Aunt Lize's cheerful voice.

" Ye can pray jest ez long 'n' ez much ez ye 're er min' ter, ef ye 'll feel any better for 't — I 've got ter see ter this bread, it 's riz too much." And then there followed such a rattling of pans, such openings and shuttings of the oven door, such a sparring-match with the dough, that it was impossible for me to catch a word of the petition.

In five minutes' time the room was clear, the man

gone, the bread at rest, and Aunt Lize offering me the camphor bottle.   Complete rout!

"Wal," she said, in extenuation of her inhospitable attitude, "I can't abide them Methody travellin' agents, Hughie; they rile me wus 'n rhubub 'n' senny; 'n' I wuz n't goin' ter hev him git track er you.   They sorter peddle patent religion, 'n' it don't set well on anybody thet 's got the real article."

Poor Aunt Lize!   She need n't count on my knowing anything about the real article — I, who have cursed God, and could not die.

I remember that week in which she took me to the camp-meeting up at Stony Brook, over Farnsfield way. I was just fifteen, and on the Sunday before "breaking-up Monday," I got religion — so they said, and I thought I had.   They prayed hard for me; — somehow I found myself on the sinner's bench, and I felt awed. Every lie I 'd told, every mean thing I 'd done, every oath I 'd sworn, lay heavy upon me and made my heart beat hard.   And before I knew it I was down on my knees, and the whole crowd groaning and praying and shouting like mad; then I caught the look on Aunt Lize's face; — that settled it.   I rose up, and said I was on the Lord's side, and felt important because the elders and the evangelist and the folks shook hands with me and slapped me on the shoulder, crying out between singing and shouting: "Glory be to God! — he 's got it!" — and I thought I had! Fool!

There was a flurry of snow this morning.   They are late with the husking.   I asked Aunt Lize if I could n't help some, and she said we would manage it, someway. They rigged me out with a bushel basket for husks beside the cot, a tin pan on it, and a horse-blanket across it. Then Uncle Shim came in with a great half-shock of corn in his arms, and laid it on the floor beside me; it piled above my head, and seemed to fill half the room.

They left me alone after that — for they were busy in the barn. I was glad to be; the nearness of the fresh-smelling leaves, the glint of yellow ears between the faded husks, the sweetness of the stalk — the first thing I did was to chew an end — sent a strange thrill of life through the living part of me; the tears came.

Yet how I hated it all, after I was fifteen! I grew so restless then; the Mountain freedom was too con-fined for me. Aunt Lize encouraged me — for she is proud of her sister's having married a professional man — to seek the nearest way out of it all: the plough-ing, the harrowing, the digging, the threshing, the hewing and felling and chopping, and become a min-ister like my father. She meant well; and I cheated myself into thinking I'd had a "call"; — *I!*

My husking did n't work. I made a great litter which it took Aunt Lize an hour to clean up. Some-how the pesky kernels got between the coverings, and the chaff and dust lay white on everything. It 's no use — no use.

The ice that formed on a sap-bucket just outside my window is an inch thick this morning. Twiddie tells me Uncle Shim is up in the pine lot near the Old

Pasture cutting four-foot logs for my fireplace.   She
has been up there too.   I saw her pass the window
just now with a big bundle of fagots on her head.   I
felt a personal interest in her legs, for they were cased
in the brown-ribbed stockings I knit for her.   I'm
on my fifth pair, but they take me longer, for Uncle
Shim's shank can be measured by the ell.

The open fire is a pleasant thing.   The fierce wind
that is raging over the Mountain drives the smoke
and flame, at times, into the room; it gives me —
even *me* — a sense of power.

Twiddie is crying in the kitchen because Aunt Lize
would n't let her go down to see the stage pass; — in
this wild weather!   What is the child thinking of?

I have been watching the night come from the east;
it is now half-past five, but dark as pitch; — the sleet
rattles against the windows, and there is alternate roar
and lull of the wind in the chimney.   The firelight is
so bright I can knit by it, and as Twiddie likes to
see the play of the shadows on the wall, rising, falling, twisting, dancing, I called her in after supper;
I don't know when anything has tasted so good —
hot roast potatoes, fresh brown-bread, and a slice of
Uncle Shim's well-cured bacon.

She 's a curious specimen.

As she sat on the rug before the fire with her elbows
on her knees and her chin in her palms, silent, — she
does n't talk much, — I wondered what she could be
thinking of.   Finally I asked her.

"What are you thinking of, Twiddie?   Tell me."
She turned suddenly, and, catching sight of her con-

torted shadow on the wall, laughed gleefully — I like to hear her laugh — before she answered:

"Thinkin' mad 'bout Aunt Lize, 'coz she would n't let me go down to see the stage — but I ain't now," she added shyly, making loops with her two hands to form a goose-shadow on the wall.

"What do you do when you go down to meet the stage?"

"I git up in the butt'nut tree sometimes, 'n' some-times I git behind the fence where ther's er patch er brakes, 'n' when I lay flat, the folks can't see me — even Uncle Jo could n't find me."

"What folks?"

"The folks I know."

"What are their names?"

She hesitated a moment. "Ye won't tell Aunt Lize ef I tell ye?"

"No."

She lowered her voice: "I make b'lieve, ye know. I learn all the letters on the trunks 'n' valises by heart — jes' ez we do in school — 'n' then I play I know all the folks they b'long ter, 'n' I go off with 'em down ter Rutland, 'n' Alderbury, 'n', oh — way, way off, most ez fur ez York State."

"How many do you know, Twiddie?"

"I dunno — 'bout twenty, I guess; ye want ter hear 'em?"

"Yes. — Curl up here on the cot beside me, or you'll have a blister on your nose." She laughed, and nestled into the hollow of my arm as she did that time when she forgave me.

"Now you can whisper, and Aunt Lize can't hear our secrets."

"First, ye know, ther's P. V. — he's real, ain't he?"

I smiled for answer, for, in spirit, the man still sits beside my cot, and at times I can feel the firm, warm clasp of his hand; his presence is more real to me than the child's beside me.

"What next?"

"Then ther's S. M. 'n' L. K. 'n' O. M.; they're all ladies, thet sit inside 'n' look out of the winder, 'n' bow to me; 'n' then ther's K. O. 'n' F. D. 'n' S. E. 'n' two H. P.'s, — they're twins — 'n' they all set up with Uncle Jo on top of the stage, 'n' take off their hats ter me jes' ez Mr. P. V. did thet day, ye 'member?" I nodded emphatically, although I had not seen him bestow the greeting.

"'N' then ther's er boy thet sets on behind where the trunks are — I mean when ther' ain't no trunks — 'n' dangles his legs; 'n' he gits down when he sees me, 'n' says, 'Miss Twiddie Lewis, here's yer mail,' 'n' then he puts the letters inter the squirrel-hole, 'n' then he jumps up behind agin, 'n' Uncle Jo cracks his whip 'n' says, 'Good-by, Twiddie, ther'll be some ter-morrer sure,' 'n' then the stage goes off, 'n' I put my hand inter the hole 'n' take out the mail —"

"What mail?"

"Why, the mail the boy leaves," she answered in a surprised tone; "'n' then I read the letters, 'n' they're from all the folks I know — thet's why I wuz cryin', 'coz Aunt Lize would n't let me go down fer it ter-day, 'n' I know ther's a letter, — one anyway."

What could I say but: "How do the letters begin, Twiddie?"

"Some on 'em begin, 'Dear Miss Lewis,' 'n' some,

'Dear Miss,' 'n' some, 'Dear Miss Twiddie,' 'n' 'nother allus writes, 'Dear Twiddie;'—but ther's one, ye won't tell?—"

"Never."

"Not er livin' soul?"

"True as you live and breathe, Twiddie."

"He allus begins, 'Dearest Theodora'" (I'd forgotten that is the child's name, for 'Twiddie' was her four-year-old pronunciation of Theodora when she first came to us, and we have always called her that), "'n' hisn are the best.   He writes every day."

"And what is his name?"

She twisted herself out of my arm and sat down again before the fire, back to me, with her elbows on her knees and her chin in her palms. "Ye won't tell?"

"Never."

"Nobody in all this world?"

"I give you my word"—as a man, I was going to say; but I sickened at the thought, and said, "gentleman"—and then I wondered at myself. But the child spoke joyfully:

"Why, thet's jest what he is!   He's H. A."

"And have you seen him on the coach too?"

She answered sorrowfully: "No, I never see him there; but Uncle Jo says he's ben there er good many times. I see his valise onct. Uncle Jo wuz takin' it home fer him, 'n' thet's how I could see the letters."

"Merciful sakes, Hughie!—what air ye keepin' this child up fer?" said Aunt Lize, appearing at the door. "It's long past her bedtime."

And Twiddie turned with a merry laugh. "Good-night, Hughie," she said, with her finger on her lips, and ran past Aunt Lize like a small whirlwind.

The wind is wild, and I can't sleep.

Curious! Long before Twiddie came to us I used, as a boy, to ride on the trunk-rack of the old Hornet, holding by the leathern straps, and swinging my legs. That was my treat, and Uncle Jo gave it to me whenever he could.

Twiddie's "folks" have been peopling the room in the dim light of the embers. Now that I have lighted my lamp to write, they are gone. I forgot to ask Twiddie whose was the letter in the yellow envelope that she brought up that day. *That* was a real one.

November 10th.

Killington and Pico are snow-capped this morning; Aunt Lize and Twiddie are raking up the leaves under the maples in the south dooryard to bank the house with. Uncle Shim has just brought down a load of hemlock boughs to lay on top of them; there is no chance for the cellar to freeze with both leaves and boughs to protect it; they keep the floors from being cold too.

Twiddie went down for her "mail" this forenoon, and it seemed scarce half an hour before I heard her back again, storming through the shed into the kitchen — but it must have been an hour and a half, for it is good four miles there and back. Aunt Lize called to her from the pantry, but she did not heed.

"Hughie, Hughie! The letter — the letter!" she cried in her clear, high voice, tearing into the room, flinging herself upon the cot beside me, panting — almost breathless — and thrusting the letter into my face. At her cry the heart of me leaped in my throat as a trout leaps to a fresh-thrown fly. I knew, without her telling me, from whom it was; and I read the address thrice aloud, to gain time before sending Twiddie from the room, for I wanted to read it by myself, — "Mr. Hugh Armstrong," — firm and solid, every stroke, like the clasp of his hand.

"Go, now, Twiddie," I said. "If there's any message for you I'll tell you; shut the door."

The child went, but not before she had flung her arms about my neck and whispered joyfully: "I told true, did n't I, Hughie?" And, for answer, what could I do but kiss her? I, who for nearly two years not only have shunned, but hated the sight of every living thing that has the wherewith to move freely on earth, in air or water — whether the sheep-dog, or the child, or man or woman, fish, flesh, or fowl.

The letter shall lie here between the leaves of this book, where lie the late violets Twiddie gave me the other day.

WASHINGTON SQUARE, NORTH,
NEW YORK, Nov. 8th, 189–.

MY DEAR MR. ARMSTRONG,

I have recently been out to St. Louis, and on my return trip stopped over for a day or two in Cincinnati. While there, I visited the School of Woodcarving for the purpose of placing an order for a friend. There are many pupils, and the results of their labor are both artistic and useful; I am much interested in it. It occurred to me while there that you also might be interested in this special handi-craft, and I forward to you one of the circulars, and a book which gives information as to the kinds of wood required for the carvings and the technical difficulties to be overcome in working them; there are also numerous plates of designs.

I often think of that forest-belt that crowns your Olympus — however did that pagan name find its lodging among the Hebraic nomenclature of Sharon, Gilead, Lebanon, that your pioneer forefathers took along as part of their goods and chattels when they followed the Connecticut upwards from its mouth? I noticed several tamaracks here and there on the way up from the butternut tree, and some fine speci-mens of mountain-ash. I have promised myself the pleasure, sometime, of a closer acquaintance with all the noble-bodied individuals of that special timber-belt that lies to the north of your land.

How is my little acquaintance of the butternut tree? Say to her for me that I am her debtor for the pleasant hour in your room, and tell her to look for a letter from me any time between now and Christ-mas. Will you express to Mrs. Lewis my apprecia-tion of her courtesy? And with best remembrances for you and Twiddie,

Believe me,
Yours faithfully,
PHILIP VANEVER.

P. S. — As an afterthought, I returned to the School and procured a set of tools sufficient to ac-complish a little practical experimenting in the art, if you care to try. Kindly let me know if your woods can be utilized for any of these designs. If

you don't care for this, give the tools to Twiddie,
for whom I shall send a box, by express, to be
used in all weathers for her " mail." I enclose two
keys, one for Uncle Jo Cheatle, and one for her,
which please present with my compliments.

P. V.

November 11th.

I gave the key and the message to Twiddie last
night — the dumb joy of the child ! It was well
worth seeing. The key is so mysterious ! She is
on the piece of rag carpet before the fire, the key
hung on a string around her neck. She is turning
and twisting it that it may catch the firelight; but she
is not in a talkative mood. Doubtless she is holding
converse with her " folks."

From the tall pine in the clearing there is a trust-
worthy echo of the post-horn to be heard, and when
the wind is in a certain direction it can be heard at
the house. Aunt Lize has promised Twiddie that
if the horn sounds Uncle Shim shall harness up and
take her down for the package.

They have been watching together in the twilight
up there at the pine, but have come home disappointed.

November 12th.

Aunt Lize says she has a " feeling in her bones "
that the things will come to-day. To help Twiddie
kill time till four o'clock I have sent her down the
road to count the larch trees, and to bring me back a
branch.

That there might be no mistake, I bade her fetch

me a piece of charcoal such as Aunt Lize keeps on hand to use in boiling cabbage, and with it I drew for her on a bit of brown paper a branch of the tough, close-grained tree.   I had the trick of a piece of charcoal when I was a little chap and drew trees and sheep and loggers' camps on the flat stones beneath the crotch set for the sap-kettles, when I went with Aunt Lize and Uncle Shim over into the sugar-bush.

She came back with an armful of the bare branches, and reported seven half a mile down the road.

After Twiddie had gone up to the pine tree, I opened the east window a crack — almost my full arm-strength has come back; — I wanted to listen for the horn.   It was still; everything frost-bound, but without snow.   Straining my ears, I heard a faint echo of Uncle Jo's signal blast; the sound unheard until now for — has it been a lifetime?

I shut the window, for I was shaking; and so shut myself in again.   Christ! — to be shut in to this, and shut out from all that!   Oh! I fight, I fight, having taken my stand, but the black thing swoops down upon me at times, and every struggle but tightens its clutch upon me.

It was like the breaking of a nightmare, when, an hour later, I heard Twiddie call joyfully: "We've got 'em, Hughie!"   Then Uncle Shim came in through the shed.   I drew a long, full breath. — It is not well to be alone, and Aunt Lize trusted me.

November 13th.

The book is a revelation, and Twiddie's box an inspiration.   It is two feet by a foot and a half; made of oak. On the panel of the door is carved a squirrel; he is cracking a nut he holds in his paws. Branches, leaves, and acorn-cups ornament the sides; the back is plain, and provided with screw-eyes for hanging or fastening. The letter-drop is a simulated squirrel-hole. I am studying the book and the tools.

Meanwhile, I'll make those meat-skewers I heard Aunt Lize asking Uncle Shim for. The tamarack wood is just the thing for them.

The fire was blazing — Twiddie on the rug before it, with Tag on one side and her box on the other — and I was whittling for all I was worth, when I caught myself softly whistling! The boy's old habit had persisted.

At the sound, Tag pointed his ears and was on the alert at once. Twiddie stole out of the room — and I, whistling all the while, took out my three-cornered bit of glass, adjusted it at the right kitchen-angle, and saw Aunt Lize listening at the door, just out of sight, with bent head and clasped hands. The tears were running down her cheeks, her lips were moving, but no sound came. I continued to whistle till I had finished a dozen good skewers.

November 17th.

Twiddie brought me this morning a few branches of the pine, balsam fir, and larch, with their cones; and all day long I have been pottering with a piece of charcoal and some wrapping-paper. I've been trying my tools, too, and have finished the book — my first in all these months.

In my answer to Philip Vanever's letter, I was ashamed to confess I didn't know how or why Olympus came by its name. I've been no better than the hogs that root for acorns, and never once know there's a tree above them that lifts its top into the blue.

November 18th.

Uncle Shim is going down to the grist-mill in Scawsville to get the corn ground. Twiddie goes with him, and Aunt Lize is putting up their dinner, for it's an all-day's job. They are going to stop on the way to put up the mail-box on the butternut tree, and Uncle Shim will make a pent-roof for it to protect it from the rough weather. I hate to see it go. They have driven around the corner of the house for me to see; Twiddie is sitting on the pile of meal-bags, and the cart, with the rack, is filled to the third board — a good half cord.

Uncle Shim used to let me ride on the corn when I was a little shaver, and root into it as I liked. It was fun to feel my legs work downwards into the yielding mass — it was like treading water.

When I wrote Philip Vanever the other day, I found myself feeling glad I had had that year and a half at the Academy. I came late to the training, but I bent all my energy to it; — I earned all I had, too, by the five years' service on the farm.

How I did long for books after I had left the district school! And with nothing but my text-books, the Bible, and my father's theological works to satisfy the hunger. I have shunned the sight of those, even, let alone the sight of living things.

I've been alone nearly all day. Aunt Lize has been busy making sausage-meat in the back shed. The fire has died down to embers; it's getting cold in the room, and outside snow is beginning to fall. I can see to knit no longer in the twilight.

Good Lord, what a coward I am! Need a man be a fool because he is a cripple? Did the log, falling on me, benumb faculties, paralyze common-sense, knock the manhood out of me for good and all? — I wish I had my legs again, with double joints into the bargain, just to be able to kick myself into trim. I'll see every Canuck that logs it on the Mountain, and every man, woman, and child that finds his way up here. I'll go to work on my Latin and French again, I'll —

That first groan must have been a mighty one, — anyway, it carried with it the burden of twenty-one months, — for Aunt Lize came running in, and a breath of onion, sage, and summer-savory came along with her.

"What's the matter, Hughie? Ye're freezin' here." She began to throw on wood.

"I've had a turn, Aunt Lize."

"Oh, Hughie!" There was distress in her voice. Then the flame leaped, lighting the whole room, and my face as well.

"Come here, Aunt Lize." She came to the side of the cot.

"I want you to take me by the scruff of my neck

and give me one good shaking — the kind you gave me when I let the woodchuck out of the trap and he ate up all your peas and beans; you remember?"

"I sha'n't fergit it soon." She laughed. "'N' I made sure fer onct thet ye'd keep it well in mind fer the rest er yer life. I know I got scairt myself, when I heerd yer teeth knockin' tergether in yer head — My! warn't I mad! — but ye wuz tryin', Hughie, ther' ain't no denyin' *thet;* allus er suthin': — baitin', er trappin', er shootin', er fishin', er whittlin' yer fingers most ter chips makin' whistles 'n' bow 'n' arrers, besides robbin' every good cock's tail I hed fer feathers ter wing 'em; — 'n' every time I heerd er squawk round the house, I knew suthin' wuz up.

"D'ye remember the coon ye treed, thet ye couldn't git down? 'n' how ye vowed ye'd watch him out till mornin'? 'n' set with yer back ter the big beech up thar in the Old Paster, watchin', watchin', with yer lantern beside of ye? 'n' me 'n' Uncle Shim went up thar 'long 'bout three o'clock, 'fore 't wuz light, 'n' found ye sound asleep, 'n' the coon gone out the back way?"

"And do you remember the screech-owls, Aunt Lize, I hid up in the back garret?" — Aunt Lize began to laugh again — "and how when you had the Methodist circuit minister to supper, one night before Thanksgiving, just as he was saying grace — " Aunt Lize was laughing so immoderately at the remembrance that I joined her.

"Oh, Hughie!" she cried when she got her breath, "what er blood-curdlin' screech thet wuz! Thet's the only time I ever see Shim Lewis's tan look yaller, 'n' the minister, he shook like er popple, 'n' riz right up, 'n' said he 'd better be gittin' erlong, he did n't want no supper. He told arterwards in Scawsville, thet the Evil One himself could n't stan' sech er racket; 'n' ye sot thar er-squeezin' yer two han's 'twixt yer little legs, 'n' wrigglin', 'n' chucklin' ter yerself!

" I never see yer Uncle mad with ye but jest thet onct. He made ye dance some 'fore ye went ter bed; 'n' I went up arter ye wuz in, — fer I had n't heerd er sound er nothin' but the cut er the ox-thong round yer legs, 'n' every stroke cut *me* — 'n' rubbed on steeped salt 'n' wormwood; 'n' then ye cried yerself nearly inter er fit. I hain't never see yer cry sence t'll — t'll — "

" Till six weeks ago? I know, Aunt Lize; it did me good too. There 's been a good deal of salt and wormwood rubbed in this last year and a half."

" 'N' it 's jest the same with me now ez 't wuz when ye warn't but seven year old — every stroke ye 've hed hez cut me too, Hughie."

She sat down on the side of the cot, and I found her knotty, toil-hardened hand.

November 19th.

A note and two books of travels christened the oak box.

WASHINGTON SQUARE,
NEW YORK, November 15th.

MY DEAR MR. ARMSTRONG,

I am glad if you can make any use of the tools. My hand has no cunning in that direction, although for several years I have been greatly interested in the wood-carvings of various countries and races; in fact, have been making a collection, which I hope to en-rich some day by an Olympian contribution. I send by this mail two books on Ceylon; I was there last year. The illustrations are excellent; please note the details of the temple carvings — you'll find some of the flora in them. Pray keep the books; I have a duplicate set. I like to think of you as travelling in imagination.

Faithfully yours,
PHILIP VANEVER.

How that thought quickens — "travelling in imagi-nation " — for me who have never been beyond the state boundary stones!

My trouble is to find woods well-seasoned, well-cured. There are two planks of basswood under the eaves in the garret, — they have been there as long as I can remember: a sufficient seasoning, I take it, for any want of mine, — and one or two slabs of cherry which Aunt Lize says her mother kept on hand in case the spindles, or spokes, of her wheels and reels should give out. I can use those after Uncle Shim has taken them down to the saw-mill and got them into shape for me.

A sure hand; an eye, not only true to a line of a hair's breadth, but open to the value of cutting-depths for light and shade to the hundredth part of an inch; a right feeling for *form* — and a *something besides.* In that last lies the art of it. I wonder if I have it.

This work is beginning to absorb me, as well as my time; I've even neglected the stockings. I've botched everything I've tried from the designs in the book, and am thrown back upon myself, which means that I must touch, feel, see, trace the actual model. I'm put to it for those now, for there's a foot of snow.

November 29th.

Aunt Lize burst into the room to-day in a state of mind bordering on frenzy, and Twiddie was behind her, clasping a half-day-old suckling in her arms.

"I never see the beat er thet old sow, Hughie; — here's yer Uncle ben gone ter the saw-mill most all day, 'n' thet's jest the time she takes ter litter — fifteen! 'n' November, 'n' cold 'nough ter freeze their tails off. Look er thar!" Twiddie held up a pink and white pigling for my inspection.

"Well, Aunt Lize, you finished your sausage-meat yesterday, and Nature must level up somehow, you know." I could n't help laughing to see Aunt Lize's discomfiture and Twiddie's efforts to warm the toes of the specimen one-fifteenth of the old sow's progeny at the fire. Such wrigglings, and squirmings, and slippings! Such infant squeals and abortive grunts! — the little pink tail double twisted like one of Aunt Lize's raised doughnuts! But Aunt Lize could brook no jest.

"Jest let it come so bitter freezin' thet every pail er hog's wash skims 'fore ye can git it out ter the pen, 'n' ther's jest 'nough straw fer the hosses' beddin' fer the winter, — 'n' thet critter, all of er suddin, presents her imperance with fifteen ter the trough! But ye let it come mild, thawin' weather 'long 'bout April, when she can git out inter the back run, 'n' she waddles round with only one, or two. I allus knew hogs wuz cantankerous — but *sows!* It's jest downright, tee-total depravity."

She bounced out of the room, — Twiddie, with her pigling, following at her heels. Poor Aunt Lize! If only I could help!

How many times I have come home from school in the early spring afternoons, to find the old sow and thirty or more shotes rooting about in the ploughed piece of land behind the house. And at my wild war-whoop and sudden rush up the Pent Road, what a lifting of snouts, a turning-to of tails, what a mad scamper for the pen — and such crowding, jostling, over-riding, squealings, snortings, and gruntings! Routed! — and I triumphant.

"Twiddie," I said, as she sat on the rug before the fire this evening, and I was knitting for dear life, trying to finish my stint — a pair in five days — "Twiddie, you never showed me that letter in the yellow envelope you brought home that day, do you remember?" She nodded.

"'T warn't er letter — not er truly one." I knew she was holding some conversation with her "folks" by the sound of her voice.

"What was it? — one, two, three, heel." — I pretended not to be over-curious.

"'T wuz ter Aunt Lize, 'n' Uncle Shim put it inside the clock."

"Did you see it?"

"No, Aunt Lize said 't warn't nothin' but er bill."

"Oh, well, then she won't mind my seeing it.   Go, get it for me, will you?"

"I'm 'fraid she'll see me, Hughie."

"What if she does?   I'm not asking you to do anything mean by Aunt Lize.   Now, hurry up — I hear her out in the shed with Uncle Shim."

Twiddie came back with the yellow envelope; it was the bill for my cot — fifty-two dollars!   White sugar, old-fashioned bureau, Uncle Shim's tobacco, the newspaper and coffee; half the taxes, and something of the interest on the mortgage!   I saw it all. I suppose I must have groaned, for Tag, lying before the fire, rose with a whine, and Twiddie tried to draw my hands down from my face.

"Don't, Hughie, oh, don't!"   Her lips quivered, and to avoid a scene I sent her out to put away the yellow envelope in the clock before Aunt Lize should come in.

December 12th.

To-day I finished the carving of a branch of larch with its little cones.   It's my fifth attempt to make something only half satisfactory to myself.   I shall send it to Philip Vanever for criticism.

There is a great racket going on overhead in the garret.   I know by the sound it's Aunt Lize getting down her spinning-wheel and the reel.   She told me yesterday she had n't but two more hanks of yarn left.   I've finished eight pair of stockings.

December 17th.

There was a light fall of snow last night, turning into sleet later on; and this morning, from my east window, I saw the sun rise over the mountain tops; its level beams caught in the ice on tree and fence, on rock and crust, and were broken into all colors of the rainbow.

3 P. M.

It is growing intensely cold, already fifteen below. The back-log glows clear red from end to end. This noon I heard the ring of an axe in the woods for the first time this season; — the sound sickened me. Uncle Shim has begun early; I know he hasn't the ready cash to pay for help, — never had; but he had me.

How often I have cut and trimmed my six trees a day. Oh! the swing of the arms, the deep " hah — hah " — that sound forced from the inflated lungs by the downward stroke! — Oh! to feel the thrill of the springing resistance of the live wood through the axe-helve! To see the slow ooze of the sap in the clean-angled gash, to smell the fresh breath of the leaping chips! To feel the coursing of the blood to the roots of the hair, and the warm moisture on the nape of the neck! Never again —

I went straight to work on my new carving — blades and ears of the corn; but the lust of the woodman was strong within me, and I hewed where I should have cut, and gashed when I tried to carve. Work ruined for to-day.

December 20th.

Twiddie's patience has nearly given out. She has been down the two miles to the butternut tree every other forenoon to see if Uncle Jo has left anything for her in the box. As yet, there has been nothing, and I saw the tears in her eyes when she handed me a letter to-day — such a letter! Enough to warm the cockles of a man's heart if they had frozen solid. Here it shall lie.

NEW YORK, Dec. 17th.

MY DEAR MR. ARMSTRONG,

I have always envied the man who can work in wood, clay, or stone, and so materialize his ideas. When I took that panel of yours out of the box, I wanted to put myself aboard the first north-bound train and congratulate you in person.

You ask for criticism — I have n't any, for it 's the larch itself, engrafted on that cherry panel! I went straight over to the Art Society and entered the piece in my name, subject to withdrawal. Of course, I knew it would be accepted, — they don't get such often, — and when I received the notification of acceptance, I went round to see the secretary, with whom I left it, and withdrew it, after promising to return it for orders. Then I went up town to see a friend of mine who is remodelling the upper story of his house, and who spoke to me the other day about a design in wood for the mantel in his den. By a stroke of luck I was just in time; he was about to send to the Cincinnati School.

Now, can you do it? Or, rather, will you? He wants the panels and lintel in the same design — larch; but he leaves you free hand in its application.

The wood is cherry. He will ship the three pieces, if you write me you will do the work. Let me know, if possible, by return mail, via, of course, the Hornet. Thanks for your thought of me.

Yours in haste,

PHILIP VANEVER.

Will I?   *Will* I? — I am unnerved, unmanned by all this.

Twiddie went down this forenoon with my answer in time for the stage at twelve. She took the small wood-sled, for the crust holds, and there is a fine coast for good two thirds of the way down the Pent Road; the bars are down for the winter, fortunately for her, for she tells me she always slides "bellybump."

Uncle Shim is over in the hemlock-bush, cutting logs for peeling. I can hear the ring of his axe, and the slow crash of the falling trees. I always used to look forward to that, and when the noble crown bowed lower and lower, the limbs strained with a groan, the mighty trunk with the last splintering crash lay prostrate — how the blood in me leaped at the sight and the sound! I felt like a conqueror.

I had Aunt Lize pop some corn, and place two Northern Spies, with a tin cup of sweet cider, on the hot bricks of the hearth against Twiddie's return. The air is white with frost — it must be fifteen below; but still, so still, that I heard a squirrel bark in the woods just now.

Twiddie came back with a telegram — my first; and my heart was like lead in my stomach when I read:

"Hold your hand with the design till you hear from me again. I have headed off the Hornet at the other end, Rutland.   P. V."

December 22nd.

Uncle Shim hitched up into the pung after four, and went down to the butternut tree; Twiddie was with him. She had a hot soapstone for her feet, and a hot roast potato in each hand. It's twenty below. I've been knitting furiously, and counting out loud like a madman, to keep from thinking — what if it should fall through, just at the moment I feel my head above water?

But it didn't! I had a note, and Twiddie had a letter, — at last. The note was a hurried one, to tell me to work into the design of the lintel the Latin verse, "*Deus haec otia fecit*."

"God hath made this a rest." So *this* is to be my first object-lesson with a block of wood!

Sometime I will carve out the face of my Fate; — it shall be beautiful, calm and noble, restful; the eyelids level; the parted lips curved in a smile — but between them I'll carve the protruding head of a poison adder, fang prominent, and the coils of its body just hinted at.

Twiddie has said nothing of her letter so long looked for, but she goes about as full of the suppressed ferment of excitement as Aunt Lize's jug of new yeast, which I hear just now blowing its stopple out in the kitchen, and raising its own row, I should say, by the noise. Aunt Lize and Twiddie are out in the hemlock-bush somewhere. They keep out of sight. Now, what are they up to? I'll get even with them.

I opened the window a crack and called:
"Aunt Lize!"
I heard her then: "Run in, Twiddie, and see what Hughie wants."
"I want you, Aunt Lize," I hollered; "the yeast's running over."
"Oh, Luddy!"
I propped the window with the crook of my staff, and leaned close to breathe the keen air: so keen, that my nostrils stuck together. I saw Aunt Lize and Twiddie dragging between them a small balsam-fir across the Pent Road and around the house to the shed. Then I heard Aunt Lize mopping up the kitchen floor.

"I never see the beat er new pertater yeast!" she said, when, an hour afterwards, she came in with my dinner. "It's jest like some folks I know — allus er-workin', er-workin' in their in'ards; never at peace with themselves, 'n' what's wuss, won't never let other folks be in peace."

I knew it was only a blind.

"What were you doing out in the hemlock-bush, Aunt Lize?"
"Me?" she said innocently.
"Yes, you."
"Oh, I wuz jest helpin' Twiddie git some moss 'n' ground-pine. Ther' ain't much snow in the bush, 'n' I fergot ter git the moss ter stuff in the winder

cracks 'fore this cold snap, 'n' 't is time 't wuz in."   I caught her hand. —

"Aunt Lize, the truth — "

"Le' me go, Hughie; I hear Shim callin' — My! but ye 're gittin' powerful strong in yer arms." I let her go, but I scent a mystery.

I 've been drawing the larch design for the lintel and experimenting with the letters. I wish I had some good paper for it; but I hate to ask Aunt Lize for even fifty cents, knowing what I do.

A curious fancy occupied my thoughts all the forenoon. I should like to carve that Fate's head from a piece of the log that laid me here; I 'll ask Uncle Shim about it. — Three months ago I wanted to hack and hew it into splinters; now, I 'd like to put it to a slow torture with these sharp tools.

December 24th.

Uncle Shim and Twiddie have gone down in the pung to meet the stage — I know by the time they take.

The door into the kitchen is shut; but I can hear Aunt Lize stirring about, and smell the hot maple syrup she is boiling down to candy; she used always to make it for me at Christmas, and I cracked the butternuts, — the blackish-brown stain on my hands for a month afterwards. How good it was! I wish she 'd open the door.

The room is red with firelight. Outside there is a still cold; the window-panes are frosted thick with silver brake and fern and raying pine leaves that catch the reflection of the flames on all their spiculæ.

There's Tag barking in the clearing; I hear the "tinkle-tankle" of the old cracked cow-bell I strapped on Prince's head-stall seven years ago; Twiddie is calling —

There was a letter, a box for me, and one for Twiddie. I opened the letter, — I couldn't wait; but the boxes are to be brought into my room and opened after supper. I have read the letter while the others are in the kitchen.

MY DEAR MR. ARMSTRONG,

All-the-year-round greetings to you on your Mountain. I wish I might see that heavy timber-belt by moonlight, in frost and snow! Tell me, sometime, how it impresses you in all its moods and tenses; I find forests have such.

The panels were shipped to-day by express. My friend finds that the price of the carving of each panel at any designer's, or Art School, would be twenty-five dollars each. Do you agree to this basis of adjustment? — for the business?

I have sent Twiddie a Christmas box, the contents of which are based on Hans Andersen's *Fairy Tales* — a book I lived on when I was younger than she. I should like to see her small face when she grasps my conception of the box. Do you help her to it and play boy again. In a recent letter she promised me some "maple-sugar-butternut" candy, and some spruce gum which she has gathered herself. Don't let her forget to send me both. There has always been a good home market for the consumption of those special articles with me.

The other box is for you, with the season's greetings. I thought you might be interested in Michael Angelo and John of Bologna, — for their trade is likely to be yours, — in Peter Vischer, and Hildesheim Bernward. I made their acquaintance several years ago, and you are eight years younger than I.

Good-night; — the traffic on the Avenue just outside the club windows is deafening — jobbers, expressmen, hacks, carriages, newsboys, messenger-boys, florists' wagons, Christmas-trees by the hundred apparently walking up town on stilts, children, men, women — confusion worse confounded; but it's two days before Christmas, which explains it all. Kind regards to Mr. and Mrs. Lewis.

Yours sincerely,

PHILIP VANEVER.

P. S. I'll put you into direct communication with my friend within a few days. That's a good idea of yours to send the charcoal designs for approval. I'm glad you enjoyed that trip to Ceylon; that lotus-flower was a thing to remember, wasn't it, as well as the trip half-way round the world? P. V.

Twenty-five dollars each! Seventy-five dollars for the three — *Seventy-five dollars!* The white sugar, and Uncle Shim's cut-plug, the coffee and weekly paper, the interest on the mortgage, and the taxes — And who is Hans Andersen? Who is Michael Angelo? Who is Bernward, and that John of Bologna? What am I — what do I know, that all these should come to *me?* —

I was glad when Uncle Shim came in with the boxes, for I was growing dizzy with the crowding thoughts.

Twiddie is quiet through sheer exhaustion from excitement. I never noticed the child's eyes before — blue-black to-night, for the pupil is so enlarged. They seem to take up the whole face. She has given me *her* letter to read.

MY DEAR TWIDDIE,

Merry Christmas! and may Hans Andersen bring you the good luck that comes to every boy and girl who loves him. You'll find your box in layers; a layer for each story. The first story you've helped to make yourself, for I know you have the little balsam-fir I told you about, set up in the room for Christmas eve. Every week I want you to read Cousin Hugh a story, and then take out a layer of the box, and enjoy it. The box ought to last two months. You'll find it is the story made real.

I'm waiting for the " maple-sugar-butternut " candy and the spruce gum — meanwhile, my mouth waters when I think of them.

Your friend,

PHILIP VANEVER.

I was as much interested as Twiddie, and, after the boxes were opened and my books had been taken out, they brought in and set up the little balsam-fir in a socket Uncle Shim had made for it. Then Twiddie, sitting on the rug, read the story of " The Fir Tree."

How my vision went roaming into the timber-belt

with the opening words: — "*Out in the forest stood a pretty little fir tree. It had a good place; it could have sunlight, and there was air in plenty, and all around grew many larger comrades, pines as well as firs.*" The resin of the little balsam was keen in my nostrils, and, suddenly, the sick longing for my boyhood came upon me.

But when she had finished with the words: — "*And the story is past too, — past, past — and that's the way with all stories,*" I pulled myself together and entered into the mute, trembling joy of the child in that first layer. Aunt Lize and Uncle Shim shared it too. It was as wonderful to them as to the child; for there lay the gilded apples and walnuts, the nets of colored paper filled with sweetmeats, the dozen little candles, red, white, and blue, a doll — Twiddie caught her breath at the sight, she has had only her rag one with brown yarn for hair — and a tinsel star for the top of the tree. Then she and Aunt Lize dressed the little fir in all its Christmas bravery, according to the fairy tale, and Aunt Lize threw over it some strings of popcorn. The candles were affixed to the branches and lighted; Uncle Shim tiptoed about, and a curious hush fell upon us all.

Christmas Day.

I waited till this evening to tell them of my good luck. Aunt Lize broke right down, and Uncle Shim went out of the room softly, in his stocking-feet. I believe I broke down too, for I felt Twiddie's arms about my neck and heard her say:

" Don't, Hughie, don't; — I *did* tell true, did n't

I?" And in comforting the child, I became again master of myself.

January 10th.

The hum of the spinning-wheel and the whir of the reel throughout the short winter afternoons and long evenings make me sleepy. Aunt Lize has been busy with the wool all the afternoon, treadle and spindle seemingly in perpetual motion.

It is among my first recollections — that sound, and the sight of Aunt Lize, foot, hand, arm, back in rhythmic movement, only interrupted by the parting of a strand or the joining of the same, her thumb and forefinger — first wet quickly at her lips — twirling and twisting the end of the roll of carded fleece. And the fleece itself! A soft, yellowish white pile in the willow basket beside the reel; — I see it all, even to the carders hanging from a beam over the garret stairs; and the old garret itself with its loom and stool, its cheese-press, its strings of red peppers and onions and dried apples, its popcorn in an old, hooded, wooden cradle that was built with the house, and has rocked me and past generations.

Oh, the work, the work! the blessedness of it! I have said as much in a recent letter to Philip Vanever. It prospers.

The cold is strengthening with the lengthening days. Everything is ice-bound. Not a sound outside except the butting of the cattle in their stalls, the thin blat of a sheep beneath the barn, and, at daybreak, the crowing of the cocks.

Twice I have heard the boom of a bursting tree-trunk and the crack of ice in a water-filled hollow. Not an egg for ten days past, — and on the latch of my door, that opens out towards the orchard, the frost is white and thick like new-fallen snow.

The windows are made snug with the dried moss in the cracks, but I roast to the fire, and freeze at my back. It's better though than the air-tight; I should stifle with that, and there is no need to spare the wood. There'll be a let-up soon.

Oh, but the work is a joy! and how the time goes! — January fifteenth, and the left panel finished. I had a fancy to cut the whole life of the tamarack into the wood: the slender spring branches with the globular buds and the catkins; the full flush of summer in its leaf; the autumn nudity with its delicate clustered cones.

Uncle Shim, with my help, has contrived a solid work-table of beech — five feet by three. It is four inches higher than the cot, and can be shoved up over it, and pushed back again over the foot when I have finished.

I have begged Aunt Lize to take up the rag-carpet that I may make all the litter I choose. She objected at first, on account of the cold floor; but I told her that, as I never set foot to it, she need n't stand for that. All she said was, "Oh, Hughie!" But she took it up last week, leaving one of the rugs for her wooden rocker, and another for Twiddie before the fire.

Uncle Shim comes in regularly to hear the stories. I don't know which I'm the more in love with — Hans Andersen or Michael Angelo; it's a toss-up. All the week through Twiddie plays her story, and lives one third in this world and two thirds in another.

Our January thaw. Whenever I wake in the night, I hear the drip, drip of the melting ice from the eaves. This morning I heard a little run start over in the sledge track on the Pent Road. Twiddie is out in the slush now, building a snow-dam across it.

January 21st.

Aunt Lize has opened my east door and let the whole world of the mountains into my room. The sun is as warm as in April, and the air filled with the running, dripping, splashing, gurgling, slipping, sliding sounds of melting ice and snow.

The chickadees are fairly singing somersaults over one another; there is a bare patch in the Pent Road.

The wind changed suddenly in the night, and this morning the sky is like lead. The chill is in the house, and Aunt Lize looks blue and pinched, even about her work. There is snow in the air, and the cold pierces to the very marrow; my fingers are too numb for work.

We are cut off from the world. It has been snowing for two days and two nights — a steady fall, straight as a plummet; but to-night the wind has risen and a gale is raking the Mountain.

What a sound that is! — the scream of the winter blast through the pines as if the needles were vibrating wires.

January 28th.

The drifts are twelve feet between the house and the barn. Uncle Shim has been tunnelling through; the wind has gone down and the mercury has dropped twenty degrees since morning.

There's another world beyond our mountains; I feel this the more I read of these great men. What a life, that of Angelo's! And his love for that woman —

I should like to see once a perfectly beautiful woman.

Linnie Lane had a pretty face; the prettiest I have ever seen: fresh skin and dimples — but I can imagine something other than that.

I must ask Aunt Lize about Linnie Lane.

January 30th.

In the sunlight I feel expansive, and reach out to that world beyond our mountains; but the firelight shuts me in, and invites to confidence with Aunt Lize.

I heard Uncle Shim snoring on the settle. Twiddie was in bed, and Aunt Lize stringing winter apples to dry for another year's store. I called to her: "Aunt Lize!"

"What ye want, Hughie?"

"You. — Come in with your apples, and I'll help string."

" It 'll make er muss — "

" Never mind.   I want to talk."

She supplied me with a darning-needle and a string, and, having placed the wooden chopping-tray of quartered apples on the work-bench, fed the fire till the room was light enough to read by, then sat down by the cot, and we fell to.

" What d' ye want ter talk 'bout, Hughie? "

" Oh, a good many things; when is Uncle Shim going to break out the road? "

" He wuz cal'latin' ter put the ox-team on ter-morrer, but he 'll hev ter plough out fust, 'n' then shovel through the big drifts."

" He can't do it inside of a week."

" No; he says mebbe they 'll break out a leetle ter help from the Farnsfield turnpike, but the heft on 't 'll come on him. We hain't been snowed up like this sence eighty-one, d' ye 'member, Hughie? the time Uncle Shim brought Twiddie home up the Mountin'? "

" Yes, I remember the snow had been setting in thick and heavy ever since noon, and you were worrying about Uncle Shim. I know I wanted to go down the Pent Road, Gilead way, to look for him, but you would n't hear to it."

" I never shall fergit thet storm; it seemed as ef the wind raised the roof 'long 'bout six; 'n' then I heerd Prince whinner, 'n' the fust thing I knowed, Shim wuz comin' through the shed with er big bundle in his arms, 'n' his face all sot 'n' blue. He walked right up ter the settle, 'n' laid the bundle down on 't, 'n' then, turnin' ter me, he says slow 'n' solemn like:

'Lize, what's thet the Good Book says 'bout sheep?'

"'N' I thought the frost hed struck inter his brain — I'd heerd er sech things — 'n' I acted kinder scairt (ye wuzn't in the room, 'coz ye'd gone out ter put up Prince) 'n' flew inter the pantry ter git some rum 'n' er red pepper ter fix up some hot drink ter thaw him out; but he follered me in, 'n' took hold er my arm 'n' led me back ter the settle, 'n', p'intin' ter the bundle, says agin: 'What's thet the Good Book says 'bout lambs, Lize?' 'n' I ter pacify him, says, 'Hev ye got er lamb thar, Shim?'

"'Yes,' he said, 'but what's thet the Good Book says 'bout lambs, Lize?'

"Then I knowed jest what he meant, 'n' says, '"Feed my lambs," Shim — is thet what ye're arter?'

"''Thet's what I mean, Lize,' he said, 'n' his voice sounded kinder nat'ral, 'n' I thought he wuz thawin' out, 'n' reached up ter take off his muffler, but he drawed back, 'n' p'inted ter the settle, 'n' says, ' " *Feed my lambs — feed my lambs,*" ' 'n' then went inter the shed 'n' kicked off his boots, while I went to work on thet bundle."

"And I found you at it when I came in with Uncle Shim, and we both watched you; how you screamed when you saw Twiddie sound asleep inside a blanket and the quilt and the buffalo robe peeled off of her! It woke her, and she put out her hands and began to cry, and when you took her up, she only cried the harder — "

"'N' then ye said, 'Give her ter me, Aunt Lize; I can't stand the young 'un's squallin' ' — 'n' took her in yer arms 'n' snuggled her head down onter yer shoulder, 'n' walked up 'n' down the kitchen with her, 'n' in er minute she stopped, 'n' she hain't shed many tears sence."

" Do you know who her father was, Aunt Lize?"

" No, 'n' nobody else. Shim hed never let on ter me thet his sister 'd come back ter Old Town Gilead more 'n six months 'fore he brought Twiddie here. He 'd took his oath ter her thet he 'd never tell who she wuz, — Shim's folks lived over 'n York State — 'n' fer them six months, she took in tailorin' fer the store down ter Alderbury, 'n' lived in half the house on the old Rowen place up in Old Town Gilead. She called herself ' Mis' Smith ' — but Shim knowed she wuz thar — 'n' when she found she warn't goin' ter live, she sent fer him 'n' gin him the child. In makin' out the death certif'cate, Shim hed to own up; thet 's how folks come ter know 'bout it."

"Was that her name when Uncle Shim took her?"

" Thet 's what she called herself; but her mother said her name wuz Theodory, 'n' Shim said her las' words wuz, ' My gift er God — my gift er God '; 'n' Shim thought she wuz wanderin', but he axed the minister down ter Alderbury thet he brought up fer the buryin', — ther' warn't no reg'lar fun'ral, — 'n' he said it wuz the child's name she wuz meanin', Theodory."

"You never told me this before, Aunt Lize."

" Wal — I hain't said much 'bout it. Yer Uncle wuz cut ter the quick with the disgrace, 'n' least said, soonest mended. But ye never took much notice er Twiddie anyway, Hughie; ye wuz allus er-plannin' 'n' studyin' how ye could git ter the 'Cademy, 'n' she knowed she warn't made much of."

"That's true, Aunt Lize; but she's a handy one to have about. She says she's going to keep my room clear of the litter each day after I get through the work."

"I'm glad on 't. She can't begin too soon, fer she's got ter earn her own livin' when she's of age, 'n' time flies. Did she slick up yer room ter-day?"

"Yes."

"I thought she'd ben here. I don't know what I'd er done 'thout her when ye wuz so sick — folks comin' 'n' goin', inquirin', 'n' sympathizin'. I could n't tend ter 'em all."

"Who came, Aunt Lize?"

She laughed softly. "How ye 've changed, Hughie! Three months ago, I dassen't so much ez tell ye Tag hed stuck his nose inter the door, 'n' now ye want ter know who come."

"Yes, all of them, Aunt Lize."

She laughed again. "Wal, ther' wuz Uncle Jo Cheatle, fust 'n' foremost, 'n' the Duddses over east-'ards, 'n' the new Methody minister in Scawsville, 'n' the principal down ter the 'Cademy; 'n' then ther' wuz Silas Strong, — ye 'member he done the loggin' with yer four year ago, — 'n' ther' wuz Lawyer Binin's son, he said he wuz in yer class; 'n' one day, two gals drove up, 'n' one on 'em said she wuz Linnie Lane from Scawsville; she wuz granddaughter to Elnathan Lane thet owned the saw-mill; he 'n' yer grand-father wuz great cronies — she come twice — "

"How long ago was that, Aunt Lize?"

"Oh, most er year 'n' er half. She wuz dressed up fit ter kill; hed on high heel gaiters made of kinder brown leather, 'n' er belt ter match, 'n' seemed real taken aback when Twiddie told her ye would n't see anybody but me 'n' Uncle Shim 'n' the doctor, 'n' I guess she took the hint.

"When yer Uncle wuz down ter Scawsville las' spring, he heerd 'em say she wuz goin' ter marry the mill-owner's son — some new folks thet come in last winter; 'n' t' other day when Shim went down to meet the stage, Uncle Jo told him they 'd hed the weddin' thet very day. She wuz purty ez er picter 'n' — " She interrupted herself suddenly. "My land, Hughie! Here I be keepin' ye up past ten o'clock, 'n' the kitchen fire most out, 'n' Shim ketchin' his death er cold on the settle, 'n' ye 're lookin' ez tired ez ef ye 'd ben drawed through er knot-hole, 'n' me runnin' on like the North Crick in er freshet — Anyway, them apples air all done. Ye 've strung more 'n half sence I set here."

She ministered to me as usual; but when the house was quiet, I could not sleep.

February 6th.

Clear and still and intensely cold. Every day the sun rises undimmed through the frost-filled air upon the white world of the mountains. Every day it wheels steadily higher to the north, yet the icicles still hang from the eaves, firm as rock crystal. Every day it sets, clear, undimmed, red, in the — to me — unseen west; but I see its crimson glow reflected in the southeast on Killington and Pico.

What a pleasure to have finished the lintel with all its summer fulness in such winter weather!

At last Uncle Shim has broken out the whole length of the Pent Road; he and Twiddie have come back with the mail — a letter, two books, and a long flat box.   My letter first:

MY DEAR MR. ARMSTRONG,

I see by the papers that you are snowed up in your region — trains and mails blocked, and stage-roads impassable, so I cannot depend upon these sendings to reach you to shorten some of the evening hours during this storm.

What you said in your last, about work, rings true. I've thought that myself — but perhaps I have thought it in just that way because, for several years past, I have read annually Carlyle's *Past and Present*. You will find it the very gospel of work — text, sermon, preacher, pulpit, all to your hand, and, I hope, to your mind.   I feel as if I had struck bed-rock every time I read it.

By the way, if at any time you should strike a workable "vein" in Michael Angelo and brotherhood, or in Carlyle, and wish to follow it up, just let me know.   Our Club has a good library for *use*.   We are glad to supply a box of books on demand for such mountain Patmoses as yours, — may the revelation equal St. John's! — I'll trust Uncle Jo Cheatle to handle anything under seven stone.

I don't know what you'll think of the contents of the long box — but I send it in good faith, trusting that a bowing acquaintance with Michael Angelo won't come amiss even in your high latitudes.

Greetings to Twiddie; I should like to see the child's face as you describe it while she is reading Hans Andersen by firelight — that is an added touch of phantasy. Let me know how the work comes on.

Sincerely yours,

PHILIP VANEVER.

I 've done nothing but look, and look, and look again — I can't look my fill at a large photograph of Angelo's *David;* the statue seems large enough to fill in the whole panel space above the mantel shelf. I shall carve a frame for it so soon as the spring shall come, and I find time. I know where some alders grow by the brook in the Hollow; they shall serve me for models — they belong to my shepherd lad and *his brook.*

What hands! like mine, and I never noticed my own till now. And the sinewy arm, and the turn of that nervy wrist; it knows its throwing power to the hundredth part of an inch. And the neck! like a young stag's — half the carrying force of that Goliath pebble lies in its power of backward brace. I know, for I, too, used to sling pebbles from our brook, long before I could use a gun.

Something in me throbs and lifts and quivers, the longer I look — You bedridden fool! Carve your little cones and tamarack branches; tend to your business; earn your seventy-five dollars, and worship — but don't aspire.

Twiddie eyes the Master's work with awe. Aunt Lize has n't made up her mind about it; but Uncle

6.

Shim said it looks better on the mantel-shelf than the coffin-plates!

Angelo's *David* drove the thought of Linnie Lane Somebody — I don't know her name — completely out of my mind. Why was it there anyway? It had no right. Oh, yes, in one respect, I am like the angels — there is neither marrying nor giving in marriage for the like of me, and I guess that's my only passport to angelhood. I curse inwardly when I think of it, for I know with the spring the sap will rise — and I am a man, cheated of his birthright.

Just a blaze of blue above, a dazzle of white beneath; day in, day out, a steady, stinging cold; the snow two feet deep in the woods for the choppers. Uncle Shim is driving the ox-sled down the Pent Road to Gilead with a load of bark for the tannery. The runners squeak and grate on the packed ice-snow; the vapor from the steaming hides frosts in a white mist about the rough-coated creatures. The yoke strains and creaks. I always like to hear Uncle Shim guide the oxen, by voice and thong. His drawling " A-hish, thar! " is a thing to remember.

February 28th.

Twenty-seven below this morning. The outside sounds are flat and lifeless. Aunt Lize said the kettle of water on the back of the stove skimmed over, although there was a good fire in the front of it. Tag came in with a frozen paw, and is lying before the fire near enough to scorch him in ordinary weather.

Uncle Shim has moved my cot in front of the fire-place, and I have managed to work an hour at a time by warming my hands on the soapstone Aunt Lize has wrapped in an old flannel shirt and laid on the cot beside me. The windows are white with frost an eighth of an inch in thickness; even Twiddie can't blow peep-holes through it.

To-night they are all in my room, huddled around the fire — a back-log of hard maple, the girth of a man, and red as a live coal to the heart of it; a fore-log of beech, with pine and birch piled high on top. Twiddie laughed and clapped her hands, rough and cracked with the cold, and danced up and down the room in the flare of the firelight on the walls.

A big crock of cider, with a red pepper bobbing about in it, is mulling in a corner of the hearth. Uncle Shim has filled the wooden chopping-tray with hot popped corn; — the smell of it tickles a man's nostrils in the dead of winter. Aunt Lize is trying to knit, but it's slow work, for although the heat from the fire warms our faces, when we turn, we can see the vapor of our breaths in the room.

Angelo's *David* is no longer white, but warmed and glowing in the lighted room.

When Aunt Lize had poured out the hot cider into the tin cups, and handed it around, Uncle Shim, who was scooping his with a good deal of satisfaction, said: " Come, Twiddie, give us yer Fir Tree. Kinder warms ye up jest ter hear 'bout thet party." That story is Uncle Shim's favorite. But I heard little of it, — the mind was seeing, — till she came to the last words, "*and the story is past, too — past, past — and that's the way with all stories*"; and I know that my story is past, nor Linnie Lane, nor any other girl will ever enter into it. I spoke out my thought, suddenly:

"Where's that log, Uncle Shim, that felled *me*?"

He shifted uneasily in his chair, looked helplessly at Aunt Lize, and rose to go.

"Guess I'd better look ter the stock agin 'fore I turn in, Lize — ye want more wood, Hughie?"

"Yes, I want *that* wood, Uncle Shim — no, no, sit down; I'm sane enough." My long arms pulled him back to the chair.

"What'd ye do with it, Shim?" Aunt Lize asked bravely, and the sound of her voice encouraged Uncle Shim, as it always does at all his unmarked cross-roads in life.

"I hauled it down inter the shed, Hughie — it give me the creeps ter see it layin' thar every time I went through the clearin'; 'n' so I snaked it down inter the shed, 'n' then I could n't abide ter tech the cussed thing with er decent saw 'n' axe, but — wal, ye'll think I'm 'n A. Number One fool ef I tell ye —"

"Go-ahead, Uncle Shim; I can stand anything after this, you know."

"Wal, the sight on 't sickened me, 'n' I felt so riled up, thet one day I heated the long poker white hot, 'n' went out unbeknownst ter Lize, 'n' branded the dummed log with er word —" He hesitated.

"What word, Uncle Shim?"

"Why, Shim Lewis!" exclaimed Aunt Lize, "what d' ye go keepin' sech doin's from me fer? —

Ye did n't swear inter it, did ye?" she asked anxiously.

"I ain't no blasphemer, Lize," retorted Uncle Shim with some warmth; "I jest burned it in good 'n' deep — I wuz feared ye'd smell the bark, Lize —"

"Fer the land's sakes, Shimei Lewis, WHAT? — I b'lieve ye grow long-windeder every day of yer life."

"Cain."

"My soul!" said Aunt Lize with an anxious look at me.

"'N' arter thet, I don't deny but thet I felt better, 'n' I rolled it agin the underpinnin', 'n' piled ten cords er hard wood on top on 't, 'n' I guess 't 'll be seasoned 'fore I need it."

"But I want it, well-seasoned, too."

"What ye goin' ter do with it?" Aunt Lize looked at me suspiciously.

"No harm, Aunt Lize. I've often wondered what became of it. It was a black birch, was n't it?"

"Yes, 't wuz thet big one we said we'd git out 'fore we went inter the woods east'ards — three foot through ter the butt."

"I know."

He went out. Twiddie had fallen asleep in the warmth of Aunt Lize's arms. In fact, the room was warmer, and when Uncle Shim came back, he reported clouds in the south and east; a sign on our Mountain, at this time, of milder weather.

The sun is running high; it will soon be time for sugaring. I have been making spigots for Uncle

Shim. The snow has settled and melted, and the woods ring with the axes of the choppers; — Uncle Shim has let out four acres to cut to halves. I can bear the sound better, and am busy finishing the last panel.

A stag and three does crossed the Pent Road just below the spruce-bush — lean-coated, gray, gaunt from famine. Tag was off with Uncle Shim in the woods, and they came down to the sheep-pen for a wisp of hay. I have told Twiddie to carry a big bundle of it up to the spruce-bush for them.

March 14th.

It's a grand book — that *Past and Present !* The lesson of the Past is the lesson of the Present, and Life elucidates Life. The horizon, yonder, has narrowed since reading it. I'd like to know more of Thomas Carlyle — I've struck one vein I'll work. And to have the books ! To be starved no longer, but to put out my hand and find food within reach !

Just to stand at the door of such a Life's smithy, and see the smith at work, ringing blow on blow upon the anvil, hammering, shaping, heating, welding, while the glowing metal, the showering sparks, the plunging hiss of white-hot iron, the clouds of acrid steam, the labored breath of the leathern bellows, toil, smut, grime, all intermingle — and a character is forged !

I've finished the book at twelve of the kitchen clock, and am still crying, " Give, give ! "

The panels went off to-day, after we had set them up about our fireplace to see what kind of an appear-

ance they would make in that distant city "den."
Uncle Shim and Twiddie took them down in the pung
to meet the stage.

Twiddie came home wild with excitement; she has
an order for spruce gum from Philip Vanever's friend,
the owner of the panels.   She has asked me to keep
her letters with mine — how selfish I have been!
Never a thought of Twiddie at Christmas!   I might
have made her a little box for her few treasures.   I'll
make good this neglect.

"Oh, Hughie, see, see!   It's comin' true!" she
cried, rushing into the room, her eyes blue-black
again, her cheeks red, her face alight with joy.   I
have always thought her a homely enough child, but
to-day — why, I rubbed my eyes; it was surely
Twiddie, but a glorified one; Ole Luk-oie must have
squirted some of his magic milk into my eyes.   She
flaunted the envelope before my face.

"Read, read quick, Hughie —;" and I read, of
course aloud, to please her:

"'Dear Miss Twiddie — '" she clapped her hands,
interrupting me:

"Didn't I tell ye, Hughie, ther wuz one allus begun 'Dear Miss Twiddie'?   The other, ye know, is
the 'Dear Twiddie' one.   Now begin again."

"DEAR MISS TWIDDIE,

"My friend, Mr. Vanever, told me when he came
back from Vermont, that you lived near a big spruce
wood, where you can find the real spruce gum.   I'm
so tired of the stick chewing-gum — you know the

kind, lavender-pink, with the flavoring in it — ["I don't, Hughie."] It does n't taste country enough, and I wish I might have some of the real kind. If you could get some for me, I should be glad to purchase a pound or two ; the price would be a dollar and a half a pound.

"Very soon I shall sit down before the new fire-place in my library, for I hear from your Cousin he has sent the panels, and look at the larch, its branches and catkins, its leaves and its cones showing so en-ticingly in the firelight, and then I shall want a good piece of spruce gum to chew — for when I chew real gum I make believe I live near the real woods ; the gum always tastes to me as the spruce trees smell — does it to you? Do you ever make believe things?

"I'm coming up some time to see you and the butternut tree and your Cousin Hugh and the real larches and spruces ; Mr. Vanever says he'll take me with him.   Meanwhile, I want the spruce gum, and am,

"Dear Miss Twiddie,

"Yours sincerely,

"RICHARD MALORY."

She breathed a long sigh of satisfaction and nodded gravely. "I shall write him I hain't never seen no lavender-pink chewin'-gum, 'n' thet I do make b'lieve lots er things, 'n' ef he'll tell me hisn I'll tell him mine.   Thet's fair, ain't it, Hughie?   I'm goin' ter git some now, 'n' p'r'aps he'd like some butternut meats, — 'n' oh, Hughie! s'posin' I should send him some maple sugar bimeby — would it help him ter make b'lieve some more?"

"I'm sure of it, Twiddie, but — hold on, wait a minute. Tell me if you've had a letter from that other chap lately, the one that begins, 'Dearest Theodora'?"

She hung her head. "No, I hain't, not fer — oh, ever so long."

"Do you think he has forgotten you?"

She shook her head emphatically, and ran away; but not before I saw the tears well in her eyes, and quench the glad light in them. She's a curious child. I wonder who her father was, or is — the gallows are too good for such, who leaves a girl like that unfathered.

How selfishly blind I've been! What must the child's little letters to men of Philip Vanever's stamp have been like? All that untrained speech of the Mountain caught from Aunt Lize and Uncle Shim — I'll begin to-morrow with her. I know how hard it was to break myself the first few months at the Academy, and the shame of it all. I've sweat many a time when I've blundered in class with the habitual "hain't" and "warn't," and Twiddie sha'n't suffer so for want of that training when she meets these men who say they're going to find out our Mountain another summer. She shall be fitted for a different life, even if she lives and dies on Olympus.

March 25th, and the first crow-caw. Twiddie's carrots, scraped hollow and filled with water, are suspended from strings in front of the south windows; they are so many hanging cups of feathery green.

She is going to the district school during the spring term.

Seventy-five dollars; I've said it over and over again, and failed to realize it, staring at the check — the first I've ever had. It doesn't mean anything to me — that slip of paper; if the money had been sent it would seem real. I think Aunt Lize is disappointed; she seems suspicious of it. But I know it's all right. I'll send it down by Uncle Jo Cheatle to get it cashed at Alderbury, and I'll write him a word or two and tell him there'll be no more shabby treatment of him the next time he gets up the Mountain to see me; and I'll ask him, as a favor, to take five or six dollars of the money, and buy a quarter of a hundred of white sugar, and two pounds of Uncle Shim's cut-plug — the same kind he uses — and five pounds of good coffee, and to pay for a year's subscription for the *County Granger*, and if there's any left, to put it into stamps and good letter paper and some coarse white drawing sheets and a half pound of pink gumdrops for Twiddie —

I stared so long at the check that I forgot the other letters. On opening one, I found an order from that Society, of which Philip Vanever told me, for two mahogany panels, larch design, to put into an old-fashioned cabinet top — they have forwarded the wood by express. Oh, if summer were only here, with its gifts of mullein and fern, of oak and tasselling corn and bearded wheat, of the wild grape, its leaves and tendrils — all models to my hand!

The other letter from my friend — *my friend!* I love to linger on the sound of the words. I have held it in my hand for half an hour, in lieu of the hand-clasp I'm wanting. He is sending a box of books, "incited thereto," so he writes, "by your hearty reception of Carlyle. He was so big a gun to fire at you without warning, that I had my doubts, but, anyhow, there's no smokeless powder about *him;* you always know when he has fired and what he's aiming at. We'll talk this over in the summer.

"I'm off now on a half-way-round-the-world trip to Japan, and shall be gone four months. In the interim, I send you a dozen or two friends of mine (consider this a letter of introduction, which they present), and so assure myself you will be in good company while I am gone.

"The fireplace is perfect; Dick Malory is showing it off to a half dozen people a day — he's near your age, by the way, and just out of college — and he told me yesterday he had two orders already for you, but you're not to repeat his special design. Dick is a bit selfish when it comes to a matter of art, but I honestly think it will be well to indulge him in this whim, unless you are put to it for models or designs at this season. In any case, if I may offer a word, I would put off the carvings for the orders, if possible, until Dame Nature can supply you with some new ideas, rather than repeat this charming design. People are willing to pay for originality. Of course, what I have said applies only to the fireplaces; Dick has no thought, no intention, nor could have any power, to restrict you as to other applications of the larch design.

"Tell Twiddie I'll bring her a Japanese teapot and a kimono. I have put in a story-book for her, —

Little Women; and for you, that you may travel with me, — you have the imagination for it, — two books on the little Japs, their country and their art.

"Greetings to one and all on your Mountain, and for yourself, a hearty hand-shake from

"Yours faithfully,

"PHILIP VANEVER.

"P. S.   Write to Dick if you strike a snag in the business while I am away.   P. V."

III

WHAT HAPPENED IN THE PEN

III

WHAT HAPPENED IN THE PEN

I WAS so excited last night at the thought of all the new life entering into mine that I could not sleep.

The box has come: a part of that other world coming to *me* — Lanciani, Hare, Ruskin and Vasari, Browning and Byron, Sand and Dumas.

And all these are strangers from over the sea, the names of but one or two known to me, who have come to me here on this " back farm " in New England and are to sit at my fireside and by my bedside to tell me of that other world beyond our mountains; to hearten me in my down hours and hold intimate converse with me in my midnight watches.

He said they were his *friends* — may they abide with me until they become mine. I 've gathered them all into my arms and hugged them close and hard.

That 's curious! I had forgotten Twiddie, to whom I had given her book, and, on looking around with my arms full of *my* books, I saw her sitting on the rug before the fire hugging her one, with both arms, too, as tightly as ever she could. She was singing to herself. I listened; it was that old verse she has caught from Aunt Lize.

April 5th.

I smell the breaking up of winter — snow-water settling in among masses of thawing leaves produces it.

Uncle Shim reports a great run of sap. Two Canucks have come over from the Duddses' to help him; it was too hard for a woman and child. Such leather-skinned, weasel-eyed runts, but tough as pine-knots! I had them in after supper, and the one they call "Toughheel" broke out suddenly with:

"Bah gosh!   Ah 'shamed."

"Ashamed of what, Toughheel?"

"Ah 'shamed ah mah legs"; and then the honest fellow gripped my hand, wrung it, and went out with a sob, like a child. We used to work together hauling logs and peeling bark.

Last night, about nine, I heard the roar in the Hollow. The warm sun and the two days' rain have loosened every little run, and the brook-ice has given way at last; a rushing torrent fills the narrow bed.

I, too, feel as if something had given way within me; he is only a Canuck, but his sudden word of sympathy is the first I have been willing to accept. I have played the coward and acted the fool hitherto. Henceforth no shirking, no shrinking, but "Tapferkeit" — the "deliberate valor" of Carlyle. I wish I knew German.

Toughheel — Toughheel, I have been saying over to myself, and it has come to me that it must mean Théophile.   I've been working "hammer and tongs" at the French these last two months and am ready for all the foreigners in my box.

The days are full, full to the brim, sometimes over-flowing with springtime, work, reading, studying, and just living. The song-sparrows have come, and a flock of red-winged blackbirds have found their way to the alders, so Twiddie says, and are minded to settle there.

"What's the matter, Aunt Lize?" I said, as she made her appearance at the east door this morning. She looked worried.

"Whar's Twiddie? I hain't see her fer more'n two hours. She wuz goin' ter help me set them Plymouth Rocks, 'n' then Shim wanted her to help him drop 'n' cover them early peas. I can't leave ter look her up, fer I've got ter tend ter my bread, 'n' — Thar she comes now, moonin' erlong; what *hez* got inter her, Hughie?"

"We'll find out, Aunt Lize; you try first."

Aunt Lize went to the door. "Whar ye ben, Twiddie?"

I saw Twiddie jump, hide something under her apron, then run round the house for dear life.

"Now look at thet, Hughie! What ails her, any-way; you don't s'pose thet t' other blood's showin' up arter thirteen years, do ye? 'n' the child's taken to deceivin'? She's allus ben jest ez straight ez er string." She went out, calling sharply, "Twiddie, come here."

Twiddie came, but through the kitchen, outflank-ing Aunt Lize, who had gone round the house in search of her. In a minute, Aunt Lize followed her in, her face red with vexation.

"Whar ye ben, Twiddie?" I never heard Aunt Lize speak so sharply before to the child. Twiddie turned white.

"Out in the barn."

"What fer, I'd like ter know?"

"Ter set the hens."

"Set the hens!" cried Aunt Lize, shrilly; "ye hain't set er hen this mornin', Twiddie Lewis, 'n' me wastin' my time waitin' fer ye ter do it — don't tell me." She laid her hand heavily on the child's shoulder, but at the touch Twiddie sprang backwards, planting her feet firmly, and clinching her fists.

"Don't ye tech me so!" she shouted rather than cried, in her clear, high voice. Aunt Lize looked at me in helpless amazement, and I saw her hand tremble.

"Ef ye tech me like thet, I'll tell ye lies." We both noticed that her eyelids were red and swollen, as if she had been crying, — an unusual thing for her.

I think Aunt Lize must have had a vision of "t' other blood showin' up," for I saw war to the knife written in her face, and I knew she would go to almost any length rather than give in to it. But she controlled herself well.

"Whar ye ben, Twiddie?"

"Out in the barn."

"What fer?"

"Ter set the hens."

"Wal, ye hain't sot 'em." Twiddie was silent. Aunt Lize returned to the charge.

"What ye ben doin'?"

" Layin' on the hay."

" What ye doin' layin' on the hay, I'd like to know, this time er day?"

" Makin' b'lieve." Aunt Lize looked horrified.

" Makin' b'lieve what?"

" Jo."

" Jo who?" asked Aunt Lize, faintly, her eyes like green gooseberries.

" Jo March."

" Who's Jo March, Hughie?" Aunt Lize looked at me appealingly.

" I don't know, Aunt Lize."

" 'Fore I'd make b'lieve boys," said Aunt Lize, trying scorn.

" 'T ain't boys," answered Twiddie, doggedly.

" Wal, who is *she*, then?"

" She ain't nobody, not truly." Aunt Lize began to look as if she were seeing ghosts.

" Ain't nobody! What d' ye mean by thet?"

" She's made b'lieve too; 'n' all on 'em, Amy, 'n' Meg, 'n' — Oh, I can't bear it!" She set up a howl that I could see would eventually drive Aunt Lize distracted.

" Twiddie," she said solemnly, and this time she laid her hand with her usual tenderness upon the head bowed into the gingham apron, " Twiddie, whar ye ben? can't ye tell me?"

" Ter the fun'ral — the fun'ral, 'n' Laurie — 'n' Amy warn't there, 'n' only Jo — Beth hed the fever — the fever, ye know, 'n' never got well — 'n' — oh, dear me!" Sobs shook her so that I began to fear for the child.

Aunt Lize was beaten.   She turned to me with the old worried look on her face I used to see there when she was watching me that first year and a half, and whispered:

"Ye don't think, Hughie, ther' could be anything here?"   She put her finger to her forehead significantly — "in thet t' other blood?   She's jest the age, ye know, fer it ter show.   My land!   I'm weaker 'n er rag; I guess I'll hev ter set down."

Poor Aunt Lize.   The bread began to scorch before she was fairly seated in the wooden rocking-chair; whereupon, she flew out into the kitchen like a hen with her head cut off.   Twiddie was still crying.

"Twiddie, come here," I said.   She came and stood by the cot, and I drew her hands down from her face.   But she hung her head when I tried to dry the tears on her apron.

"You don't want to trouble Aunt Lize, do you? She has enough to do and to fret her with me here; she must n't have you, too, on her hands."

She gave her head a dissenting shake.

"Won't you tell me what you were doing out in the barn?"   She found her tongue then, and the words fell over one another.

"Jest readin' *Little Women*, Hughie, out in the barn, 'n' makin' b'lieve Jo; 'n' Beth hed jest died, 'n' I fergot Aunt Lize wanted me fer the hens, 'n' I fergot 'bout Uncle Shim 'n' the peas, 'n' — ye hain't" ("Have n't, Twiddie," I corrected,) "have n't," she repeated obediently, "ye have n't" ("You, Twiddie, remember,") "you have n't read it, but when ye" ("You, Twiddie,") "you do read it, Hughie, *you'll*"

("That's right, Twiddie,") "cry too, 'n' fergit" ("No, no, — forget,") "forget things like as I do" ("As I do,") "as I do." She began to smile.

"I'll read it, Twiddie, but I won't promise to cry; there are so many real things to cry over."

"But you'll, *you'll*" ("Yes, I hear,") "think they're real, 'n' thet's all the same."

"I haven't made up my mind about that yet, Twiddie. Now run and help Aunt Lize."

Those little Japs are a wonderful people. I have finished the two books Philip Vanever sent me. I get an inward vision of them set among their plum and cherry blossoms, their miniature waterfalls and yellow chrysanthemum blooms — the blue sea encircling all.

What is the sea like, I wonder? Sometimes, when of a morning the valley of the White Branch is filled with blue-gray mist that rises and falls as if some great heart were beating beneath it, and, beyond, in the east the mountain tops heave dark blue against the horizon, with half-shut eyes I narrow my line of vision and say to myself, "That is like the sea." Sometimes I fancy I see a sail, but it is only the sunlight catching on the bellies of a flock of swallows that wheel suddenly at an acute angle in mid-air.

Sunday, May 2nd.

Cherry blossoms, chrysanthemum blooms, visions of blue seas! What joy do they give me comparable to the sight of Uncle Shim in clean shirt-sleeves sitting on the step of my east door and smoking like a blast furnace! And *I* earned the cut-plug, and with my two hands can keep up the supply, I hope indefinitely. —

I miss Twiddie. She is all day at the school, and the house is alone with me. Aunt Lize is helping Uncle Shim, for it is lambing-time, and the ewes have dropped naught but weaklings this year. Uncle Shim says it was the steady, bitter cold of February that did it — never a day on which at noon the mercury was over five above. There's one now! He's been lying in the clothes-basket by the kitchen fire since yesterday afternoon, and Aunt Lize has been feeding him. By the sound, I'll bet he's on his feet this very minute — "Ca-duc, ca-duc — "

Oh, my God! and I used to call them at the lower bars of the Old Pasture, and love to feel them crowd me with their soft, warm bodies —

At my call, the day-old idiot actually came staggering on its wabbly legs into my room, and blatted at me, and rubbed against the cot. When I put my fingers to its mouth, it took them all in, and sucked, and sucked, as if it could never have enough!

The dumb fool of a beast — no more fool than I; for I found as I watched it, that its fleece was turning all colors of the rainbow, and my cheeks were wet.

Twiddie gave me no peace until I read *Little Women;* and now, in the long May twilights, we talk together of Meg and Jo, of Beth and Amy, of Laurie — lucky dog; and the little woman on the doorstep lives in another world, and I have the key that unlocks the door by which she enters it;

if I had n't, I should be a "shut-out" as well as
a "shut-in."

What an old house this is! — Every clapboard
weather-blackened and browned. — I 've been thinking of what Philip Vanever wrote about coming up
here again in the summer; I believe he meant it.
Then Twiddie's friend, Mr. Richard Malory, whom I
call Dick Malory because I like the name and he is
near my age, wrote her he was coming too. I wish
I could make the old house beautiful for them; if
only —

I have it! I 've been hatching plans as fast as the
White Brahma, that has stolen her nest in the depths
of the spruce-bush, has been hatching her chickens
to-day, — eleven thus far, Twiddie reports.

We 've a lot of spruce boards and two or three
bundles of laths, and if I can ply Uncle Shim long
enough with cut-plug and keep him answering questions as to how he did things when he was a boy over
in York State, I 'm sure I can get something knocked
together; and if, in addition, I can rouse Aunt Lize's
enthusiasm and Twiddie's curiosity, I 'll fetch it.

We 're hard at work. Uncle Shim laid the flooring yesterday; to-day we 're finishing it. It 's just a
big latticed porch like one I found in an illustrated
book on Holland that Vanever sent me: the gable of
my end of the house extended ten feet and supported
on four stout cedar posts; a big flooring laid beneath
it on a level with my east door, and boarded up for
two feet and a half to form an enclosure. One end,

to the south, I have left open for an entrance.   Coarse lattice fills the triangle of the gable and follows down the sides of the posts.   I'm going to cover it with vines, fill the shelf around the three sides of the base-board with Aunt Lize's plants, and so make a bower of greenery for her and Twiddie to sit in, and for Philip Vanever and Dick Malory to see when they come by the end of the house.   Perhaps they will smoke a corn-cob pipe there with Uncle Shim.   I'll make some in readiness.

To-day Twiddie brought me up another order that fairly staggers me.   It is from the Society, and nothing less than the carving of sixteen oak panels, six feet by one and a half; the designs to show forth our New England spring, summer, autumn, and winter!   Four panels for each season.   Nature will have to hustle to keep up with me now.

Aunt Lize has left her work to go down with Twiddie into the hollow where the brook-alders are in blossom.   They have been gone two hours; I hope nothing has happened, the rocks and stones are so wet and slippery.   There they come now, loaded with alders, dogwood, and great branches of cherry blooms.   I see the white stars from here; they must have been up into the woods beyond the Old Pasture.

The SPRING entered my room with them and filled it.

This morning Uncle Shim came in and began to move my cot across the room.

"What are you going to do, Uncle Shim?"

"Goin' ter give ye er breath er air. I measured the door 'n' the cot yisterd'y unbeknownst ter yew, 'n' it fits ez neat ez er thole-pin — jest shaves through. See thar now!" He was triumphant, and hollered to Aunt Lize who was sorting beans in the back shed:

"Lize, come here!"

She came running into the empty room — Uncle Shim does n't often holler like that — and cried out in a frightened voice:

"Shim, whar's Hugh?"

"Here I am, Aunt Lize, I can't run far —" It was a dead failure; for Aunt Lize sat down suddenly on the platform and began to cry softly into her apron. Uncle Shim disappeared round the corner of the house, and I swallowed lumps at the rate of two-forty a minute.

So I'm out here at last. I have drawn my first full free breath.

I never knew such a last-of-May morning! There is not a living thing on or above the Mountain that is not making some kind of a noise. The lambs are bleating in the Old Pasture, and the cattle lowing at the bars — they have just been turned out; the hens are *chuck-churring* about the dung-heap behind the barn; even the old sow is grunting because she has been let out into the run.

I hear the brook in the Hollow, the plunge of the waterfall, the wind drawing through the pines, the drone of the bees in the orchard which lies like a sunrise cloud on the slope. The swallows are screaming like mad as they turn, and wheel, and dive around and over the barn; the crows are cawing in the forest, robins calling, pewees crying; now and then a song-sparrow down in the lilac-hedge along the Pent Road bursts into melody.

Uncle Shim is ploughing in the corn-patch and hollering to Prince, who is neighing like a colt; Aunt Lize is churning, and Tag's tail whacks in time to every *chug-chug* of the dasher. I'd like to yell — but it would frighten Aunt Lize.

Another day in the open. The sun warms, the air quickens, but not to work. It is enough to be here, and just look and breathe and feel — that part of me which can still feel. Curious! I have never known a spring that intensifies life like the present one; it is as if there were sensation even in my finger-nails, in my hair —

Twiddie is grubbing with might and main for clematis and hop roots; Uncle Shim has just put out a stout wild grape-stock at the entrance to the Pen, — I call it that, — and Aunt Lize is mounted on the step-ladder, staining the whole structure with butternut juice, — a good blackish brown that just matches the weather-stained timbers of the house.

How the Pen will glow in due season with its climbing nasturtium and morning glories, with its riot of color in Aunt Lize's geraniums, begonias, and fuchsias, — all her house plants massed against the greenery of grape and hop and clematis, and set in the black-brown frame of the latticed porch!

Twiddie is wild with delight, running in and out of the Pen, and Aunt Lize, who has just finished the last bit of trellis, is standing around with her apron rolled over her bare arms like an animated exclamation-point. She was preparing to do her baking when I called to her this morning to come and help, and now it is four o'clock and we 've stopped only for dinner — a makeshift one — baked potatoes and cream-pork gravy. I 've never known Aunt Lize to omit her Saturday baking before.

7 P. M.

Whew! — there 's a blue smoke of burning fat coming in from the kitchen; Aunt Lize is thumping out doughnuts in the pantry; Twiddie is paring apples for pies; Uncle Shim is down cellar fishing for a piece of corned-beef. I smell gingerbread and fresh-baked cookies.

"I say, Aunt Lize, what are you doing?"

"My Saturday bakin'; I hain't never missed one onct sence I married Shimei Lewis, 'n' I ain't goin' ter begin now. I ben foolin' round all day, 'n' all yer fol-de-rols won't feed ye over Sunday. I 'm goin' ter bile thet piece er beef ef I set up all night ter do it — Twiddie, go down cellar 'n' see what yer Uncle 's up ter; I b'lieve my soul he 's pokin' round in the salt-pork bar'l; tell him it 's in the little keg 'longside er the pertater bin."

This first day of June has brought me a letter, the paper so thin that it is like the inner skin of the young white birch; and the strange stamp! I hold it to the light, and think how it has travelled to me from out the Land of the Sun — winds, ocean, forge, fur-nace, steam, electricity, stage-coach, and Twiddie's willing feet, the bearers of this friend's greeting.

KIOTO, May 1st.

MY DEAR MR. ARMSTRONG,

A word of greeting from Fuji-san to Olympus!

I take it for granted you have read the two books, so spare you any description of this, after all is said, indescribable country; only, I want to say to you right here, that if I don't turn up in Farnsfield by August 10th, — the 1st is the limit of my Japanese trip — you may telegraph to Dick Malory to put a tracer on my track, and he'll be apt to find me among the wood-carvers of a little village just a few miles north of Kioto. How I wish you were with me! I've purchased some pieces to take home, and as for the workers in iron, and the ancient sword-guards — I'll have to bring some up to show you.

There is one I picked up for you — of the eighteenth century; it is three inches in diameter, yet it pictures a great cliff, full six hundred feet high, a river flowing swiftly at its base (you can see the current), a man poling a boat against it, inshore, and a tiny full moon of hammered silver the size of a small pea that lights water, cliff, and boatman. I've seen nothing here more wonderful in art than these.

Did the books arrive safely? And have my friends made themselves agreeable? And how is the Wood-carver of Olympus himself? I fancy, from what you wrote last, that you are impatient for the fruition of summer; yet the spring should yield you some grist for your mill. Sometime I mean to see it come there in that New England of yours.

Tell Twiddie I've bought her a kimono, and should like to see her with it on come flying down the pasture-slope as she came that day last September.

My trip is resting me by giving me new interests.

For the past three years I have had some rather large affairs on my hands — the trip to Ceylon was a business one — besides the settlement of my father's estate; it was well to narrow my life for a few months to the Japanese dimensions. But I couldn't breathe long in this atmosphere! Neither could you; and I'm going back to my own country with increased respect for its national and social ozone. I am already looking forward to August. Till then, believe me

Yours faithfully,

PHILIP VANEVER.

How such a letter heartens! A cold rain is falling; the mountains, valley, birch-hill — all blotted out. From my window I see only the spruce-bush shining gray with rain-and-mist-beaded branches. The alders are growing beneath my hand more rapidly than by the brook in the Hollow.

With the help of my dictionary I am reading *La Mare au Diable*. I wonder if George Sand is a woman? I should like to know so many things. He, or she, says "the four-lined verse" (that heads the preface) "in simple naturalness is profoundly sad."

I, too, should find it so, had I not had my two years' object-lesson in enforced idleness, and learned by experience that deprivation of labor is death, — work only, life. I have Englished poorly the little verse of old French:

> "In the sweat of thy face
> Thou shalt earn thy scant bread,
> Toil and moil with the race,
> After — feast with the *dead*."

There's Twiddie coming home from school; I can hear her singing — singing in the rain like that robin somewhere in the orchard yonder. I wish she'd choose something else, anything but that:

> "'Change me, O God! my flesh shall be
> An instrument of song to thee,
> And thou the notes inspire.'"

But I know she likes the tune; Aunt Lize used to sing her to sleep with it.

June 6th.

Such a morning! Clear, sunny sky with high white clouds rising over the timber-belt and sailing over the roof of the house, across the Hollow, and vanishing behind the birch-hill. Every grass-blade and leaf glittering with raindrops; robins, swallows, bluebirds are drunk with the joy of life.

While waiting for Uncle Shim to move my cot out into the Pen, I have been looking at my David, and thinking what George Sand said on the next page or two of that wonderful preface: "No, we have not to do with death, but with life." And a little farther on, it is said of the true artist: "His aim ought to be to make people love the objects of his solicitude, and, upon occasion, I should not reproach him for embellishing them a little. — Art is not a study of positive reality, but the search for ideal truth."

I, even I, Hugh Armstrong, such as I am, can understand *that*. I have looked at my Shepherd David, and it has been revealed to me by something not of the marble, but in it. Something, too, is being cut into my alders and dogwood, that shows the mounting spring joy in every living thing; — it does not detract from the truth of reality, it but enhances it. If — if —

"Ye ready, Hughie?"

"Uncle Shim, can't we get the work-bench out into the Pen?"

"Jest ez ye say, Hughie; I'll have ter git Lize ter help h'ist it through the door."

"Where is Aunt Lize?"

"Makin' scarecrows fer the corn-patch; the corn's jest prickin' through, 'n' them thieves hez their weather-eye open every time, — durn 'em."

I like to see Uncle Shim cross, he is so shiftless about it; his "durn 'em" would n't scare a one-eyed crow.

I work daily now in the Pen, while this settled June weather lasts. It seems as if I could hear things grow; there is such a thrusting, pushing, upreaching, unfolding, expanding process going on about me. The new pine tops grow green, green, greener; the new spruce tips thick, thick, thicker; the corn-stalks high, high, higher; the tasselled birch on the oak panel more and more satisfactory — but in the midst of it all, I smell the spruces in the sun, and something grips me at thought of the little fir tree and the "story that is past." Perhaps I've thought more of it because Twiddie's teacher is coming up the Mountain to stay over Sunday with us. Aunt Lize asked me if I minded. At first I felt like begging off, but the look on Twiddie's face warned me in time. It's the first time I've had to face a girl since this happened.

I dread her coming; I dread to see a girl anyway.
Sometimes I wish, almost, I had n't read *The Devil's
Pool* — I fear to be bedevilled, for it 's the flood life-
tide of the year, and I 'm human.

Monday.

I need n't have been such a coward!   I 'm glad she
came, and I hope she 'll come again.   She 's a quiet
girl, wears eye-glasses; she was graduated from the
Academy last year.   She says Twiddie is the smartest
child in the school.   She did n't seem to notice my
legs, or act as if anything was the matter with me.

Twiddie and I have struck a bargain.   She asked
me the other day if I would n't teach her French;
— French and Twiddie!   I never thought of that
combination.

"Why, Twiddie?" I asked.

"Oh, 'coz."

"Now, Twiddie, tell me why."

"You won't tell?"

"Never; here 's my hand on it."

She took it, straightened out each of my long fingers, crooked them again, then doubled my fist and
suddenly squeezed it between her hands.   She looked
at me with shining eyes, and a rich red was in her
cheeks.

"'Coz" ("Because, Twiddie,") "because I 'm goin'
off some day."

"Off where?   To the Canuck country where Toughheel came from?"

"Stop teasin', Hughie."   She turned away with

a pout — positively, Twiddie is growing pretty. I
caught her hand, and tried to pull her down beside
me, but she drew back, and, pointing over to the
mountains, said earnestly:

" Over there, Hughie, to see the places I read
about in *Hans Andersen* and *Little Women*, where
Amy went; I make b'lieve I go every night, 'n' now
the folks are beginning to come again in the stage
from Alderbury, it seems real. I wait after school
every day now, 'n' make b'lieve I 'm goin' off in the
stage; — don't you remember 'bout the princess in
Hans Andersen? 'n' how Amy 'n' her folks talked
French over there? — " she pointed again beyond
the mountains — " in Europe, you know. I want to
learn; Jo did n't, but she was awful sorry afterwards.
Won't you learn me, Hughie? "

" Yes, I 'll *teach* you, Twiddie, if you 'll learn to
speak English first — yes, I know you 've tried;
you 're doing well too. Now, that 's a fair trade,
is n't it? "

" You don't think Aunt Lize would mind, Hughie,
if I speak different from her? "

" Bless your heart, no, Twiddie; only, you 're never
to notice how Aunt Lize and Uncle Shim speak.
Ladies never do that, and I take it that is what
you 're going to try to be — like Jo and Amy? " She
nodded emphatically.

" Well, then, Lady Twiddie — " But she interrupted me:

" Lady Theodora, Hughie; that 's what I make
b'lieve." I humored her.

" Lady Theodora then, let 's begin to-night. I 'll

8

give you a French verb to learn, and you stop saying
'learn' for teach, and 'ter' for to, and don't drop
your 'g's,' and don't say ''coz' and—"

"I 'll try *to*, Hughie," she interrupted, laughing
merrily, "but 't is n't fair to make me do all that
fer" ("For, Twiddie,") "for jest—I mean just,—one
verb."

"No more it is n't, Lady Theodora." Hearing
that, she grew so radiant that I was minded to gaze
after her as she ran out of the Pen and around the
house, Tag barking at her bare heels. How she
is shooting up! As slim as a willow-shoot. She's
getting too big to run barefoot like that and swing
on the butternut tree when the stage goes by. I
must speak to Aunt Lize about it.

The four spring panels were sent to the Society
last week. I wonder whose they are to be? I'm
behindhand with my work; there are the two fireplaces for November.

I have had word to-day that I need send no more
designs on approval; this leaves me free hand and
eases me up a bit.

Aunt Lize and Twiddie are off to a swamp down
the Pent Road, Gilead way; it lies in the corner of a
pasture where the brook leaves the Hollow, and some
back water sets in there. I told them they would
find it by the two black ash trees that grow by the
fence. The great blue-flag is found there three and
four feet high. I was bound to get my swamp
somehow into the panels,—this design will fill one
nobly.

The wheat in the roadside-field by Farnsfield will come later, and August will bring the larger brakes and the Canada thistles. So, in time, I shall manage to have them all for the panels — swamp and mountain-slope, roadside-field and thicket. Who, who is to see it all? It is getting to be a labor of love. I shall make bold when I shall have finished the sixteen panels to ask the Society; they have given me until February.

July 4th.

I sent down by Uncle Jo Cheatle to bring up some torpedoes and fire-crackers for Twiddie to celebrate — for me, too. I love it — have always loved it. After I was a youngster of five, Uncle Shim and Aunt Lize always made a bonfire on the Mountain for me; folks used to say they could see its light for miles. I've asked them to make one to-night. Uncle Shim has fastened grandfather's old flag to the post of the Pen. — I wish I could have voted once for president; I should feel more of a man for having done so. An American, his mark; that's what an honest presidential vote should be to a man.

July 18th.

Something was in the wind; I knew it as I sat working in the Pen. I heard Tag barking furiously, and Twiddie *hoo-hooing* wildly from the clearing; in a minute the two came racing around the corner of the house. Twiddie flung herself full-length on the grass before the Pen, and Tag flopped, panting, beside her. I waited till she should get her breath.

The shadows were growing long and I laid aside my tools; I had been at work all day like a beaver with my chips. The Pen is looking as I hoped it might; hops and clematis are flourishing, and nasturtiums and morning-glories are in full bloom. It is good to see Aunt Lize's joy in it.

Finally, Twiddie sat up facing me, her knees drawn up to her chin, her hands clasping them.

"It's all coming true, Hughie," she said dreamily.

"What!   More folks?"

She nodded.   "Real ones this time, though."

"Tell me about them, Twiddie."

"I will if you'll b'lieve me, Hughie."

"Believe you!   Every word.   Did n't your letters come true?"   She gave me a grateful look.   Suddenly, at some thought, her face grew scarlet and she hung her head.

"I disobeyed you and Aunt Lize."   I could scarcely hear her.

"Come, speak up, Twiddie; out with it."

"You won't be mad, Hughie?"

"I? — no; what should I be mad about?"

"I'd took off my shoes 'n' stockings — I hate 'em so!   I only wear 'em to please you 'n' Aunt Lize — 'n' was swinging on the butternut tree waiting for the stage."

"Oh, Twiddie, they did n't see you up there with your long, bare legs!"

She nodded, but looked so shamefacedly penitent that I had to laugh.   At that she brightened up a bit.   "Yes, I was, 'n' they look different than they did, 'coz, ye see" (in her excitement her English was

going all to the dogs, but I did n't correct her, thinking the story was of more importance), " I hain't gone
barefoot for so long thet the tan hez come off 'n' left
'em awful white, 'n' Uncle Jo 's got er new leader,
'n' I never thought 'bout my legs swingin' so fast 'n'
they bein' so white, 'n' all of er sudden, when the new
leader see 'em, jest ez Uncle Jo reined up under the
tree, he give sech er jump thet he went clean over
the traces, 'n' Uncle Jo hollered at me awful, 'n' all
the ladies —"

" What — ladies ? "

" Yes, *ladies*, real ones, this time.   They called ter
me ter git down, 'n' I dropped right off the tree 'thout
stopping to swing down by my hands, 'n' fell in the
grass, 'n' one on 'em said I must be hurt, 'n' they all
got out while Uncle Jo wuz fixin' the leader, 'n' — Oh,
Hughie ! ef ye could jest see *her !* "

" Her — who ? "

" The one thet thought I wuz hurt — but I wuz n't.
She saw the box, too, 'n' asked who made it ? 'n' I
told 'bout the things ye make.   They all talk so different, Hughie, more like you do, 'n' she —"

" Who, Twiddie ? "

" The one thet said it wuz charmin', 'n' 'nother
said it wuz 'n idea — no, 't warn't thet —"

" Ideal ? "

" Yes, thet 's it, 'n' one er the gentlemen —"

" Gentlemen, Twiddie, and you in your bare legs ! "

" I never 'll do it again, Hughie, never — but they
did n't seem to mind, 'coz I squatted on the ground
'n' tried ter hide 'em.   They jest talked 'bout the
scen'ry, 'n' one on 'em said it made him think of —

of — I can't remember where 't wuz; 'n' one on 'em gave Uncle Jo er cigar 'n' they all lighted theirs, but first they asked the ladies if they might, — think er thet, Hughie! jest ez ef they wuz princesses, 'n' all the rest wuz swineherds jest like in *Hans Andersen*, ye know."

"What did the ladies say?"

" Oh, they wuz willin'; they said they'd ride inside 'n' leave 'em the top all ter themselves, 'n' one er the gentlemen — the one thet give Uncle Jo the cigar — came up ter where the ladies wuz all stan'in' 'bout me, 'n' said, 'Come, Madeline, give me a chance ter look at thet box,' 'n' then he see me close to, 'n' took off his hat, Hughie! — his *hat*, quick, so quick, 'n' laughed and said, 'By Jove, it's Twiddie!' 'n' held out his hand; 'n' I wuz 'shamed, 'n' 'fraid he'd pull me up, 'n' I did n't want him ter see me bare-legged, so I jest squatted harder, 'n' made b'lieve I did n't see him."

" Oh, Twiddie! "

" 'N' then they all laughed, 'n' he put his hand under my chin and made me look up, 'n' said, 'Is n't this Miss Twiddie Lewis, who sent me the spruce gum?' 'n' — 'n' — Oh, Hughie! — "

I saw her chest begin to heave, and I felt for the child. "What did you say, Twiddie?"

" *I said I wuz n't.*"

"Why, Twiddie Lewis! What will Aunt Lize say?"

She sprang up, and I saw her set her teeth in brave effort to keep back the tears; then suddenly the scarlet flame leaped upon her throat and ran over neck, face, temples to the roots of her hair, and she cried out shrilly, stamping her foot:

"I did n't lie! I ain't Twiddie Lewis — I ain't, I *ain't!* I heard you 'n' Aunt Lize talkin' thet night ye thought I wuz ter sleep — I 'm Theodora Somebody, 'n' ye don't know who, 'n' Aunt Lize, nor Uncle Shim, nor nobody knows who, 'n' teacher licked er boy fer twittin' me of it last week — 'n' I ain't er-goin' ter school any more, 'n' I ain't er-goin' down ter see the stage — "

She was sobbing uncontrollably, and I do hate a scene.

"Twiddie, come here." But she flung herself down upon the grass again full-length and sobbed face downwards into it. Tag whined and nosed her. I thought, after all, it was better to let her have her cry out. Poor little Twiddie! I 'm the shut-in and she 's the shut-out; — which is worse? I 'd like to thrash that boy within an inch of his life.

July 19th.

She cried herself out yesterday afternoon, and then I sent her down into the Hollow to get some ferns, and to wash her face in the cold water of the pool.

After supper, while Aunt Lize and Uncle Shim were salting the sheep in the Old Pasture, she sat on the cot beside me — we were out in the Pen — and we talked together (it did us both good) — I the shut-in, a man who has known suffering for two years, and must live with it the rest of his life, to a child — hardly a child any longer — the shut-out, who is just entering into the same heritage of suffering, only with a difference.

Yes, it must have been Dick Malory. I wish he had n't passed me by. I asked Twiddie if he replied to her, and she said he did not, but that he turned away and got up on the seat beside Uncle Jo, and she heard him ask him something, and Uncle Jo said, " Yes, thet 's her, thet 's Twiddie ; " and she had not dared to look up again, nor to get up in order to run away, because of her bare legs ; so sat there in her shame and misery till the stage had disappeared. I am glad school is over. She is trying so hard with the English, and takes to French like a duck to water.

July 20th.

Twiddie came rushing in early this afternoon with a letter, the one I had been looking for from the Society for a week past. I had proved to her that all her trouble came to her the other day through her diso-bedience, — and the bare legs. She was sensible enough, and offered to go down as usual for the mail. Now she has come back with the astounding announce-ment that they are all coming up here to-morrow, Uncle Jo says, and we must be ready for them ; — coming up Gilead way to see the view, and so on through the clearing and down over the Mountain, and back to Alderbury !

This thing has never happened before. They have chartered the Hornet, and Uncle Jo is to drive ; Silas Strong is to take his place for the day, and carry the mail and passengers in the big, three-seated wagon.

To see the Hornet again! To hear the horn! To see people from that other world — to touch Life again in its fulness to others, real men, real women! My hand shakes; I can't work. I am as excited as Aunt Lize and Twiddie, but I keep it under, and, as a result, am less useful.

We have been concocting ways and means. It's my house, and I'm not going to act the coward this time. Aunt Lize says they ought to have a treat, and I say so too; a steep climb of five miles from Gilead on a hot July day is no fool of a job for man or beast.

Uncle Jo asked Twiddie to come down and open the first bars below the house; it's no place to stop, for there's a bad pitch there; — and then she is to ride up on the rack for a treat.

She and Aunt Lize are out picking late wood-strawberries; the ground, they say, is covered with them up near the timber line; there is plenty of cream, and Aunt Lize is going to make some of her soft, sugar cookies. I'm glad we can have all the white sugar we need. Twiddie has swept the Pen as clean as a whistle, and I'm going to stay inside and leave it clear for them to sit in and eat their strawberries; the sun turns early, and the shade in the south dooryard is deep.

July 21st.

Oh, the horn! Uncle Jo never blew such a blast before, and never will again. How it rang among the heights, repeating itself for full twenty seconds, the last faint echo seeming to die away somewhere near Killington and Pico; at the sound, every fibre of me thrilled with sick, excited longing.

I could see the old Hornet from the south window, the horses straining to that last pitch, and Twiddie at the bars; the men were walking up; I saw the movement of the green and white parasols of the women on top. As they drew nearer, I heard them talking — the sound carries at this height — and exclaim at the view, and at last cry out when they caught sight of the Pen and all its glowing mass of color. They were within a few hundred feet of the house when I caught the words from Uncle Jo:

"Yes, thet's Hughie's work; purty good fer er cripple, hey?"

Then a woman's voice — such a voice! do women of that other world yonder often have such voices? —

"I wonder if he has a soul commensurate with such beautiful expression?"

Dick Malory — I knew it was he — came into the yard first, where Aunt Lize was standing in the shade, and, behold! Twiddie was with him, laughing gleefully. And then Uncle Jo pulled up, and called out:

"Where's Hughie? we've come ter see Hughie," and Twiddie answered joyfully:

"In here," and brought him in, while Uncle Shim tended to the horses and the men helped the ladies down from the top — four of them, gay, bright, smiling women. They were chatting with Aunt Lize as if they had always known her, and all the time Uncle Jo was talking, my ears were strained to catch that voice. Now and then I heard it — Aunt Lize was asking them where they came from, how they got here, how long they were going to stay; she was in her glory, but I was sorry, knowing they came from that other world which is unused to ours of the Mountain.

Somehow, within a few minutes, — I don't know how it came about, — the other three men were all in with me, and Dick Malory was gripping my hand, and telling me of his friendship with Philip Vanever. He's my age nearly; but I felt, as I looked at him and heard him praise my friend, of another and an older generation. But the blue eyes, the hearty way with him, the straight back, square shoulders, and clean length of shank! He was good to look upon as a man.

Then Uncle Shim came in and gave me away, saying: "Ye don't seem ter be in yer right place here, Hughie; the Pen looks kinder lonesome 'thout ye."

"But, Uncle Shim, we planned to have the ladies eat in there, you know."

For answer, Dick Malory laid his hand upon the cot to help Uncle Shim move me out, and, looking to the deep shade of the elms and maples in the dooryard, I saw *her* for the first time. She was helping Twiddie set out the old, two-leaved cherry table with saucers and the best spoons, the glass jug of cream, and my grandmother's willow-tree bowl of blue crockery heaped to the brim with the wood-strawberries. Twiddie was setting on a plate of the sugar cookies when Aunt Lize said:

"Git the six-quart pail, Twiddie, 'n' go down ter the spring fer some good cold water."

Hearing that, Dick Malory called out: "Madeline, come here, and keep Mr. Armstrong company. This is my cousin, Miss Cope," he said, as she came into the Pen; "I'm going with Miss Twiddie to the spring," and he was off with a bound that I, too, knew of old.

July 22nd, 4 A.M.

It is light, but the sun is not yet over the mountains; it will rise to-day for me out of a new heaven upon a new earth. I am still here in the Pen; the night was so hot I stayed out for air. I could n't sleep, and have been watching for the dawn.

She is so different from the others; even I, unused as I am to many women, can see that. She is neither a shut-in nor a shut-out, but carries her head in a free, glad, uplifted way, like a red deer breaking from cover at sunrise. When she spoke, she was the voice; when she looked, the eyes spoke for her, and when she smiled, the face grew radiant, like the eastern horizon as I write. What is it that illumines a human face like that?

She is tall, too; I calculated swiftly as she stooped to enter the Pen, that the dark head would come a good bit above my shoulder, and I am six foot one.

How interested she was in the work! The others exclaimed over the summer panels I have finished; she said never a word, but just came back to them again and again, as if she could not look her fill. Twiddie took her in to see the David; "An old friend of mine," she told me afterwards; — and there on the shelf she found the books, and lingered within, handling them; and I knew by her manner with them that she, too, cared as I care. I wish I might have talked with her of them. But the time sped; there was the Hollow to see, and the sheep and lambs in the Old Pasture, and the north path through the forest-belt — a trail I blazed four years ago when I went into the woods with Toughheel; it is green twilight there even in the brightest summer day. Then Twiddie must needs beg Aunt Lize to let her show them the garret — her play-room — with the loom and cheese-press, the wheels and reels; and of that neither Dick Malory nor she could have enough.

While they were rummaging about, I was left with the old yellow Hornet for company. Uncle Shim had taken out the four horses to bait and water, and he and Uncle Jo were smoking in the cart-shed. — I have seen it standing like that so many times before the tavern at Alderbury; but then it was empty. Now, as I looked, it was filled with memories of my boyhood; inside, outside, baggage-rack, driver's seat — everything taken by a tow-haired, barefooted boy, who used to watch for its coming down by the butternut tree, and dream of the time when it should take him away from the Mountain and its pent life.

They were with us three hours. When they left, Dick Malory said he would blow the horn once in the clearing, and two or three times down the Pent Road. I strained my ears the last time — they were at the butternut tree, so Twiddie told me afterwards; she had ridden down with them — and as I caught the last echo, a longing came upon me unlike anything I have ever felt.

But I have touched her hand. She came the last to me to say good-by. I was awkward enough, for I not only clasped the hand held out to me, but, having it once within my palm, looked long at the slim, white fingers, that could give pressure for pressure — at the nails, the markings, and wondered at the delicate strength. When I looked up, a light red had mounted into the clear white of her cheek; but she smiled down upon me so womanly-kindly! — she is no longer a girl, but a woman of Philip Vanever's age, with a young grace of figure, and a child's heart shining out of her dark eyes. — To work, to work!

August 1st.

How full my life is — of summer, of work, of thoughts, of friends.

August 6th.

Aunt Lize says that Dick Malory told her that they were on a coaching trip through the Green Mountains, and had been stopping at Wynnegate Inn for a week; that he had proposed that they charter the Hornet for a two days' trip over the Mountain and take in Olympus on the way. Philip Vanever had told him about the views; and, moreover, he wanted to thank me for the fireplace carvings. So she is his cousin.

A hot haze covers the mountains and the valley, limiting the range of vision; but the inner eye's horizon line has widened since July.

Madeline, Madeline Cope; I say it softly to myself while at work, and when Aunt Lize and Twiddie are up in the pasture picking blackberries, and the house is empty save for the buzzing of a blue-bottle, I speak it aloud, and the sound of my own voice lingering on the name soothes for a time, then inspires me to new effort. Why, I cannot say.

I feel as if all the world had come to my door that day.   There was one among them, a professor — Waldort, if I caught the name — from one of the great California universities; as tall as I, fair-haired, ruddy-skinned, blue-eyed — a geologist.   I liked the man and had the curiosity to ask him how he had found his way to our mountain-corner of New England; and I liked his answer:

"I have found that a man who travels on a trunk line does not know the American people, and I have learned that it is not in the highways, but in the by-ways, one gets beneath the surface; that is why I have found out this New England corner of yours."

That was two weeks ago.   Yesterday I had a letter from him ; — what am I that all this should come to me ? I, who have cursed God, and man in his likeness?

I like to think of filling these pages, that have been a reflection of my own life, with the thoughts of others as they express themselves to me in these rare letters that find their way up here.   It's pleasant reading, and lets in daylight.

OAKLAND, CALIFORNIA, August 5th.

DEAR ARMSTRONG,

I am sending you a box of books that, I hope, will compel you to think oftener of me than would

otherwise be the case.   You know I am your debtor
for an Olympian hour or two on that perfect midsummer day.

I'm still pig-headed enough at thirty-six to believe
that every new man I meet — and like — is just as
interested in the rock-ribs and outcrops and vein-
ings of this earth-mother of ours as I am — forgetting that all men were not born in the " diggings ";
for I am a miner's son, a Californian by birth, and have
had among other things " stones for bread." Your
trade is akin to mine; your trees break rock in
the subsoil; — hence the kind of books I have sent
you.

Will you remember me to all your people? and
say to Mrs. Lewis, please, that throughout the length
and breadth of this big, Nature's prodigal of a state
of ours, there are no strawberries that can compare in
flavor with those delicate wood waifs to which I paid
natural homage that day.

Across continent greetings from,

Yours sincerely,

FRANZ WALDORT.

They went down for the box after chores were
finished, and on their return brought the whole round
earth into my room and my life.

There they lie on the bench, — six noble volumes
of Élisée Reclus's geographical works, and two of the
professor's on the mineralogy of the Pacific Slope.
Strange!   He, a breaker of stones, to me, a whittler
in wood.

Oh, the world beyond my Mountain is not so wide
after all!   And what a world it is!

September 18th.

I was interrupted in my last entry by a voice answering Twiddie's joyful outcry — Philip Vanever's!

A month has passed since then. What a month! He was with me as guest in my own house for a week, and the close companionship of such a man has been a revelation; we are Hugh and Philip for each other now.

It came about in the silences of the night, when the smoke from our corn-cob pipes curled about the roof-timbers of the Pen, the moon rose behind Killington, and the valley in the August haze looked, so he told me, like a southern sea.

It came in the brief speech of the morning, when the Pen opened its flowers to the kindling eastern light, and the dew lay heavy on grass and corn. We had our breakfast together on the bench in the Pen, — blackberries and cream, coffee and Aunt Lize's good Johnny-cake, and for a top-off, buckwheat flap-jacks and maple syrup.

It came in the hot noons, when he lay beneath the maples in the deep shade of the dooryard, and Twiddie, in her blue and white kimono, read to us his favorites of the Andersen tales — "The Fir Tree," "The Wild Swans," "The Old House," and "The Storks."

Dick Malory, too, came up for a few days' trout-fishing — I might say, with Twiddie; for they were off together with a basket of lunch by the day, and Twiddie showed him all my haunts, — the deep pool in the heart of the North Creek glen, where, beneath the shade of a big rock overhung with alders, I have

found a two-pounder, with his nose rubbing the rock
shiny; the trail up the Hollow, where the brook picks
its way among the moss-covered boulders, that
nourish in their crevices the fronded ferns, to a little
run that gets a fair start away from the rocks and
whirls into a sand-pocket across which lies the trunk
of a monster pine. Just there the water will dartle
suddenly; — there's a flash of silver, a spurt for the
little run — where am I?

He also satisfied me in regard to himself; as he
said, "opened the windows a little."

One night when all were gone to bed and the moonlight transfused the crowding birches on the face of
the hill over against the Hollow, we spoke of Madeline Cope. I asked him if he knew Dick Malory's
cousin, the one who was with him on the coaching-
trip.

"You mean Madeline Cope?"

"Yes."

"Yes, I've known her for five years — that is,
off and on. She is a Baltimore woman; Dick's
mother and hers were sisters, both of them Maryland
women, and my father's aunt was their grandmother.
Now, make what you can of that relation. We claim
a distant cousinship — that's safe under the circumstances. I haven't seen her for a year."

"She's about your age, isn't she?"

"Why? does she look it, do you think?"

"No — but she's different from a girl."

"She's a month or two younger than I; — interested in the carving, wasn't she?"

"I'm sure of it, but she did n't say anything about it."

He knocked the ashes from his pipe and refilled it before he answered:

"That's like Madeline. She's demonstrative enough over anything that pleases her fancy merely; but let her be really touched, and all the king's horses and all the king's men can't draw an expression from her."

"But I know she liked them," I persisted.

"Why should n't she, Hugh? She'd have to be blind not to see the beauty of them, and if ever a woman had an artist's eye, true for line, and appreciative of color, she has. By the way, have you chosen your designs for the new fireplaces?"

It is pleasant for a man to hear words of praise for his work from the lips of his friend, and, somehow, he switched me off the track, and I heard no more of Madeline Cope — and I would so gladly have heard more!

The fall rains have set in early. Uncle Shim is behindhand about getting in the corn, and Aunt Lize is fretting for fear of mildew in the shocks.

It is so dark, so overcast, that I have had to lay aside my work, the designs for the autumn panels — oak branches, corn in the ear, vines of the hop and wild grape.

Aunt Lize came in a few minutes ago; I knew by the way she sat down in the old rocker she was out of sorts, discouraged. I don't blame her, Uncle Shim is so shiftless.

" What ye doin' in the dark, Hughie? "

" Thinking thunks, Aunt Lize," I answered, knowing that my announcement of this occupation gener-
ally put her to rights.   Not so to-day.

" I wish ye 'd speak ter yer Uncle," — she broke
out fretfully — " he hain't no notion 'bout seasons 'n'
their doin's; he 's allus queer 'bout some things, 'n'
it 's more 'n flesh 'n' blood can stan'."

" What 's the matter, Aunt Lize?   He 's churning
now, I hear him out in the shed; is n't it pretty late
in the afternoon for that? "

" Oh, yes, he 's churnin'," repeated Aunt Lize with
all the scorn of which her voice is capable; " he 's
churnin' fer the second time ter-day."

" How does that happen? "

" Jest ez everything happens in this house —
through clear, downright shif'lessness.   Ef he wuz
er woman, I 'd call him er slattern, but he hain't jest
thet nuther; he 's clean 'nough, Shim is, 'n' allus
changes his shirt 'n' overalls 'n' boots when he sets
out ter churn; — but this mornin' — I dunno but
't wuz part my fault — "

Aunt Lize was weakening; that 's the way she
always does when she is finding fault with Uncle Shim
— ends by laying all the blame on herself.   It riles
me.   I 'm afraid I spoke up pretty sharp:

"What's he churning for anyway at this time of
day?   He 's going it two-forty a minute — " Aunt
Lize began to chuckle, then to shake, and at last
she laughed so hard that she had to wipe the tears
away with her apron before she could speak.

" Ef ye 'd only seen him, Hughie, ye 'd carry the

sight with ye ter yer dyin' day. My senses! I wished I'd hed one er them new-fangled ambrotype boxes thet the folks hed up here, thet ketched me 'n' Twiddie while we wuz talkin', quicker 'n' ye can say Jack Robinson." She began to laugh again.

"He wuz out in the shed where he allus sets, ye know; I'd skum half the cream 'n' hed er big mess, 'bout six quarts, 'n' he wuz churnin' erway kinder half 'n' half, thinkin' the Lord knows what; — I ain't blasphemin' nuther, fer Shim hez got the slowest workin' mind fer er man I ever come ercross; 'n' I wuz stewin' 'bout the corn mildewin', 'n' s'posed he wuz lis'ning. Purty soon, I heerd er cur'ous noise, 'n' the kitchen door bein' open, I jest laid my eye ter the crack 'thout stoppin' jawin', 'n' thar he sot — both han's graspin' the dasher, goin' it chuggety-chug, 'n' his two eyes raised e'en-a-most heavenwards ter the shed timbers, 'n' his old cowhide boots, he'd fergot ter change with his shirt, all flooded ter the vampin' with my good cream — 'n' most ter butter too!" I began to laugh immoderately.

"What did you say, Aunt Lize?"

"Say? — nothin'; I jest let him keep thet dasher er-goin' till he come to, 'n' found he'd somehow managed ter git the bottom out er the churn. *He* said 't hed warped — but 't warn't no sech thing. Six quarts er good thick cream! I can't git er cent erhead ef I git up fore cock-crow ter do it."

Poor Aunt Lize. But I could see she felt better for the telling of her trial. She began to rock comfortably.

"Let's make b'lieve, Aunt Lize, as Twiddie does.

What would you like most to have in all the world if you could?"

"Me, Hughie? I hain't no time ter make b'lieve; but I guess ye know the fust thing I 'd want."

"What's that?" She leaned over and stroked my tumbled hair with her hard, work-worn hand. The hair caught on the roughened skin.

"Guess it 's most time fer barberin', ain't it, Hughie?" There was a quaver in her voice, but her hand went back and forth, over and around, smoothing my hair.

"It 's about a year ago you barbered, Aunt Lize; do you remember?"

"I hain't fergot; ye 've changed er sight sence then."

I laughed. "Grown in grace, have I?"

She nodded emphatically. "Ye 'member he come jest ez I 'd finished?"

"I shan't ever forget *that*."

"It 's them folks hez changed ye, Hughie; give ye new life, 'n' put new marrer inter yer bones — "

"Only so far," I interrupted, pointing to the dead end of me; then, seeing the look on Aunt Lize's face, I could have kicked myself for having shown the white feather. "Not the new people wholly; *you* trusted me first with the darning-needle, — do you remember? — and Twiddie forgot to be afraid of me. No, no, Aunt Lize — you and Twiddie first."

For answer her hand rested on my head for a moment, then the sound of Uncle Shim's dasher suddenly ceased. Aunt Lize flew up.

"I must go — the butter's come! quicker 'n it ever

did before; I guess thet scoldin' did n't hender it any."

October.

Work fills the seven hours of daylight out of the ten; the rest I give to reading. Twiddie has been out gathering butternuts; Uncle Shim is just emptying the bushel basket on the garret floor overhead. How that sound stirs every fibre of my Past! — Sometimes I think I 've conquered; then, of a sudden, a sound like that! — and I 'm undone again.

The barberry bush lives once a year in its color. How it glows against the big, gray boulder that crops out just above the hemlocks! I wish it might lend itself to wood and tools — but it does n't, I 've tried it.

November.

The fireplace panels are off, and I 'm having a vacation of a week after my fall working-term. I 'm tired, and rest by looking at my David and the iron sword-guard; by reading of the lands till now unknown to me, of other races, their development dependent upon the physiography of their habitat, their differentiation and points of contact. It is wonderful what these volumes of Réclus have opened up to me.

On a bitter night like this I am far away in the lotus-land of India; in the few days of Indian summer, I roamed the Canadian forests and rivers with the old French voyageurs.

The mind is unfettered, reading so; — the bound body forgotten, tenantless when its in-dweller roams.

Two checks for seventy-five each have come this week. We have decided to lift the mortgage little by little; when the whole nine hundred shall have been paid off, we can draw a free breath — and celebrate Thanksgiving in old style.

In part, this is " making believe," like Twiddie, for how do I know that work will be given me? It has been just a run of luck thus far.

Day before Thanksgiving. — How I 've laughed over the revolt of Aunt Lize; laughed and —

Yesterday afternoon at dusk I heard a wild commotion in the hen-house. Afterward Twiddie rushed in with my supper — a bowl of fresh hulled-corn and milk — nearly spilling it in her flutter, and then tore out again, slamming the door behind her; that means I am shut out from something. But I would n't give her the satisfaction of asking her a question ; if I wait long enough, she 'll always tell.

But she did n't! I read till ten o'clock, then I rapped pretty sharply with my crook on the wall, and Uncle Shim instead of Aunt Lize appeared to settle me for the night.

" Halloo, Uncle Shim; what 's up? "

" Yer aunt 's got er spell, Hughie."

" What kind? "

"Oh, fixin' things."

"What things? "

" Oh, kinder gin'ral mussin'."

"Come, Uncle Shim, out with it."

"I dassen't, Hughie, I gin my word."

"What was the trouble in the hen-house last night — skunks?"

"No — 't warn't er skunk."

"Fox?"

"No — can't say ez 't wuz er fox."

"Uncle Shim, I'll never knit you another pair of double soles to go stocking-feet in if you don't tell me what Aunt Lize is up to."

"I dassen't, Hughie ; I gin my word."

"Tell Twiddie to come here."

"She's jest gone up ter bed, Hughie."

"What! without saying good-night to me? — She never does that."

"Guess she dassen't nuther; she gin her word ter Lize."

"Shim Lewis!" called Aunt Lize from the pantry, "ye've hed time 'nough ter put Hughie ter bed ten times over — I never see sech mortal slowness; come here ; I want ye."

And Uncle Shim went, chuckling.

It is Thanksgiving morning, old style, — bleak and gray, ground frozen hard, a spitting of snow with a rising wind.

Aunt Lize came in before it was fairly light and raked out the coals, piling pine brush on the split wood. Then, when the flames leaped, she rose from her knees on the hearth, and, coming over to the cot, stood by it a moment without speaking, but rolling the corner of her apron between her thumbs and

forefingers — a sure sign with her of a perturbed
state of soul; I've seen it before.

"What is it, Aunt Lize?" I asked in surprise.

"I've got ter speak, Hughie, even ef 't is yew."
Her voice trembled.

"Go ahead, Aunt Lize; don't mind me."

"I can't help it, Hughie — Oh, I can't help it even
ef ye be er cripple — "

"What in thunder, Aunt Lize — " I believe if I
could have reached her mouth I should have stopped
it.   She has never called me *that* before — and just
to-day!

By the light of the fire I saw her lips twitch, then
tighten, before she went on; — no tremble in her
voice this time:

"Yes, er cripple; 'n' I ain't goin' agin the mercies
er my God any longer jest 'coz ye be one.   It 's goin'
on nigh onter three year sence ye wuz laid here, 'n'
all this time I ben sayin' my prayers under my breath,
'n' thinkin' ter deal with the Lord kinder left-handed;
'n' Shim hain't said grace onct, 'coz we could allus
hear ye cursin' 'n' blasphemin', mutterin' 'n' swearin'
ter yerself agin the God thet made ye."

I think I must have felt for the handle bars to raise
the cot, for Aunt Lize drew back, and put out her
hand as if to ward off something; but she went on
steadily:

"I ain't sayin' He put ye thar — mind *thet*, Hughie;
't warn't God, 't wuz the log; 'n' anybody thet 's got
common sense ain't goin' ter lay nat'ral things onter
Him; but He made ye, body 'n' soul, 'n' I ain't goin'
ter deny Him in His merciful kindness any longer

erlong er *yew*, nor Shim nuther; 'n' now thet ye 've stopped cursin' — leastways I hain't heerd ye aloud — I 've changed my mind 'bout waitin' ter hev Thanksgivin' till we 've paid off the morgige, 'n' I 'm goin' ter hev er reg'lar dinner jest ez we used ter hev — turkey 'n' chicken-pie 'n' all the fixin's, 'n' Shim 's goin' ter say grace, 'n' I want ye ter be moved out on yer cot 'n' eat with us — won't ye, Hughie? "

I could not answer; it had come upon me like a lightning-bolt out of a clear sky — and struck. She went on:

" Ther' ain't no use er folks thinkin' they can morgige their futer, 'n' cal'latin' ter pay int'rest on 't arterwards; — ther' ain't nothin' but jest *now* thet 's ourn, 'n' I, fer one, be er-goin' ter make the most on 't. We can afford ter make Thanksgivin' this year, 'n' I 'm goin' ter make it."

" Where be ye, Lize? " called Uncle Shim. She turned, threw on more wood, then hurried out of the room.

Such a paring, and chopping, and beating, and whisking, and rolling, and patting, and stewing, and boiling, and roasting, and basting, as went on for the next seven hours! Then they moved me out into the fragrant, Thanksgiving-filled warmth of the old kitchen, and we had dinner together. Aunt Lize and Twiddie were radiant, and Uncle Shim said grace, but in a husky voice, — the same he used to say:

" O Lord, we thank thee fer life and victuals, 'n' fer thy mercies everlastin'; Amen."

" Amen! " said Aunt Lize, triumphantly.

" Amen! " echoed Twiddie, joyously.

Aunt Lize and I have been knitting together in the short December twilight. We have decided it is not best for Twiddie tò go longer to the district school; what happened early in the summer influenced us. I told Aunt Lize what the child said to me that night we talked together:

"But we always have mothers, don't we, Hughie? They can't twit us 'bout not havin' *them ?* "

"Ye call her er child, Hughie, but she's growin' up fast," said Aunt Lize when she could speak, " 'n' ther' ain't no use puttin' her inter places whar she'll hev ter suffer more'n she need ter.   I knew she'd hev ter know sometime, but I never thought 't would come thet way — I'd oughter told her, but I was er coward. I hain't dared ter tell Shim; he's slow 'bout sensin' sech things, but when he *hez* sensed 'em he holds on ter er grudge like er dog ter er bone.   Ef he'd known it, I dunno but he'd er killed thet boy."

"I'm glad you kept it from him; we'll manage somehow.   I'll see to her sums and geography; and, in time, I hope to get enough books together to help her out.   She learns French so quick — she beats me; and yesterday, she was begging me to teach her Latin.   We'll manage somehow; don't you worry."

"I dunno, Hughie, what we should all dew 'thout ye."

"How about you, Aunt Lize?"

"Me!   Oh, I don't count much."   She beat the patch-work cushion in the rocking-chair till I thought the feathers would fly, " redded up," as she says, the hearth with the turkey-wing brush, and then flew out to get a hot supper for Uncle Shim, who has gone down to Scawsville to take some logs to the saw-mill. Twiddie is with him.

She came back, overjoyed. It is a fact that Twiddie is growing handsome; even Aunt Lize spoke of it the other day when we had our talk. She had had a note from Madeline Cope asking her to tell her what books she would like for Christmas, as she was going to send her a box.

I have the little note in my hand, — have kept it a half-hour under pretence of having forgotten to give it back. What a fool a man can be when there is no one by to see!

We are nonplussed, both of us; we don't know the names of any books — that's the trouble. I've advised Twiddie to write that she would like Miss Cope to send her the books *she* liked when she was fourteen. I pulled one string for myself in this.

To show her approval, Twiddie danced up and down the room, clapping her hands, and making such a racket that Aunt Lize came in to see what was the matter.

After supper she wrote her letter; she has improved much in her English, only dropping a "g" now and then, or mispronouncing a word. When she had finished it, she grew strangely quiet.

" A penny for your thoughts, Twiddie," I said.

She looked up; the firelight caught on the thick waves of her reddish-brown hair, and the profile against the flame showed as pure as the David's.

" Hughie, Miss Cope isn't a mother, is she? "

(What a thought leaped within me!)

" No, Twiddie."

" And she is n't married, of course?"

" No, of course not."

" But, Hughie, I don't understand. I had a mother, did n't I?"

"Why, of course; Uncle Shim's sister."

"But she was n't married either, was she?"

" No, Twiddie." I began to grow hot and wish Aunt Lize were in the room.

" But she was different from Miss Cope; — how, Hughie?"

"Why do you ask such things, Twiddie?" I tried to speak sternly, but failed; for her blue eyes — nearly black with inward excitement — were raised to mine with a look in them like that in the brown ones of a doe with fawn that I shot once by mistake.

" Because — don't I say it nice now, Hughie? — " (" Yes, Twiddie") "because I wish — you won't laugh at me?" — (" Not I.") "I wish she could be my mother; I love her so!"

I was dumb.

I shall be careful how I ask for the girl's thoughts again. Yes, undoubtedly, Twiddie is growing up.

What weather! Clear and crisp; sunshine from sunrise to sunset; enough snow to blanket the ground, yet not so much as to prevent work in the deep timber-belt. Everywhere there is the ring of axes. I 've been able to hire ten Canucks for a week this year; Aunt Lize feeds them, and Uncle Shim spends his time sledding food to their camp beyond the clearing. I've lived in a perpetual stew this week, for Aunt Lize has cooked from morning till night— brown-bread, boiled corned-beef, baked beans and pork, doughnuts by the hundred dozen, I should say; I know the appetite that is whetted as the axe dulls. —Whew! The air!

I've envied Twiddie up at the edge of the woods beyond the Old Pasture with Tag for company. She is gathering greens, ground-pine, ground-hemlock, and bitter-sweet to make into Christmas wreaths for Philip Vanever, Dick Malory, and Madeline Cope.

Miss Cope wrote her again to ask her to gather as much ground-pine as possible, and send it to her in barrels. She says the price in the city is five cents a pound, and she will pay Twiddie that for all she gathers.

How joyous the girl is! She and Aunt Lize are making "maple-sugar-butternut" candy in the kitchen. Uncle Shim and Toughheel, who has been helping Twiddie with the greens for half a day, are cracking butternuts before my open fire, each with a flat stone on his lap, and a cobble for a cracker.

It was Twiddie's idea to send a box of the candy to each of our friends, not forgetting Franz Waldort in California, and mine to carve a bit of our New England winter— bitter-sweet and partridge berry — into the wood of each. The house has been like a beehive in consequence, and Twiddie's joy in it all is contagious.

She flew into my room just now, and flung down a huge bunch of bitter-sweet upon the bench; her cheeks match the red of the seeds.

"Oh, Hughie! I never had such good times in my life."

She seized my face between both mittens, and gave it a well-meant, if somewhat rough, rubbing.

"There now! I 've put some winter red into your cheeks! Do you know what you are?" This with a parting scrub.

"Come back here, and play fair, or I 'll —"

"You 're a *bijou !* "

"Twiddie, come back just for a jiffy —"

For answer, I heard her laugh in the kitchen with Aunt Lize.

There is no denying it; — Twiddie is growing up.

I went to work again on my boxes.

I 've worked like a beaver these last two weeks. To finish the boxes, I 've put aside the winter panels, but the designs are ready — pine and cones, mountain-ash, larch, and last, — but I like it best of all, — being put to it for a fourth winter design, I bethought me of the little chipping-sparrow's nest in a spruce tree yonder in the bush. It is in full sight, and I have put branch and empty nest, just as I see them, upon the panel. — That 's winter with a vengeance.

Now look at that! The very day on which Uncle Shim carried down the barrels of greens and the pack-ages as far as Scawsville, he came back with some mail and a book parcel; I can't get ahead of them, do what I may.

DEAR ARMSTRONG,

That letter of yours had the right ring; I glory in your grit. Sometime, if it comes right, I 'll tell you a bit of my own experience. I find that social life is no botch-work, no hit-or-miss affair, but subject to natural laws like those that govern the trend of strata, outcrops, faults, and the like.

Meanwhile, I 'm pleased enough that the books please you, and because I want you to know us better, us, who have only " Forty-niners," for an ancestry, I send you, with the season's greeting, a year of the *Overland Monthly*, — I don't believe you know it, — the poems of our Joaquin Miller, and two volumes of Bret Harte. I add to them a little volume of verse by Sill — do you know him? and have marked a poem or two, " April in Oakland," and " Eastern Winter "; I think of you in that environment at present; if I am wrong, tell me.

As we Westerners don't stand particularly on cere- mony when we 've struck a vein — or staked a claim — of anything, I am shipping to you to-day, with- out so much as asking your leave, two planks of our best redwood. I told a friend about those carv- ings, and he would like you to fill this order, if you can, by May 1st. I say if you can; for you may not find it workable; but possibly a broad treatment may show results. He wants the redwood for a fire- place for his " shack " back in the mountains of Santa Barbara — all New England designs; he leaves you free hand in everything. Of course we grow every- thing out here that any one else grows, but we don't grow it in quite the same way as you do in that New England corner of yours — I have n't forgotten those wood-strawberries.

Set your price, and don't mind my saying "shack."
He owns a mine or two, and can pay with a "gold
brick" (no joke) if necessary. His "shack" has
seventeen rooms, and the fireplace is for the living-
room.

The season's greetings to your people on the
Mountain, and turn to page 28, last verse, of Sill, for
I want you to see by the aid of the mind's eye what I
am looking at this winter night in California.

Yours of the Overland,
FRANZ WALDORT.

> " Away
> Across the bay, the city with its lights
> Twinkling against the horizon's dusky line,
> Looks a sea-serpent, crawled up on the shore,
> With rings of fire across his rounded back,
> And luminous claws spread out among the hills —
> Above, the glittering heavens.   Magnificent ! "

Dare I say longer that this is a " run of luck " ?

Aunt Lize's attitude toward all this work and litter
of mine amuses me ; to her it is merely "whittling"
and " chips," nor can she understand why I get such
pay for it.

The Canucks have gone, all except Toughheel,
who is to help Uncle Shim haul logs. Saturday
night, after six, they filed into my room to get their
pay, — a squat, black-browed, brown-faced crowd ;
before they left, I read to them from Réclus the river-
songs of the old Canucks that they sang to ward off
evil from their craft :

" ' Un noir corbeau, volant à l'aventure,
    Vient se percher tout près de ma toiture —
.   .   .   .
    Va t'en manger, laisse moi en repos.' "

How the beady eyes sparkled, the strong yellow-
stained teeth came into full view, the gold half-moon
earrings twinkled as they nodded emphatic approval!

But when I read them the other, which most of
them had sung on some lumberman's lugger in the
rapids, they one and all, led by Toughheel, fell into
a kind of swaying motion, keeping time with their
feet and jerking their arms, and broke forth in shrill
cadence:

" ' Nous avons sauté le longue Sault
    Nous l'avons sauté tout d'un morceau —
.   .   .   .
    Roulé, roulant, ma boule roulant,
    En roulant ma boule roulant —
    En roulant ma boule ! ' "

It did me good to hear them sing the old catch,
and they were as frankly pleased with their per-
formance as children.   But Aunt Lize and Twiddie
were frightened, and fled to Uncle Shim in the barn
with a woful tale.

Two days before Christmas.

Uncle Shim remembered the fir tree of last year,
and came in to-day with a little beauty; he has set
it up in my room.   Aunt Lize, too, has caught the
infection, and trimmed my room with greens.   Twiddie
has made wreaths for every window in the house.

Three Christmas boxes have come, and she is

tense with curiosity and excitement. My own small gifts I have had to make and procure on the sly, for Twiddie has had eyes in the back of her head these last two weeks.

Christmas night, 11 P. M.

All abed, and I am writing by the light of the fire. The little tree, so green and sturdy, stands at the right of the fireplace; its fragrance fills the nostrils pleasantly.

The bench is covered with remembrances from that other world; they were too many for the tree. I touch this and the other, and North, South, East and West strike their palms into mine; — the blood tingles, thought quickens, the heart throbs high at the contact.

Another box of books, two boxes of the best cigars, another photograph; I've scarce been able to keep my eyes from it. It glows warm in the firelight like the David on the mantel-shelf. The figure in the photograph stands full three feet — the Venus di Milo! Who is she? What is she? Has she taken all men sensuously captive as she has me? I can't wait to know more of her — but wasn't Aunt Lize shocked when she saw her!

"It's downright pagan-heathenish, Hughie."

"Then I'm a pagan-heathen, too, Aunt Lize." I had to laugh at the look on her face.

"I don't deny but she's well-made, Hughie; I s'pose there be jest sech women, but I wish ter decency she'd h'ist her shift er leetle." I roared, and Aunt Lize went out of the room in a huff.

I noticed she was back again mighty quick, and did her share of the looking. Uncle Shim was stupefied into an open-mouthed "I vum!" Twiddie thinks she is beautiful, and so shows her sense of what is fine. — I wonder if *she* is another friend of Madeline Cope's?

A Christmas note from *her* — my first! It lies under my pillow, to be read and re-read in the night-watches.

MY DEAR MR. ARMSTRONG,

I have purposely delayed writing to you in acknowledgment of your Mountain hospitality on that never-to-be-forgotten summer day, because when I wrote, I knew I should have to make a confession as well as ask a favor. — Now is n't that the depth of humiliation for a woman? I 'll put my favor first, as a kind of moral breastplate for the confession.

My aunt and I are going to Florida the first of March; and before we go a sale is to be held at our house. Do you think you could find time for the carving of some small articles — book-racks, magazine-cutters, or photograph frames — for my table? If I 'm asking too much, don't hesitate to say so; I know what steady application you have given to *my* panels — Yes! They 're *mine!* I do so hope it's a surprise to you. It all came about in the simplest way. I was in New York after the holidays at my uncle's, Dick's father, and before I had time to take off my hat, Dick dragged me up three flights of stairs to his den to show me the fireplace. Dick has called me a Vestal Virgin ever since, for I knelt right down on the hearth to examine, and remained to adore.

I think I know the very larch you modelled from;

— it's on the right-hand side of the Pent Road on the north side of Olympus, about half a mile from your house — isn't it? Dick, having dragged me up there rather against my will, had to drag me away for lunch, wholly and entirely against it.

Of course, I determined on the spot to have some of those lovely carvings to live with permanently. Dick directed me to the Society, as I wanted to preserve my incognito you-wards, and I'm waiting for my last panels.

How could I help stealing back into your room to see the designs for the autumn panels and the finished summer ones! Thank you so much for giving me an opportunity, while living in a crowded southern city, to breathe on your New England mountain-top.

The panels are to be set in my own little morning-room, where, after breakfast, my aunt and I linger to read letters, write them, or sew for a while. Sometimes our club, the one that is to give the sale, meets there, and I don't know what the girls will say when they get a sight of those four seasons — alders, dog-wood, birch, and cherry; iris, thistle, wheat, and fern; corn and oak — ear and acorn — climbing grape and twining hop; for winter — what? I have tried to imagine, but failed. Don't keep me in suspense too long, even if you have to neglect the things for the sale.

Will you remember me most kindly to Mr. and Mrs. Lewis? and tell Twiddie I have sent her special greetings with the box.

The check for the panels would have been sent long ago, had it not been for the rules of the Society, by which, as a purchaser through them, I am bound as by the laws of the Medes and Persians. So for a time I must still remain your debtor for the panels — and ever and always for those three hours on the heights.

Sincerely yours,

MADELINE COPE.

P. S. We will have no middlemen after this — will we?

How like her! Frank, open-hearted, with a kind of buoyancy making itself felt in every line; one feels that in her presence.

No, — we will have no "middlemen" hereafter in anything, she and I. Twelve by the kitchen clock.

IV

WARP AND WOOF

IV

WARP AND WOOF

July, 189–.

NOT an entry in this book for more than two
years, yet Life has been so full, so enriched with work, friends, love; — I dare
write the word, now that I have grown used to living
with it in thought. Indeed, I have another record of
these thirty months of far more value than anything
I might have written here; for I have led two lives
during this time: one the life of a working shut-in — the
work growing more earnest every day, the art more
dear; the other, through the many letters, that of a
traveller in foreign lands, with a congenial companion
— sometimes a man, but oftenest a woman — by my
side. Journeyman years they have been in the true
sense of the word.

Beginning with the Florida note that came with the
orange flowers packed in gray moss, and made known
to me our Sir Galahad of poets, Lanier, I have read
through the entire record for these years.

All this forenoon I was busy selecting, arranging,
combining the hundred or more letters that would
fill a quarto were I to attempt to transcribe them
here; and, during all the time that, in spirit, I was
across the sea, roaming with Her the purple-heathered

heights about St. Fillan's and Lochearnhead, or the golden-purple heaths of North Germany, seeing with Her the unspeakable beauty of Venetian sunsets, or the ineffable but faded glories of Veronese in dark San Sebastiano, satisfying my craving for the real with the ancient carvings of Bernward's Hildesheim, or letting my soul bask in the sunlight of the divine serenity of the Madonna faces of Holbein and Raphael, I was aware of Aunt Lize at work with the old hand-loom in the garret overhead. I heard, as an accompaniment to my thoughts, the rick-rack of the swift shuttles, and the jar and rattling crash of the frames every time Aunt Lize shifted them. It has given me food for thought.

How incessantly the shuttles have been flying these last years, interweaving our life-threads — Madeline Cope's, Waldort's, Philip's, and mine! Nor yet may I trace the pattern. — Strange!

This afternoon I am alone, and have been re-reading a dozen of the letters that are entirely personal; transcribing them also, as well as a few extracts from the many descriptive ones. In them I have found the loose ends of several strands; the strands themselves, which I mistook at first for single threads, I find to be duplex, triplicate, yea, multiplex.

While busy transcribing these letters I have felt as if I were working at the Loom of Life, watching the plying shuttles, taking a hand now and then in shifting the frames. Once or twice I have caught at an end — a mere " thrum " — and tried to unravel a little way to find its connection with the pattern of the whole; but I have been balked in my purpose, and met only bewildering entanglement, labyrinthine intricacy.

Oh, Waldort! Heart of oak that you are; you have deserved better of Life; yet your last word shows you sound to the core, and the grain of the wood fine, fine!

MOUNT VERNON PLACE, May.

MY DEAR MR. ARMSTRONG,

Here we are at home again; but only as birds of passage, for we sail for Europe in June, and shall probably remain there two years, seeking the by-ways — and browsing by the way.

You may trust me to be on the lookout for all sorts and conditions of carvings. I mean, if I can, to keep you in touch with all the blossom-side of life over there. I am going because I have found a thorn among my roses over here, which is a rather unpleasant surprise for a woman of thirty-two.

I am so glad you like Lanier; I thought you would; that is why I sent him to you. Does n't it seem to you as if the key to that wonderful spiritual genius of his lies in the fact that it begins and ends in God?

I am perfectly sure that neither Grampians, Alps, nor Apennines can give me fuller enjoyment than your New England mountains gave me on that ideal summer day. —May I come again, invited, sometime when I shall be again in America?

Tell Twiddie I wish she would write me often; the child's letters are unique. Dick says she has promised to write him. Did you know he is going? All letters may come care of Baring Brothers; you see I am taking it for granted that the Hornet's mail-bag will carry some with that address; that's a woman's privilege to take things for granted, — or is n't it?

Sincerely yours,
MADELINE COPE.

SAN CHRISTOVAL, CALIFORNIA, June.

DEAR ARMSTRONG,

The redwood fireplace is a triumph. I am guest in the shack, resting after an extended trip with my post-graduate class into the Sangre del Cristo mountains of Colorado — for the moraines of Grape Creek. Tough, back-breaking work it has been; but I have welcomed it, for I have noticed that when a man's " nerve," not nerves, is overstrained, the best restorative is a set of muscles dead-beat through overwork.

The truth is, Armstrong, there's been an upheaval in my life of late. I knew it had to come, — it's been coming for years; but when it came it was a regular convulsion of nature; and, just at present, I'm played out, and have come away up here to draw a long breath and get a new grip on Life. It's a good place for it.

I wish you could see it. The shack is located on a grassy plateau in the apex of a triangular gorge, the base broad and open to the plains and the sea. Behind us the gray walls of rock, weathered and eroded into massive sculptured pillars, rise sheer a thousand feet. There is a brook at all seasons tumbling into the depths beneath us, but in the rains it is a white leaping torrent. The gorge is filled with pines and their shadows, and we look over them down and away to the Pacific.

Mine host has a history; all men have who are lucky enough to have been born out here in the sixties. He has made and lost a half-dozen fortunes — but is solid now. I met him in Europe, and he has never failed me; but he does n't "open up well," as we say of a vein, when it comes to the eternal things of a man's life. We get on well enough with the transient — quotations on stocks and bonds, land prospectus, mining, etc. So I turn to you there on your New England mountain-top, sure of finding with you what I can't with him.

Don't ask me to define the "what," — I'm not strong on definitions; but give me a good fact like a geode, and I can crack away on it with the best of them.

I can't help saying I do admire your pluck, Armstrong. I should be a devil if I were in your place. You have the kind of courage I admire more than any other; I have n't it. Let me know how you're coming on. — I hear Miss Cope is going to Europe for two years. I met her there, too. In fact, but for mine host, I should never have seen her — and I take it she's a woman worth any man's seeing. But I'm aware that I'm speaking in the dark to you. I'll fulfil my written word of telling you something of my experience later on, as you have shown such kindly interest in the Forty-niner's son.

But I'd like to know what the deuce you mean by taking such liberties in legitimate business, as to send back half the amount of that check and saying it is over-pay! Did n't you know we Californians dropped Troy weight in the diggings?

I had no lie ready when mine host came in with your check in his hand and a thunder sign between his eyebrows, so I told him the truth about the proverbial squeamishness of the true New England con-

science, etc., etc. But it was no go; you'll have to
take it; besides, you earned it fairly and squarely —
so don't be a fool. With which personal admonition
the case for the plaintiff is closed.

Yours fraternally,

(I hope you appreciate this signature after the
admonition.)

FRANZ WALDORT.

(Oh, Armstrong, I've been such an awful one!)

— Why won't the Gloire de Dijon roses bloom in
America as they do here, like great yellow moons
flattened against the gray stone lintels? Why aren't
there lochs instead of lakes? Why aren't there
mountains, purple with heather blooms, that shadow
the lochs which gleam like huge opals in the after-
glow? Why can't we live in one-roomed gray stone
huts, with a kitchen grate in one wall and a noble
red-draperied bed in a cosy alcove in the other?
Why can't we have pewter bowls and platters and
spoons, and from them eat delicious green-goose-
berry jam, and curds and cream?

Why, oh, why? . . . To all your Mountain deities
greetings from over the sea from a — just at present —

Fair Maid of Perth! (St. Fillan's)
M. C.

Here's a photograph of the "'Prentice Pillar" in
Rosslyn Chapel — a bit of real carving in stone
worth some hours of worship. I feel as if it were a
desecration to eat "cold kale" even "on Friday"
after seeing this. — Why can't we Americans apothe-
osize the hop-vine in some such way? You, at least,

are the pioneer in wood. Do use it all you can,
won't you?   M. C.

DEAR ARMSTRONG,

That letter of yours did me good. If there are
others among your friends who are lucky enough to
get that kind from you once in a lifetime, they may
well be envied.

How do you reach out into all that — cut off as
you are from the world, the flesh, and the Devil?

Yes, I am glad to tell you something of my own
life; you put it kindly enough — that it will help you
to elucidate yours. I think it is the other way round.
I can't promise it will be pleasant reading, — but
here goes.

In the first place, I was n't started fair, for I don't
know who my mother was. Just turn to one of those
volumes of Bret Harte, and find " The Luck of Roar-
ing Camp " — you 'll get it all there in a nutshell,
without annotations on my part, which are n't necessary under the circumstances.

My father was a German from the Harz region,
who had worked in the mines in Saxony, and run
away, shipping at Hamburg for the States, to avoid
conscription.

My eyes opened on the " diggings," and for fifteen
years my range of vision was limited to them. Unlike the "Luck" in Bret Harte, I had for mother's
milk, curses, blows, and desertion.

I can't say how and when my father disappeared;
I have no recollection of seeing him after I was nine.
Some men told me he was carried off by the typhus
in San Francisco, where he went yearly with his bags

of gold dust for a grand gambling and drinking bout.
A dirk knife with his name on the handle, — the name
is mine, — a Colt's revolver, a "lucky pig" (a German
trifle he carried in his pocket), a bag of gold dust
worth a hundred dollars, and twelve Spanish doub-
loons were delivered to me tied in a shirt-sleeve by
the men who came up from 'Frisco with the news of
his death.

How I kept that heritage, I fail to understand,
except that at eleven I was past master in the use
of the dirk, as quick as a weasel in my movements,
and as unexpected, which meant "hands off," and a
good deal of respect shown me in the various camps
where I found work.

I had panned gravel, broken quartz, washed gold,
dug, picked, mined, frozen, starved, baked, feasted,
and rioted, — all before I was fifteen. Then, something happened.

I was going down the gulch one night to get my
canteen filled at the settlement shanty at the lower
end; in reality, it was bar-room, grocery, post-office,
gambling-hell, and miners' bourse, all in one. The
moon was full and the night cold — December in the
Sierras.

As I bore down the trail, I heard, high above
me, the wickering squeal of a pack-saddle mule; —
that meant news from the coast. In a moment, I
saw the flare of a camp-fire, and, boy-like, wanted
to know what was up.

I was hampered in climbing by my heritage, which
I carried with me night and day, hung around
my neck beneath my shirt; but I risked it: toe in
one crevice, dirk in another, a pine root, hand over
hand, a trapeze act or two, — and I lay out on a

branch on a level with the camp-fire and the group
about it.

I have been told, Armstrong, that there is in every
man's life a moment for conversion — whether he avail
himself of it or not. That was mine.

It would be wholly impossible for me to formulate
the change that took place in me; but change there
was.

A man was reading by the light of the fire the
story of "Little Nell." For four nights running, I
crawled up there at the risk of life and limb, and
when at last they laid *Her* away, Life, for a time,
was a blank to me.

By the next train of pack-mules I went to the
coast. There had come upon me a madness of longing to get away from it all; to roam, to wander in
other lands, of which I had heard so many tales by
the camp-fires in the mountains; to see something of
the world besides the Sierras, the gulches, the placer-
mines; in fact, something other than the "diggings."

I worked for six months as stevedore for the coast-
wise vessels at 'Frisco, then shipped as cabin-boy
on a brigantine bound for Australia. But I was no
true salt. Arrived at Melbourne, the old life laid
hold of me again, and drew me back into the Aus-
tralian Alps, into the "diggings," and there I squan-
dered life and substance for another year. Again
came the longing to roam, and I fled, shipping for
Singapore and the Straits Settlements. In Singapore
I got hold of a half dozen of Dickens' works —
second hand. *Old Curiosity Shop* was among them
— and a well-thumbed volume of *The Subterranean
World*. All the books looked as if they had been
through the cholera and black plague combined, but

I knew I'd struck a vein which I proposed to work for all it was worth. And then I turned another corner.

As I wrote you once, I had had "stones for bread," for playthings also; for a pillow, as well as a defence, ever since I could remember anything; — and what was more natural than that I should look to stones for my future?

I can't say how it came about — it was an adolescent process, I suppose, but the result was plain enough. I familiarized myself with the physical features — especially the mountains — of every new country upon which I set foot. I shipped again, for Borneo, and its gold mines kept me six months. While there I fell in with a Dutchman, or more properly a Boer, and from him I caught the South African fever. I had it hard, and the Kimberley diamond diggings held me chained for two years — but what am I thinking of! It is late, half-past one in the morning!

A full moon silvers every pine-top in the gorge; — Do, Armstrong, read that immortal poem of Bret Harte's in the second volume, "Dickens in Camp." It belongs to the world, but to me especially, as a Californian — and tell me if for true, inward humanness, there has been, in America, its equal.

> "Above the pines the moon was slowly drifting,
>   The river sang below;
>   The dim Sierras far beyond uplifting
>   Their minarets of snow."

Armstrong, I tell you, a man knows the good of being a man when he feels that uplift. Thank God, I was born a Californian!

Yours,

F. W.

I'm sending just a word, in season, to bespeak from Twiddie another box — a much bigger one — of that "maple-sugar-butternut" candy such as she sent me last year.

I had to give in when that melted in my mouth; — we can't furnish that in California; you New Englanders go ahead of us there.

Tell Twiddie, for me, that for the box of candy — I take it for granted she will send me some — I propose to trade with her on reciprocity terms; a box of our Brobdingnagian fruits for a box of her butternut candy. How is that, Armstrong, for a compromise with free trade?

I send the box by express to-day; it is well-packed, the shippers say, to withstand anything above zero. I shall write soon.

Yours, in haste,

FRANZ W.

SAN CHRISTOVAL, December.

It's about as you say, Armstrong: — every thinking man has a hard row to hoe between twenty-three and thirty, I don't care whether he's a *Porphyrogenitus* or a *gutter-genitus* — it's all the same in the end if he use his head-piece as an instrument for any modicum of soul he may have.

You did n't feel me grip your hand the other night, did you, about eight, Eastern time?

Well, I did. I reached right out across the continent, after reading your letter, and gripped hard, for it was the only way I could express rationally my feeling of fellowship on the subject of your own outreaching for more light in that other world of what other men have thought, felt, known, suffered, enjoyed, proved, tested, examined of Life's heights and depths and everyday levels since recorded Time — in a word, books, whether of parchment, papyrus, brooks, mountain-folds, or stones.

I'm with you there every time.

It was that craving, that longing to be in touch with some other life than that to which I had been born, and which I perceived — but only dimly — to be attainable for me through books and study, that, in the end, put a stop to my rovings and anchored me for four years.

From Cape Town I took passage to Amsterdam, and from there to Gothenburg. I wanted to see the iron mines of Sweden. I had made my little pile of a thousand dollars, and had I eschewed gambling and drinking, I should have had twice as much.

There in the iron mines of Dannemora I worked for three months side by side with an American — a son of one of our Iron Kings: a heavy-featured, big-headed, persistent sort of a chap, who was learning the trade root and branch. He spoke Swedish fairly well, and when he found I was an American with a sneaking fondness for the contents of our Mother Earth's bowels of mercy, he spoke a good word for me with the superintendent, and so gave me a boost.

I shall never forget the first time I went over to his rooms on invitation. I quit work, washed up, and changed my shirt, and then went over to dinner at seven. He had his own ménage, — a half-dozen rooms and two servants, — and I sat down for the first time in my life at a gentleman's private table. A year or two ago I dined with him in his own mansion in an Eastern city, and I assure you, Armstrong, all its elegance made no such impression upon me as that modest dining-room, the salon, and the little library with its book treasures.

I sweat through the first two courses, for it was my initiation, remember, and I was awkward with the tools! But after that I felt better, and forgot myself so far as to stretch my long legs under the table, put my shoulders against the chair-back, and get my hands out of my way. A good smoke in the library afterwards made it all plain sailing.

When we were well on with the third pipe, that chap began to talk to me like a grandfather. He was about twenty-four.

He said I was n't making the most of my opportunities — I 'd have drawn my dirk on a man in the "diggings" for less plain speech than that; but, you see, the environment made the difference, and, moreover, it was after dinner — that I had the natural endowment, and all I needed was the equipment; that it was my own fault if I did n't get it; that if I could n't get a university education, I ought to approximate to it by study and travel; that I had such a gift for languages I ought to try Latin and Greek. Finally, he wound up with advising me to buy a good Scotch tweed suit, English make, and slough off the miner's garb after work hours.

I want you to realize, Armstrong, that all this was from a multi-millionaire's son to a scion of the Sierra gulches. Moreover, all this advice was gratis — he drew the line right at the pocket, for he made no offer of a pistole towards furthering this much-to-be-desired consummation.

When he had finished, I opened fire on him by asking him from what university he had been graduated.

You should have seen how he wilted, Armstrong! And I asked all in good faith, too.

But he owned up fair and square that he had been expelled for high jinks in his second year, and could n't take a degree from any university. That's why he was there, trying by his devotion to the business to make up to his father for the thing his father had set his heart upon — and could n't have. We got on still better after that, and the upshot of it was, that when he left for America, I stayed on for two years with the use of all his books, and a letter of introduction to a professor of science in Upsala University, which unlocked for me treasures untold.

I began to count my wealth from that time. Acting on the advice of the professor, I decided to take the four years' course of mining and engineering at the famous School of Mines in Freiberg, Saxony. To this end I worked like a Turk, and went thither when the professor thought I was sufficiently prepared, and spent my time, during the summer that followed, in the Harz region, whence came the man who begot me. I worked for a while in the various mines there, and acquired a knowledge of the whole region, including the smelting stations.

How I wish all this were by telephone! — then you could "ring off" to shut me up. I don't seem to know when to stop. Sometimes I think I 'll save all this to say through the smoke of our corn-cob pipes in the Pen next summer; but the disturbance from that upheaval I mentioned is still very great, and just at this time this opening up to you gives me a necessary vent.

I am glad all of you are enjoying the fruits; there is a largeness, a natural amplitude about them that,

somehow, belongs to our state — but don't think I'm
boasting! I'm humble enough when I think of those
wood-strawberries, and the delicious New England
candy.

If you could see my state from the Sierras to the
Sequoias, you'd know what I mean. Greetings to all.

Yours,

FRANZ WALDORT.

HILDESHEIM, GERMANY.

Christmas greetings to all on Olympus! How
would it seem, think you, to live in a carved house
that stands on a carved market-place, its nine-story
houses wrought and painted to the apex of the gables,
and its huge stone fountain sculptured into quaint
forms?

And the carved market-place is in a carved town
where post and lintel, frieze and cornice, gable and
casement run riot with carvings of animate and inani-
mate things — grewsome, graceful, grotesque! Hildesheim is the illuminated initial letter in the missal
of German art. How I wish you might see it!

We are here for the fair. Oh, if Twiddie were only
with me! In the box I have sent for all of you on
Olympus — in the care of my uncle, Mr. Malory — I
have put some photographs of these ancient carved
buildings. Bishop Bernward set his people the good
example more than eight hundred years ago. — There
are the vesper bells ringing from his cathedral, which
is ten minutes' walk from here. I must be off to that
service; — Catholic? Yes, but it's all one to me so
long as the stones were raised in His name. —

I'm just back from the service. I like to think of
you as a young Bernward living out his idealism in

Art's service away up there on your New England mountain-top. Indeed, dear friend, if these detached bits of the mosaic of my life over here give you the pleasure you say they do, — as you express it, " enrich my life beyond measure," — be sure I shall keep right on sending them to you.

Perhaps I, too, am a debtor — to you. But I'm not going to tell you how. That is n't playing fair, is it? Well, perhaps, sometime — I don't know. I told you it was a thorn. —

I have thought so much of what you said in a recent letter. You say you are convinced a man has nothing but his will with which to meet Life; that " deliberate valor " is the only safeguard against temptations that beset a man's weaknesses. True — but — Well, I wish you would look for just one verse in your new volume of Browning; seek for it, please, and when you will have found it, learn it, and say it over to yourself in those night-watches of which you write me; afterwards, ponder it in your *heart*. Here it is:

> " All I could never be,
> All, men ignored in me,
> This, I was worth to God, whose wheel the pitcher shaped."

That is what I felt when I saw you.

OAKLAND, CALIFORNIA, January, 189–

DEAR ARMSTRONG,

I had such a letter from Twiddie the other day! Enough to warm the cockles of a childless man's heart through and through. Give her my love, and tell her that if a small Christmas gift of an Indian basket can give her such pleasure, I shall send her without delay a Navajo squaw's blanket to match the basket. That will mean, of course, on the reciprocity principle, another long letter from her. —

I don't know, Armstrong, — I don't know about that last hypothesis of yours. We get hammered into shape, or out of shape, whether we will or no, and in the end — But, God knows, I've no right, as a man, to measure myself with you.

All this talk about "ordained dimensions" sounds well; there's a set of men — an Eastern importation — here in the University, who ring so many changes on that theme, that the soul grows deaf; — how stands it with the deeds? With the facts?

In any case, let me know if your hypothesis prove a working one. It looks that way now, and I am ready to be convinced.

I'm beginning to understand, through your letters, the satisfaction a man may get in looking at himself under the microscope just once in his lifetime. I don't take much stock in those men who spend their strength in self-analysis; they wabble too much to suit me and my views of life. But, just at this time, I count myself fortunate in having a friend to whom I can "open up"; Olympus can keep its own counsel, and — Jove reigns.

It was in my third year at Freiberg that I met Her, — no need to write the name; it's a nasty wound, and just to see the initials opens it afresh. I suppose you've thought all along that a woman's hand has been on my lever.

It was in the Saxon Switzerland, just above Dresden. I had been tramping through it for a month, enjoying to the full the summer vacation — it was such a fine, free life! — and one day, as I was strolling up a valley that in its ascent to the heights narrows to a ravine, chipping and ringing with my hammer here and there, as is always my wont when examining a new crease or wrinkle in Dame Nature's wonderful mantle, I stepped aside from the narrow, rocky path to allow passage for a train of mountain horses coming up behind me.

I heard the gay voices of girls, the merry jest and laughter, and recognized my countrywomen of whom I had seen but few and known not one during my years of roving. Then I heard the voice of " mine host" greeting me. I must say, that man has never failed me. He did n't then. His father was off in Leadville somewhere, working to let his wife and children splurge in Europe. They knew how to do it too. " Mine host" was a student with the rest of us in Freiberg, but lived like a swell, — big bachelor apartment, two servants, etc. The mother and three sisters had been in Paris. Consequently, I had never seen them.

He had been running up to Dresden pretty regularly once or twice a week during the last winter, but I never suspected why, until I saw the look on his face when he introduced me to the girl whose horse's bridle he was holding. That was enough. I knew he was hard hit.

He found out later that " the golden key unlocks all doors but Heaven's " — and that, I take it, Armstrong, is a true woman's heart. At least, that's my idea of Heaven — all I care to know of it. He has never married; could n't, in fact, until the last two years, for he has had his whole family to support, and in a luxury to which they were not born — far from it! That's what makes me mad!

From the moment I saw her, Armstrong, there in the Amsel Grund, that queer blank that was left in my boy's life when they laid Little Nell away under the pines of the Sierras beneath the December moonlight, was filled, and it seemed to me as if I had but just begun to know the thing called Life.

In the fall, "mine host" gave a lunch to half the young American colony in Dresden, and the few Americans among the students acted as ushers in the inspection of the silver mines. Then I saw her again, so joyous, so interested in everything, with a charm of manner beyond any I have ever seen since in girls.

You have seen her on Olympus. The face and figure have changed but little, only, the promise of her girlhood has been richly fructified, and the woman's charm has been enhanced a hundred-fold.

I fairly gambled with happiness, Armstrong, and grew as reckless in the new dispensation as I had been in the old — only, with a difference. I bought a dress suit and accessories — my pile had diminished to three hundred dollars during the student years; I contributed to the ball fund; I took private dancing lessons; I borrowed a book on etiquette from one of our mess, a Californian like myself; I made a clean sweep of my beard and mustache, and, at last, at the Freiberg ball which we gave in December to the American girls ("mine host" was leader in all this, and set the pace) my courage failed me — and I did n't ask her to dance!

How that girl — she was only nineteen — managed to open up her world to me, I can't say. I had a note from her aunt, a gracious Southern gentlewoman, asking me to make one of a party at the skating carnival in the Grosser Garten in Dresden during the December holidays. And when that was over, there was a little dance at her house, and afterwards a ball for " mine host's " sisters. I was there every time.

Time and again, during those days, I had an inward vision — of myself as a factor in the midnight orgy in the settlement shanty, or as a reveller in the purlieus of Melbourne, and a terrible soul-nausea would attack me. I began to realize I was handicapped by my ancestry, by my early environment, by the years of dissipation — and I suffered; but, I thank God, it was the travail of re-birth.

You see, Armstrong, I had n't come into any realization of my Americanhood. I had gone from the Pacific coast ten years before, unwitting that behind the rocky wall of the Sierras lay another America, to which I was a stranger, — to its customs, to its traditions, to its civilization. In entering Europe by way of Asia, I had found before me the Chinese wall of caste separation reared by the hands of a hundred generations; and between those two ramparts my life of twenty-five years had been spent.

A man's rough exterior may lose the point of its angles in contact with other men — it 's only a woman's hand that can use the rotten-stone, and polish.

What that girl did for me! I don't believe she knew she was doing it, either.

Her kindness to me and thoughtfulness of me were just the simple surface drainage of an unspoiled, unselfish, genial soul. She was an art-lover — not a dabbler in art, like the thousands of women of to-day, but a true worshipper of the best in painting, literature, music. And the best belonged by right to her.

You'll think I'm idealizing in this — but if you could know her!

So I was drawn by the best of leading-strings — a gentlewoman — to the best in Art; and the Dresden Gallery, the music, the opera and concerts, the wonderful collections of porcelain, and treasures wrought in silver, ivory, and gold, became mine for a trifling sum.

That's one of the glories of that old country — Life's doors swing *outwards* for the Poor into the regions of Art.

A year after she left Dresden I took my doctor's degree, and the first thing I did, Armstrong, was to go down again into the Saxon Switzerland, into the Amsel Grund, and there, on the spot where I had first seen her, vow to make myself worthy of her; to purify my life in act and thought, and to keep myself unspotted from the world — if there was strength enough of manhood in me. It was only so that I could realize to myself my love for her.

My funds were, by this time, at lowest ebb, and I took what work I could find wherever it could be found, — anything, everything, to earn an honest thaler, till I made my way down into the Dolomites — a region I had long wished to examine — and from there into the Oetz Valley, where I lived with Tyrolean peasants, one with them if not of them — a simple, quiet mountain-life in the higher Alps. Two years I gave there to the writing of those volumes I sent you. I got them printed in Berlin, and they opened the scientific fraternity to me. Thus equipped, I turned my face homewards, entering America this time by the front door, and knocked at the portals of the young University of my native state. They let me in;

and I thought then, "Now I've just a straight road, with no turning, to Her!" But I did n't know, Armstrong, — I did n't know. How could I, born and bred as I was?

You'll think by this time that I have a talent for waiting; so I have, — that belongs to my trade. Mother Earth writes large with aeons of patience, and a man may well learn a lesson or two from her.

Good-night; I'm dead tired — I know you must be by this time. FRANZ W.

Easter. — Good-morning! Just look over your valley towards Killington, and if you should see a bluebird or a swallow fleck the sky between you and it, imagine it my Easter greeting.'

I have celebrated this year in my own way. — Church? No, indeed. Did it ever occur to you that on that first Easter day they did not find Him in any sepulchre of stone, but abroad — on the road?

I, too, think I found Him, at least in a by-way of the road. M. C.

DRESDEN, ALT STADT.

— I am so glad you have that special work for the University! No, indeed, don't look to Europe for designs. I am sure you will find enough native inspiration on Olympus. — No wonder you love Franz Waldort. I do! I feel I may say that to you and be understood; for when I meet with such sincerity, such straightforwardness of purpose, combined with such a queer, old-fashioned chivalry of manner towards all of us women, just because we are women, I find it refreshing, and, without exactly flattering me, it makes me feel at peace with my entire sex, the world in general, and my own world in particular. He is a friend of whom any man or woman may be proud. I met him in Dresden years ago, and knew he would be heard from sometime.

— And you *do* care for those few lines of Browning? And they would mean so much more to you if you could see what I saw the other day at Meissen.

We were at the famous porcelain works. As I stood by one of the workmen, I marvelled as I saw the rough mass whirl, and bend, and curve into concave and convex surfaces, and assume its beautiful shape, although broken again and again on the wheel by the skilful hands.

The old words came back to me: "But now, O Lord, thou art our father, we are the clay and thou our potter; and we are all the work of thy hand": my friend on the distant New England mountain-top, that nobleman, Franz Waldort, the potter beside the wheel, the men and women and little children that should drink of the cup — for it was that which was being fashioned from the clay of which I am next of kin! Oh, Hugh, dear friend, I wanted you there beside me to feel the force of that object-lesson!

Did it ever occur to you that a physical disability is the least of Life's handicaps with which a man must reckon? — But, oh, when I say all this, I know I should n't. What am I to speak of these things to you who have suffered such deprivation? I, who have had everything except the one thing a woman must have to be wholly content. But what am I writing, and why? It was the potter at his wheel that has broken me in thought. — May I have a letter soon?   M. C.

DEAR ARMSTRONG,

You may well ask, as you did in your last, why I
have n't let myself be heard from the last two months.

You did n't consider that order I sent you in
February to the point then?   Now, I thought I was
doing a mighty friendly thing to get the committee
to give it to you!   I told them I knew a man East—
this is always a good bait for us Californians, I confess—who could give them something worth while;
that so long as they were about it, they might as well
perpetuate their names by giving the University a
lasting memorial in real and, at the same time, in-
digenous Art.

You have been in correspondence with them, so
you know what they require.   It will be your monu-
ment, Armstrong, and mine also, in that I have such
pride in your work.   So "Glück auf!"   You say
you 're bothered about designs for the ceiling, and
are looking to Europe to help you out.   My advice
may be worth nothing in this matter, for I am such a
rabid American that I never can see the use of borrowed plumes when we have our own ostrich-farms!
But don't you think it would be more to the credit of
all of us to keep on this side of the Atlantic?

You can do it.   You say it will take you a full year
and a half, steady work—and I am glad to know it,
for I shall soon be off to South America for a year or
more.   I welcome this.   It 's my first sabbatical year,
and I 've always wanted to tread in Humboldt's footsteps and make acquaintance with the Cordilleras.   The
planning for this—arranging the courses which my
substitute is to give, marking out the work for the
post-graduates, two of whom accompany me—has
filled my time.

Then, too, I have delayed a little, knowing I should close, with this letter, the chapter of my life I have opened to you.

Until She marries, Armstrong, I shall be only a sleeping volcano; I know this, and have accepted it. But, meanwhile, I want to give Nature a chance to cover me with her own gentle, softening growths, and I'm going to do all I can to give her that chance.

When She marries — and I know she must, sometime, no woman like that should be without a mate — the volcano will be extinct; but the surface growth will, I trust, supply sustenance for another, a domestic love, or loves. I want a home, Armstrong; a true woman to love me; I want children to play about my hearth; I shall want a change from the homeless, unbound life I have led so long in my faithfulness to an ideal. I shall want to be bound by the ties of a quiet, domestic affection.

If there should come a time when some woman might need my protection and my love, she should have both; but not until I had told her what I have told you, — what I tell you now. She shall know *all:* know that a part of me she can never possess, and that part — God help you, Armstrong, if ever you give that part into a woman's keeping, for she will hold it in this world and the next, if there be one!

There's no use; — when one *soul* lays hold upon another, there is no escape, and the worst — or best — of it is, one does not wish for it.

Two years ago I went East for the first time. I had never heard from her directly. She had gone back to her own, and even "mine host," who had swallowed his bitter pill like a man, had ceased to mention her. But I took a Baltimore daily, and so kept track of her comings and goings in that " other world " of hers, between her own city, New York, Washington, Annapolis, White Sulphur Springs, Bar Harbor, and Newport.

In spirit I fought the Navy and Army combined, challenged the East to single combat, and cudgelled the entire South simply to keep her intact — for me. For I, too, felt myself a man; I had won my spurs like a man, and I was n't going to knuckle to any one with a pedigree even if it were as long as the missing-link's tail.

I had some work for the Government in Washington, and I stopped over in Baltimore to see her. I found her the same genial soul, glad, so she said, to renew her Dresden acquaintance. She informed me, considerably to my surprise, that she had been keeping track of *me!* — that she was so proud of my record; and would I give her the pleasure of allowing her to present some of her friends to me — and more of the like. What is the use of repeating it, even? A woman like that has everything at her command for a man's enchaining — and I had been hers already so long.

But she was so true with it all, so kindly, so friendly, the girl's bright charm softened, yet enhanced to a woman's fascination! What wonder that I lost my head?

I have been East every summer since, and have spent some portion of each where she was. Little by little, I began to see what her environment was, what her traditions were, what it meant to come of a family that struck root into America's soil over two hundred years ago, and during that time had given the best of its manhood and its womanhood to the up-

building of this country in its Government, its Judi-
ciary, in its Defenders by land and sea.

But it was the woman I loved — realizing all the
time as I did, more and more clearly, that just this
woman was a product of her ancestry, her environment. Yet such was — and is — my faith in her,
that I knew — and know — that where her heart goes
she will follow.

But then another curious fact made itself plain to
me, — " fixing " in my consciousness as a film is set on
a sensitive-plate, — that she could and would love only
along the lines of her heredity, circumscribed by her
environment; and that even herein, she was not
narrowed in the worldly sense.

Her aunt was gracious; her friends, men and
women, were gracious; they could n't be otherwise,
for they were all true Southerners with the blood that
warms and tempers our national life to a humanness,
which, when it is once known and understood, shows
that national life at its very best.

It was a curious process; — there was throughout
no disillusionizing, only a gradual perception of conditions, before unperceived, and with it, a gradual
weakening of my power of will to achieve that which
I had set before me.

At last I gathered myself together — it was after
that coaching-trip through the Green Mountains —
and when I got home, I wrote it all out to her; I
knew I could never say it face to face — not *my* life.

And I had such a letter in return! that — Well,
Armstrong, all I can say is, paradoxical as it may
sound, that letter, while true to herself and her
womanhood, true to me and my manhood, has made
it possible for me to love some other woman, some-

time, I hope, the better for it.   More I need not say;
— not of this.   I shall never mention it again.

But I do want to say, right here, that it has been
to me a help to say this to you.

Once, in the China Sea, our vessel was struck
by the typhoon, and all hands took to what they could
get.   There was a man in the crew — second mate
— I'd nursed through the Java fever; he was still
weak from it, but he had a wife and two children off
in one of your New England seaports waiting for him,
and as there wasn't room enough for all of us who
had taken to the catamaran, and like to be less with
the madness that was coming upon us through drought
and famine, I slipped off behind with a plank and a
marline as the dark fell, — quietly enough, I thought;
but in a second there was a splash beside me, and a
hand gripped mine: " No, you don't, Waldort!   If you
go, by God, I'll go too! — Here — hold on to me."

And that hand helped to save me, for, knowing
his weakness, I fought twice as hard for us both during the next twenty-four hours, till we were picked
up more dead than alive.

Your letters have been another such hand.   God
bless you.

I sail next month for the Isthmus.   Tell Twiddie
she may order anything from South America for
next Christmas from a parrot to an electric eel — I
am hers to command.   I am looking forward to this
work; but my letters will be irregular and far between,
for I go inland at once, away from the ordinary
channels of communication.

By the way, the committee have told you they
want California redwood, New England cherry, and
South American mahogany?   How do you like the

combination? Let me know if I can do anything at my end to help you.

I leave the fifteenth— send me a good stirrup-cup of a letter!

Yours (consider your hand gripped just here),
FRANZ WALDORT.

FROHE ALP, FELSENGARTEN,
VALLEY OF THE OETZ, IN THE TYROL!

At last I am looking down upon your two-thousand-feet-high Olympus from a superior height of three thousand feet, and am, in turn, looked down upon by the Wildspitze, one of the monarchs of the Tyrolean Alps, with its hundreds of attendant peaks; so it is in vain I try to feel any superiority.

Oh, what a mountain-peace this is! This little hamlet of Felsengarten lies on a narrow plateau two thousand feet above the river, that looks like a mere thread of silver interwoven in the black depths. At this height not a sound rises from the valley, although the water foams and leaps and rushes downward with a deafening roar through its gorges and ravines.

Behind the hamlet, which consists of a dozen or more houses straggling along the plateau and climbing, at one end, to the small church built of dark-timbered fir, rises the Frohe Alp, or green, wide-stretching mountain pastures where the goats and cattle browse. On the slope of this Alp is the farmhouse of a well-to-do peasant, Nicodemus Bendl — now, how do you like that for a sturdy mountaineer's name? He has given us two rooms for our own, and, I fear, crowded himself and wife out of the house; I have yet to discover where they sleep.

My room is — don't be shocked — over the cow-

shed, and I mount to it by the cow-shed stairs! But
a cleaner, sweeter, wholesomer little room does not
exist in the civilized world. For you must know
our cows are washed and scrubbed, and, for aught I
know, perfumed; their sweet breath rises to me in the
early morning, and, at night, their beds of fresh straw
give forth a warm scent as of dried herbs. I can't
express it or explain it, but it's just the wonderful
breath of the Alps, pure with the purity of virgin
snows, and sweet with the delicious growths of these
high, untainted pastures.

The room is about eight feet by ten. I have in
it a chest for my clothes — a carved one, too, — a
small washstand, a high-backed chair of some dark
wood, and a narrow bed furnished with two coarse
sheets, white as the driven snow, a moss-and-straw-
filled mattress, and a feather-bed for my coverlet
cased in dark blue, loosely woven woollen. On the
wall, over the head of the bed, is a wooden crucifix.

My one window takes up half the narrow end of
the room, and is provided with a kind of wooden
eyelid that opens in the roof and is propped on a
stick set in a wooden socket. I keep this eyelid
open all the time, and the view from it is the moun-
tain-sea of the Oetzthaler Alps, the white crests of
its great rock waves caught in marvellous folds and
plications. Just to see the morning come, kindling
its light from beacon peak to beacon peak till the
whole serrated horizon flashes with rose and gold —

There's no telling it.

Tuesday.

But there *is* telling of the simple life here; of our
black bean soup — what if we do eat it from wooden

bowls? — of the delicious roast goose stuffed with apples and plums, and the plums, themselves, purple for the stuffing, and golden, big as goose eggs for my breakfast, which consists in addition of a bowl of goat's milk, a new-laid egg, a square of black bread and a small morning churning of unsalted butter. —

Wednesday.

I have been wanting to send you something that would bring this mountain life nearer to you, but *what* has puzzled me till yesterday, when I went into a low-ceiled room in one of the village houses where a chamois-hunter, crippled for life by an accident on the glacier of the Donnerjoch just above our house, was carving the Liliputian figures of chamois, goat, dog, and hunter. Tiny? You will see by what I send you; for I have chosen a dozen of the frail things, packed them in cotton wool, and sent them by post, in the care of my uncle on account of the customs. The whole collection can be set up on the surface of a silver dollar; — and such strong, big-knuckled, brown, peasant hands that carve the dainty things!

I thought of you, and told him of your work and your mountain home. He was delighted, and has sent you a chamois-beard he used to wear in his best cap; I have put that in the package. He said when I left him:

"You'll tell him, — won't you, Fräulein Madeline? — that fine fellow over yonder, that when a broken chamois-hunter like me thinks of him, I take good courage again to live." — I am sending you to-day a little German Tale, *Der Herrgottschnitzer von Ammergau*. There is a translation, I believe, *The Cruci-*

fix-carver of Ammergau, but you will enjoy it more in the original. I am so glad you have conquered the German. — Grüss' Gott!

— All that you say makes me feel humbled in the true sense of the word. Isn't it queer? Just the moment we free ourselves from conventions — and the soul is bound by them at times as with an iron ring — the good begins to work, unwittingly to us, but surely, both to ourselves and others.

Now see how all this came about. I knew I was eight years your senior, knew that your horizon line and mine had never coincided, knew that it would need but a word to deprive myself of the joy, which, with only a woman's intuition for an excuse, I foresaw would be mine in that remote, mountain-companionship of yours — and I neither spoke the word, nor have I written it since. I *couldn't* — and I don't know why either.

I saw that you were a thinking, feeling, suffering man, and a thinking man's age is not to be measured by years; so I cast that barrier to the winds. That you had a heart that trouble and deprivation had not been able to embitter was shown to me in a dozen ways during those three hours on Olympus; for was there not the expression of yourself in the lovely " Pen "? and your manner towards Twiddie and your " Aunt Lize "? and the carvings, with the seasons' life almost visible in them? and the books and the David?

That you had suffered, both physically and spiritually, was plain enough, written large in your face. Then, too, your Aunt told me how black the shadow had been that had rested so long upon you, and because upon you, upon them, — for they adore you;

(if you could see Twiddie's letters! — but you can't).
Yes, they do; and when Mrs. Lewis told me, with
tears in her eyes, that our coming would bring new
life into your life, I just squeezed her hand hard, and
tried to say that perhaps the indebtedness was n't
wholly on our side, which I have long since discovered
to be a fact.

That hand-squeeze, which we two women gave
each other, and — yes, I will confess everything —
that quiet holding of my hand in the *way* you held
it when I said " Good-by," broke the last rail of any
imaginary fence that was hedging me in.

I know all this is n't the " thorn," — but I don't
feel thorny to-day. I am going down with Nicodemus
to Felsengarten to see my chamois-hunter. I 've
ordered a quantity of those figurines to send home to
various people for Christmas, and he is to carve a
crucifix for you, to illustrate the Ammergau story.

He is the dearest fellow! Sings at his work,
plays the zither to distraction, and makes loving,
longing eyes at the prettiest Sennerin in the village.
She ought to wear a bright skirt with an embroidered
bodice, and yards of silver chain about her neck;
but, instead, she goes gowned in plain linsey-woolsey,
barefooted, to drive the goats of the high-peasant, for
whom she works, up to feed with Nicodemus's, now
that the pastures are failing. I see the kernel of a
romance in this, and shall prepare the ground in the
most practical way — enrich it with a prospective
bride's dowry for Trudel; that 's her name.

I know she loves him, for she told me so! — up
there on the Frohe Alp, at the very entrance to the
ice-world, where we opened our hearts to each
other.

"Now, you see, Fräulein Madeline," she said, brushing aside a little heap of snow to let free a tiny blue gentian, "the world is n't all ice and snow, and warm hearts make sunshine enough; and if I had a herd of goats and a cow, I 'd marry him to-morrow in spite of himself — that is, if he 'd have me — but he won't *speak*, Fräulein Madeline! So what am I to do? With no goats, no chest, even," (that is the peasant-girl's linen-dowry) "only my two willing hands, my ready feet, and one loving heart — "

Of course I made up my mind it must be, — I simply can't leave here till he *speaks;* besides, I have a strong fellow-feeling with Trudel — and all because of that "thorn," of which surely a prick in my next letter.

Nicodemus is ready with a kind of wooden creel strapped on his back. He brings home his weekly provisions in it.   Yours,

M. C.

So you, too, are interested in this romance of the higher Alps? — Well, I intended you should be!

Two weeks since my last bulletin — and still he has not *spoken!* I 've tried wile, diplomacy, bribery, stratagem, subtlety, archness, which is not becoming to my years, and artifice, which is foreign to my constitution — all to no purpose as yet.

But I have n't lost all hope — oh, no! Meanwhile, Trudel is actually growing thin, and her face shows pale through the tan. The sound of the zither is heard no longer from within the low-ceiled room; the lovely melody:

" Behüt dich Gott,
   Es wär' zŭ schön gewesen — "

sounds no more in ringing tenor down the village street of a pleasant autumn evening. He has spoiled more than a dozen of my figurines, and if this state of things continues I am sure he will be incapacitated for work. *But what can I do?*

Yours distractedly and, vicariously, in despair,

MADELINE COPE.

P. S. I am too busy extracting Trudel's thorn to think of my own.

Another week! I packed my trunk on Tuesday because I felt *sure* by certain signs that the longed-for word would be forthcoming, and, moreover, Aunt is growing uneasy in the thick cold mists and flurrying snows that hover and settle around us day and night. We are lost in a cloud-world that is confusing to sight and hearing.

Trudel weeps quietly when we walk and talk and consult together — even the six goats I have given her (we went with Franzl over the Donnerjoch to another " Hof " to purchase them) fail to give comfort, although the yield of milk, she says, is *enormous !*

The strain of the situation is becoming tense — even Nicodemus feels it, and is grumpy.

M. C.

October 22nd.

Yesterday I bought a cow with Nicodemus's aid, and we drove her — I say " we," for Trudel, Nicodemus, Franzl, and I had taken advantage of a half day of sunshine to go to Ilsengau, three miles down the mountain, to buy her — up through the village street just before sunset.

Of course, we had to pass His window. He was there — poor fellow, he is always there of necessity — and I said to myself, " *This* will bring it about; it *must* — six goats and a cow ! " But I reckoned without my host.

Well ! For all the obtuse, fossil-hearted, obdurate, stiff-necked specimens of humanity, commend me to this chamois-hunter of Felsengarten !

I had wild thoughts of begging Nicodemus and Franzl to buy eight or ten cords of dressing from somewhere, and having it hauled through the village street in his very face and eyes, placarded " For Trudel " ; — for be it known unto you, that the precious " muck-heap " is the peasant's Bank of England consols. But all was brought to naught by Trudel, who came up to me after supper, and begged with scarce articulate lamentations that I take back the goats and the cow and make her poor again ! ! ! Did you ever ?

I tried reason — but I might as well have reasoned with the wind.

"Oh, go and tell him I'm poor," she said, " poor as I used to be — go, Fräulein Madeline, go — do, *do*, if you love me ! "

Of course I went — this morning — as fast as my two legs and the momentum acquired by the rapid descent of a precipitous alp could carry me, and with outward calmness inquired how the work was coming on.

" Fine, Fräulein Madeline."

I saw the brown hands tremble a little.

" I want to see just these last two or three finished before I go — I shall leave Monday."

" So? — I am sorry, Fräulein Madeline."

That was all, but the dark eyes rested on me with a look that somehow made me feel blood-guilty, and I saw the strong hands begin to shake.

"Yes," I said cheerfully, "and I may take Trudel with me — she's such a *dear* girl, and needs some one to protect her; she's too young, too alone in the world," ("Stand that if you can," I was thinking to myself), "too poor — "

"Poor, poor did you say?" He gave a scornful laugh, but I heard his voice break, "With six goats and a cow — that is not true, Fräulein Madeline; a Sennerin is rich with that, and can choose among the high-peasants."

"Oh, but she hasn't any goats and cow — that's village gossip," I hastened to explain. "They're mine; that is, — I'm coming back again next summer, and Trudel has promised to take care of them for m— "

"Fräulein, Fräulein!" he cried out, dropping his work and burying his handsome face in his hands, "I've been a purblind fool — tell her — tell her — "

"What, Hansl, what?" cried an eager, loving voice behind me. Of course it was Trudel's. I made my escape, but not before such a "jodel," full, ringing, joyous, like the "blowing up of the trumpet in the full moon," resounded along the village street, that all the children, men, and women ran together at the Post thinking a brief had come up from the Emperor. Even Nicodemus on the Frohe Alp heard it.

"What was that, Fräulein Madeline?" he asked, the moment I came in sight.

"Hansl's announcement to Felsengarten that he is betrothed to Trudel."

"Herr mein Gott!" exclaimed Frau Bendl, clapping her hands, "that's a piece of luck for the fine fellow."

"But the goats and the cow, Fräulein?" said Nicodemus, anxiously.

I smiled. "Oh, I'm going to hire Trudel to take care of them for me till I come again next year, Nicodemus."

"Praise God," he muttered, crestfallen. I know he wanted them himself.

I've packed my trunk for good and all, and on Monday we leave for Italy, faring over the Brenner Pass. Really I feel the reaction from this awful strain. To think of that fellow's pride! He wouldn't ask her because she was suddenly become rich, and he is what he is — "cripple-lame" as he expresses it. — Good-night.

— Venice in winter! You can't imagine it. Just now a queer bronze mist is driving in unexpectedly over the Lagoon, and the wastes of steel gray waters are furrowed with black. We have had letters from Rome that urge us to spend the winter there. But to one and all we say, "No." We have promised, however, to go down for a month before Easter; we must sacrifice that to the family, for a cousin of mine is in the embassy. But it will mean for me a round of balls, dinners, receptions, conversazioni — I know it all, and am tired and sick of it.

But till then, this fascinating, unmolested corner in Venice, and intimate acquaintance with my favorites. If it be a possible thing, I am going to make you *see* all this. How, do you suppose? I am going to

revel in the carvings and sculptures of this city of the
waters, and, as I make acquaintance with the most
beautiful, write out an account of them, and then mount
a photograph of some exquisite detail, and so form
an illustrated book of Venice's handiwork along *your*
lines.

Imagine my pleasure in all this! — The close, daily
companionship with the realized ideals of these
masters; the companionship in spirit with a certain
Wood-carver far away across the ocean, and by means
of these ideals the communion of All Saints, which I
shall have gratis for my work of love. Your letters?
I'll not tell you what they have been to me — not
yet, for I have still to strip myself of that thorn. I
find there are compensations — There's my aunt.

M. C.

VENICE, CORTE SCARLOTTI.

DEAR FRIEND,

Once when a monk was showing us through the
cloisters of a Cistercian monastery in northern Italy,
I saw him gather a branch of roses that was set with
strong thorns, and crush the stem in his palm. Directly after I saw the blood trickle from his clenched
fist, and I spoke impulsively: "You have hurt yourself with the thorns."

"I did it for remembrance," he said sternly, turning upon me, a worldling, such a Last-Day-of-Judg-
ment look that I quailed in spirit. But I have often
thought of that and wondered what its entire signifi-
cance might be.

This letter seems to me a symbolic repetition
of that act on my part; for just to remember, to re-
live certain experiences, will draw blood like that

monk's thorn. You will wonder why I do it then? Have n't you found that in the crises of Life the soul needs a little blood-letting as well as the body? That's why. Moreover, unless I tell you, you cannot know what your letters have been to me these past years.

You know something of the shadow that fell upon my life when I was fifteen? A shadow that has never wholly vanished. I was an only child, and when I was just entering into the joy of young girlhood, I lost both father and mother within two weeks. It seemed for a time to blot out the whole life of my affections; but my aunt was all to me that a woman, not my mother, could be; I was young, and the joy of life came back to me gradually, but never undimmed as it was before.

And I have so disappointed that good aunt! She had settled all my future for me, along pre-natal lines, if I may so express myself, and her ambition knew no limits. We not only entertained largely in our own city home and our summer one, but were entertained in turn. Consequently, it was a round of gayeties for me for the year and a half after I came out. Then, yielding to my importunings, my aunt took me to Europe. A cousin of my mother's had married in England, and I can credit, or discredit, my life with a full London season. We went directly from there to Germany, and settled in Dresden; in the comparative quiet of the city on the Elbe, I found time to draw a free breath, look about me, and begin — to think.

If I had married at nineteen, like so many others of my acquaintance, and a little child of my own had led me, I might never have cared to think of Life's meaning to others, only to my own, — perhaps not even to myself; I don't know — these things are hidden from us.

But I did know that, although I had entered into all the gayety of the life about me in America and England, I never felt one of it; I don't know why. There was never a balcony-door opened, but that I looked for some indefinable release from something I could not define; — never a new acquaintance appeared in the drawing-room that I did not idealize him for ten minutes — or more — and was disillusioned forever after. Yet people said I had everything; — I knew better.

In Dresden, that quiet back-water where the current of cosmopolitan social life makes scarce a ripple, I had time to think. At first, through Art and Music, then through German thought and German books; and before I knew it, Hugh, I was dragging anchor, losing the dear, sweet, child-like faith I had kept as my best heritage from my father and mother, a Christian gentleman and a Christian gentlewoman, and with it, losing much of the spontaneous joy of life.

It was then I met our friend, Franz Waldort. He was one of the American students in Freiberg, and already making his mark, the professors said. He is a splendid-looking man now — but I wish you might have seen him then! " Balder the Beautiful," was our name for him in private. He was just like a young Norse god; and he brought into my life a breath of that other "elemental world" which had yet to be discovered by me, a Human. I did n't stop to investigate; I tumbled head-first into Science. This strenuous effort to comprehend, not the law of the crystallization of a mineral, but the *why* of the mineral itself, brought about confusion worse confounded in my ideals of life, and the eternal things thereof.

I realized that the lenses, spiritual, social, must be readjusted before I could "see deep enough to see musically," but I was too young to do it; — I had to grow to that. Meanwhile, I grew restless, and roamed for four years, dragging my devoted aunt from Algiers to St. Andrews — from Andorra to Odessa. Then we returned to Baltimore, and there, literally on the threshold of my own home, I found what I had been seeking! . . .

But I must stop for to-day. My aunt is ready, and our gondolier, Beppo Cortelli, is waiting at the foot of the water-steps. It is a day of days; a sky the color of the Virgin's mantle; the waves of the Adriatic alive like sapphires in the sun. — Give my love to Twiddie. Tell her that last letter made me long to taste some of the quince preserve she is "doing up." I hope she received the box for Christmas day. I wish I might see her in the white serge! Won't she have her photograph taken for *me?* Dick writes me he has a tintype of her taken last summer. He won't send it to me, but says he will show it to me when he meets me in Rome. Positively, I'm jealous. —

What will you ask next! Why do you want to know what gowns I wear at these receptions, balls, and dinners? — I was at the Russian Embassy last night, and wore a gown of dark blue velvet made perfectly plain, with a square neck, and angel sleeves lined with pale blue silk — Oh, what does a man know about angel sleeves! Well, you must use your imag-

ínation; anyway, they fall a yard below the hips. I
tell you this that you may not delude yourself into
thinking they extend horizontally from the shoulders
backwards! With this modest gown I wear no jewels,
but a single "red, red rose." — Dick took occasion
the other day to show me that tintype of Twiddie.
Why, Hugh, how beautiful she has grown! Dick has
put the poor tin plate into a dainty velvet case, and
the girl's face, even with that queer combination,
rivals in feature and expression many an ivory I have
seen here.

I thought of her at the conversazione which my
cousin gave for us at the Villa last evening. I could
see just how she would grace some of those exquisite
gowns I saw in the columned salon — Oh, you want to
know what I wore? — heavy, corded silk, ivory-white,
with a bertha of Venetian Point, a pearl necklace and
girdle of my mother's, and a bunch of yellow tea-roses
fastened in the clasp at my belt. Does this find favor
with Olympian Hugh?

Dick and I spoke of Olympus when we found
time, after our guests had gone, to go out on the
terrace and pace there in the moonlight for half
an hour. We talked of you and Twiddie, and Dick
said, pointing to a group of ilex and cypress just
below us:

"What wouldn't I give for one full inhalation of
that forest breath on Olympus!" —

— Yes, you have a right to know of my "seeking and
finding." I should be no true woman if, receiving as
I have the assurance of your feeling towards me, I
did not draw aside the veil of my Holy of Holies once
at least; for only by a glimpse of that can you understand what you are to me — and why. But not

now — not here. This air proves miasmatic for my
soul ; — I can't expose it in Rome.

Good-morning, for it is that.

M. C.

CAMALDOLI, NEAR BIBBIENA,
AT THE INN OF THE SANCTUARY.

Where it is so beautiful that one understands the
meaning of the Holiness of Beauty. This Forest of
the Camaldoli is the true sanctuary.

With the advent of Lent we fled from Rome.
Having done the whole of my duty, I felt entitled
to live for myself for a few weeks, and under the chestnuts of the first sanctuary, Vallombrosa, I sloughed
my society skin, and cleared my soul of malaria,
Rome-engendered. Goodness, how that city oppressed me !

I stopped in that dear city of Saint Mary of the
Flower — how I love it ! — long enough to order for
you a set of book-shelves, carved in the black oak in
which the Italians work so much. The Florentine
carvings are all a joy, whether in marble, wood, or
precious metals. I have also forwarded to you, by
freight via Leghorn, — of course, in the care of my
uncle, — two planks of Italian walnut, that you may
try your hand at it, and in the same case I have sent
two hats for Twiddie ; one is a broad Leghorn, the
other of light Tuscan straw made by the peasant
girls of Fiesole. The book of Venetian Carvings
goes with them, as also some photographs of the best
Florentine work. And do you mind my putting in
two of the pretty Florentine blankets made of refuse-
silk — one a deep blue, the other the color of a cactus
flower?

I thought one would look cosy on Twiddie's bed, and the other might lend a bit of fine color to your room in the firelight, if thrown over the cot of a bitter winter night.

I am glad you like the Browning poems the more you read them. What you say of them is what I have always thought but have not been able to express: that you feel "not only the jar of Life in them, but its adjustment." The touchstone of his world-humanness is that you realize the truth of that which you have said of him, just as forcibly here in this solitude of Camaldoli or on the top of your distant Olympus, as in the Ghetto at Frankfurt, a Roman salon, at the curtain of a confessional-box in a cathedral, or in the rush and roar of the thoroughfares of our New World metropolises.

I like to imagine all those books you have been gathering and making yours on these special shelves. From what you write, I know so many of my friends must be among them. I believe in the end you will make your room as fascinatingly beautiful in its way for the shut-in months, as you have made the Pen for the uncaged ones.

I am writing in the loggia, or roof-porch of this mountain-inn, and our landlord is placing our dinner, which we take at five, on the small round oak table by the balustrade. It is temptingly simple — two fat potted pigeons, a kind of purée of boiled chestnuts, two huge artichokes stewed in olive oil, two strips of pulled white bread, a dish of olives, a small flask of the red wine of the country, and a basket of mandarins. For the last touch, he has brought in a square, deep jar of coarse, green majolica filled with long-stemmed narcissuses.

The forest lies below us, about us, above us, and through the clearings there are ravishing glimpses of purple Apennine and sun-misted plain.

À-Dieu.   M. C.

EASTER SUNDAY,
FOREST OF THE CAMALDOLI.

DEAR HUGH,

You write that your life has been a slow resurrection for the past four years, and that your soul had lain for nineteen months in — worse than the tomb. I, too, thank God that there can be a resurrection of the life of the heart after it has lain long in the winding-sheet.

Such a resurrection has come to me through the beautiful love you have given me, Hugh. And just as parched lands welcome refreshing showers, I accept it; accept it as you give it, feeling all, understanding all, realizing *all*. The knowledge of it has revivified me; but that I have been to you all that you say, I fail to realize. It humbles me; but, Hugh, you have idealized me.

I told you I would tell you how I " sought and found"; but, indeed, I did n't find, not really, for all my seeking. It was *revealed* to me. I have often had in my thought the truth of those words, " Who by seeking can find out God?" Does one ever find Him out just by seeking? I doubt it. But to the true seeker, I am sure He is revealed; revealed to each individual of the seeking multitudes in some one of His infinite ways — by a word, an inspiring thought, a moment of anguish, a flower blooming on the grave of some belovéd; through the scourge of a sin, in the star-filled sky, in the miracle of a kernel nourished in an earth-clod; by the law of the spheres, of the earth, and all things thereon — of ourselves; but most perfectly of all — may I not say most transcendentally of all, through the agency of the Human as the most perfect expression of Himself?

It was revealed to me *so*.

It is easy to say all this to you, here in this forest quiet, which is a singing silence of leaves stirring in the tree-tops; — and on just this day, too!

Above me I can catch a glimpse of the sanctuary's walls — a centuries' old sepulchre of a long unrisen humanitarianism. But the resurrection has come, even here, and one finds one's Master no longer in cell and cloister, but abroad — on the road with his people, in brotherly converse and the breaking of bread.

There was a friend of some friends of mine, whom I met for the first time on my return. I had heard much of him, and all in praise. Can a woman ever tell, in real life — fiction is another thing — *how* she comes to love a man? Why, perhaps — but *how?* I doubt it.

When I saw him, I *knew*, and a great peace came with the knowledge; I felt intuitively that my quest was over. There is no need to tell you in detail; only, for several years, I saw much of him and heard often from him. I learned to look upon his thoughts as my thoughts, his ways as my ways. In what I learned from others of his way of life, I knew that he was true, pure, upright, with a largeness of heart and an humility of soul that found its best expression in walking side by side with the outcast, the forlorn, the sinned-against of God's earth.

Unknown to him I had opportunities, and made them, to acquaint myself with his work. It is far-reaching. I know of lives, some enriched, some de-

veloped, some rescued, some protected, some turned
God-wards through him; and, at last, the purposes
of God through Christ stood revealed to me through
this man — His image.

Woman-like I worshipped His creature — how
could I help it? I had waited so long; not willing
to accept any lesser thing; and I don't know why —
I suppose it sounds conceited, egotistical, but, indeed,
it is not meant so — but because I loved him with all
my heart, I thought that he, being free, must love me,
— and *so*.

But, Hugh, I was mistaken. I waited, and waited;
he never called me " friend," but we drew close, so
close in purpose, in sympathy, in thought — and our
life-lines, too, ran parallel. (My aunt saw, and almost
openly rejoiced.) But the word, for which I was waiting, longing, — yes, praying, Hugh, never was spoken.

At first I was amazed, then indignant, then humil-
iated when the letters grew infrequent, and he was
off and away across the ocean with only a few words
to make known his change of plans. Hugh, I have
been " very vilely proud," and that my love, my first,
true, deep woman's love should be unrecognized, unsought where I feared I had shown it all too plainly,
I felt to be an insulting humiliation. Even my family
had speculated upon it — and such speculations are
a sensitive woman's worst defeats.

Once, and once only, during the years I knew
him, I had let my heart leap to my eyes when I bade
him good-by, and I *knew* he must know, must understand, must see through that one look the very soul
of me. And I — I saw a response that I trusted; but,
as it appears, in vain.

Shortly after his return, before I had opportunity

to see him, I determined to run no more heart-risks, but burn my bridges behind me and set a limit, if I could, to the suffering of soul-humiliation, by putting the ocean between us. But I was n't only cowardly, — I was n't good, Hugh. With the knowledge that I had given my love, as it appeared, unsought, came a feeling of vengefulness, of " don't care," of *laisser-aller*, and I did just as many another woman has done; " If I can't have what I want, I 'll amuse myself with what I don't want," was my thought, and my life followed suit. Oh, Hugh! the awful humiliation of all this! It was worse than the first. I know of many marriages, — fairly happy ones, — both for men and women, that have been founded on the rebound of a disappointed love; but I knew myself well enough not to take that step; for, with me, there can be no such thing as a " fairly happy marriage." But I erred — sinned, if you will, in my heart, and suffered in consequence.

This is my " thorn "; and now you know why I had so strong a fellow-feeling with Trudel.

But before I went I met you, and a strange mountain-peace, an influence for good, seemed all about me and around me that day. I was glad to know you; and because through my own heart-suffering I had come again into an attitude of child-like trust in the Father, because I saw how best I could serve Him by serving others of His children who are less fortunate than I, who have suffered more, — indeed, been deprived of Life's best; because I felt that you, too, wished it, I entered into this friendship, this companionship, which has been so much to me during these two years of finding myself through losing myself in others.

There, dear Hugh, you have it all. If, after this confession, you can still love me, just keep on telling me so; it won't harm either of us — not *this* love; for, Hugh, I am older than you, and because older a little wiser in the ways of love, for the reason that I have loved as a true woman loves but once. There are other ways, I know; and this of my loving you is one of them.

Sometime you will see for yourself just what I mean; till then, I am going to ask a favor of you. Will you, in the future, destroy, after reading, the notes I shall send you? You say you have kept all my letters of the last two years to read and re-read — but, please, not the others I shall send you. The time will come when I can tell you the reason; till then — trust me, will you?

We make our way northward to the lakes, and again to Venice for the white roses over the wall of the Corte Scarlotti; then across the Adriatic and the Semmering Pass to Vienna and Gastein, where we meet Dick and some friends. From Gastein back for a day or two to our beloved Joyous Alp and Trudel's wedding, when the goats and the cow are to be hers " her heirs and assigns forever." Dick goes with us, for he is as interested in that romance as you are. —

Have you heard from our friend, Franz Waldort, since he left for South America? My dear love to Twiddie, and for yourself — I think you know all there is for yourself after this.   M. C.

MOLLENDO, COAST OF PERU, May, 189-.

Now look at that, Armstrong! When I got to the coast last October, I left a box and some letters to go by the next steamer and the Overland to you. I wanted Twiddie to get the South American trifles by Christmas without fail; and now, after seven months in the clouds and a recent drop of fifteen thousand feet from the quicksilver mines of Hauncavalica into this miasmatic hole, I find the letters and the box safe in the ship agent's office — they were forwarded from Callao — waiting for some one connected with the government to " viser" them.

I can assure you, Armstrong, there has been an irruption of the natural volcanic order that has surprised some of the numerous asinine officials — they 'd fumigated those letters, too! But what can one do? The *laisser-aller* of this people is as stupendous as their country, and that, Armstrong, is incomparable. —

I count myself fortunate in having received an extension of leave in order to give me time to do some tall-game stalking in the Andes.

Tell Twiddie, with warm thanks for her charming letters which I found awaiting me, that she may imagine me henceforth shooting butterflies as large as dessert plates with a shotgun loaded with mustard seed, stampeding electric eels in the back waters of the Orinoco, or peaceably milking cow-trees, peeling Peruvian bark, or smoking rubber in the Amazon regions.

Thanks for your letters. — I was anticipating them. They keep me in touch with the normal conditions of Life-as-it-should-be-lived.

I can't say where I shall come up next to breathe, but probably on the Brazilian coast near the Amazon; I want to travel in Humboldt's footsteps for a while.

Is n't it rather remarkable that a girl of Twiddie's age should interest herself to the extent you say she does in making a collection of the rocks and minerals of your region? Is n't that due to your teaching rather than to my books? I am afraid, though, I want to think the latter. What a way girls and women have of interweaving a man's interests in their sheltered lives! The sex continues a wonder to me.

I 'm satisfied with the amount of work accomplished. As you know, I 've been working off steam, and the results are rather surprising, even to me. —

Do you know, I still have an ideal? Don't laugh; — I want, sometime, to go to you on your Mountain for five months under a flag of truce with Life, and busy myself in the wholesome serenity of that atmosphere, domestic and otherwise, with my two prospective books. I 've a curious unreasoning feeling that Life has n't played my Ace of Hearts yet! God bless you, Armstrong; I know the worth of this friendship of yours. My love to Twiddie.

Yours,
Franz Waldort.

V

THE LOVE OF MAN

V

THE LOVE OF MAN

I SHALL try to set it down as it all has happened since that day in midsummer when I finished reading the record of those two years of travel, my journeyman years that have enriched my life beyond telling. — Happened, did I say? "As it was ordained" from the beginning, would be better.

Twiddie had been down the Pent Road towards Gilead to get me some blue-flag in the swamp by the two black ash trees. I was putting the letters back into the box where I keep them, when I heard her "hoo-hoo."

"Ship ahoy!" I shouted without looking up, for I wanted to get the letters out of sight before she came into the Pen. I had noticed several times that she seemed irritated, almost resentful, if she found me re-reading them.

"Look, Hugh!"

I had kept my head down purposely; I like to make her come sometimes more than half way. Then I looked up suddenly, full in her face. She was leaning against the post at the corner of the Pen. The rapid walk up the hill had quickened her breath and deepened the rich color in her cheeks. Her beauty startled me. In truth, I have caught myself marvelling during the last year at its ever-varying charm. She has a new face for a new day, and the artistic element in me is sufficiently selfish to rejoice in the pleasure it affords my eyes.

But as I saw her so, standing at the entrance of the Pen, beneath the vine that moved softly above her in the light breeze, her hands clasping the long, angled, dark-green stalks of the iris, the superb blue of its petals touching the damask of her cheek and matching the eyes that looked down at me from under the shade of the broad Leghorn hat that Madeline Cope had sent her, I found myself wishing there were others there to see, or that the girl's beauty might have its chance, and not be wasted for me here on this Mountain; — I did n't feel it to be right.

Suddenly she laughed merrily: a fresh, sweet sound, as when a bell-wether shakes his head in exuberant life. She laid the bunch of iris on the bench.

"I shall be careful how I ask you to look again, Hugh, if you keep on looking that way much longer! What 's the matter with my face, anyway? Pollen on my nose? —"

She looked cross-eyed with a frown down the ridge of that little straight member, and, raising her gingham skirt, gave it a thorough polishing.

"There now! It 's nothing but a freckle; I 'm bound to have them, Leghorns or no Leghorns. — See?"

She knelt by the cot and held her face up for inspection. The texture of the skin was so fine that I marvelled the more upon nearer view. But there was a freckle, sure enough, on the tip of her nose.

"A beauty-spot," I said, smiling down into the upturned face, and fanning it with the Leghorn hat which she had thrown aside. "Was it hot down there in the swamp?"

"Hot! No name for it. I oozed in and I oozed out; I had to wade, Hugh."

"Wade? Do you mean you had actually to take off your shoes and stockings?"

"Yes, I did — and if I let those flowers lie there another minute, I shall have had my pains for nothing. Whew! — " She seized the hat from my hand and began to fan herself vigorously. Suddenly she flew up.

"I must get that big stone jar down cellar that Aunt Lize keeps the boiled cider in winters; that is just deep enough for those stems."

I heard her about the house, filling, it seemed to me, all the rooms at once; for I heard her first on the cellar stairs — then at the water-butt — then in the pantry; at last, she was off through the wood-shed, — then silence.

I knew her ways so well! She would be off to the hives to see if the bees were thinking of swarming; then away to the Old Pasture bars to pat the Jersey yearlings on their velvety black nozzles; mayhap, she might gather a bowl of raspberries for supper before she came back — What was she doing? She was back again so soon, and I heard the tinkle of ice — she had been to the ice-house!

"Oh, Twiddie," I cried, "you're a gem of a girl! How did you happen to think of raspberry-shrub?"

"Simply because I'm melting — now, no nonsense,

Hugh, or you'll get none!" She lifted the tray, with its huge, old-fashioned goblets filled with the rich red juice, high on her hands above her head, beyond reach of my long arms, and all the curving grace of her young figure was thrown into relief against the darkened doorway of my room where she stood.

"Give, give, I cry you mercy," I pleaded. But she was obdurate, shaking the tray till the ice tinkled deliciously, thirst-tormentingly against the glasses.

"Now wait, Hugh; there's no hurry. Here, I'll set it down on the bench under your very nose, and you can tinkle the ice to pass the time till I come back —"

"Torments of Tantalus!" I groaned.

"I'll be back soon," she said appeasingly, relenting a little, "but not a taste till I come, — promise."

"One swallow, Twiddie — just one —"

"Not one, at your peril."

"A sup —"

"It'll be your last!"

"Just a drop, then, for love of me — hold on, Twiddie —" I caught her skirt and held her as she was about to flee.

"For love of you!" she repeated with mock earnestness. "Oh, that's quite another matter; — here, open your lips. One drop —"

She dipped her finger, and holding it above me, let *one* drop slowly gather at the tip and fall upon my tongue; — then she was off, and in another two minutes was back again from the barn with two fine, large straws. Our equipment was complete, and we "oh'ed" and "ah'ed" like two children, while we drew up the cooling drink through the yellow tubes.

"Goodness, Hugh! we have n't half enough. I 'll run up into the pasture and pick some fresh berries to make some more for Aunt Lize and Uncle Shim — it 's most time for them to be here. Won't Aunt Lize be primed with all the news of Scawsville?"

"Here, take your hat, Twiddie; remember the beauty-spots." But she laid it on the bench.

"This will do just as well." She laughed as she broke a piece off the grape-vine and tied it, kerchief fashion, over her hair and under her chin.

"Raspberry stains won't hurt this — I won't be gone fifteen minutes; they 're as thick as spatter." She reached for a strong-handled, flat basket that hung on a peg in the post, laid it with leaves, and started up the hill.

The minutes passed without note of time on my part, for across the Valley of the White Branch, the mountains loomed blue and high in the soft haze, and, in my imaginative vision, they were metamorphosed into Alps and Apennines, Grampians and Cordilleras — mountain homes of a foreign life, but human in its every appeal to me. Suddenly I was aware of footsteps — not Twiddie's — and voices — neither Aunt Lize's nor Uncle Shim's — at the turn of the house, and behold! — Philip Vanever, with Dick Malory, whom I had not seen for three years; not since his three days' fishing with Twiddie.

"Oh, I say!" I shouted in my joy at seeing them, and, having no cap of my own to toss up, threw up Twiddie's great Leghorn flap, which the breeze caught

and landed at Dick Malory's feet. He picked it up
and came in with it. Then we all talked together, —
hand grasping hand, — and the fellowship of the Pen
wrought upon us all to the forgetting of Twiddie —
at least, on my part.

"Where is Twiddie?" said Vanever at last, pointing to the empty glasses with the straws still in them.
"Is that her work?"

"Yes; Twiddie is the same hospitable little soul —
what a surprise this will be for her! She is off in the
Old Pasture after more raspberries; it's time for her
to be back — there she is now!"

We heard her singing as she came down the Pent
Road behind the house, at the very top of her voice
too; a curious, hodge-podge of a catch she learned
phonetically years ago, when she first came to us,
from an old Canuck who used to chop wood for
Uncle Shim. When she is in her gayest spirits, she
is pretty certain to sing it. We listened.

> "'Roky tummy me là, là, *là*,
> Came put a dee de *là*, de *là*,
> De lil ol chou,
> De mikum, makum, lemma nata jou;
> Szumme lumme me là, lemma nata jou.'"

How the clear voice rang out, beginning again:

> "'Roky tummy me là, là, *là* —'"

Round the corner she came full tilt, then stopped
short, voice and all — breath, too, for a moment.

I looked at her once, and took it all in; — would
have looked again had not the faces of the two men

before me as they caught sight of her claimed my whole attention. I never saw such a contrast.

I recall distinctly her gown of dark blue and white gingham, simple enough but enhancing the fairness of her skin. Her face was still flushed from exercise; the bronze brown hair, disordered among the raspberry bushes, caught the level rays of the sun and showed golden on the roughened curves of the thick waves; the wilted leaves of the vine framed the entire face, and the stem was knotted beneath the firm, delicate oval of her chin. In one hand she held the flat basket filled with the luscious red of the fruit; in the other she was dragging a branch of maple with a curious fungus growth upon it.

I saw something leap into Dick Malory's face, the like of which I had never seen before in any man's — it transfigured him; and, suddenly, I, too, *saw*. But over Vanever's face there crept a slow, ash-gray wave, I can't explain it otherwise; and I noticed that his hand shook as he lifted it slowly and closed it a minute upon his eyes, as one does to clear a blurred vision.

Twiddie, leaning into the Pen, set down her basket on the bench, and held out both hands, one to each, with a joyful welcome in her eyes — but tongue-tied, like the others. I came to the rescue.

"A surprise-party for you, Mistress Theodora; what can your hospitality offer for supper, for Dick says they saw Aunt Lize and Uncle Shim as they came through Scawsville, and Aunt Lize sent word she would not be at home before dark."

"Just hear him, Mr. Malory!" she exclaimed joyously, and pouncing upon me, as is her way when she is a bit excited, with an energetic manner of her own that is captivating. She put her finger under my chin and lifted my face.

"Honor bright, now, Hugh; do you, or I, keep the spindle-side of this house?"

"Neither of us; Aunt Lize seems to be the special spoke in this domestic routine."

"Aunt Lize!" There was scorn in her voice. "You'll see how big a spoke she is — but what is the use of arguing about what I can do? The supper's the thing; that's my strong point in the argument, isn't it, Mr. Vanever?"

"We'll wait till we see," he answered, willing to tease her. She turned with a pout to Dick Malory.

"You'll help me, won't you? — for we have fished together."

There was a kindling light in Malory's eyes that was dangerous, and I was sure he welcomed the diversion.

"All I ask is that you will let me help you till we can confound these unbelieving scoffers; they ought to starve in penance. — Tell me, can you make as good buckwheat flapjacks as you used three years ago?"

"Better — you'll see to-morrow; I'll make some for breakfast. Come and help me with the table; we will set it here next the Pen, then we sha'n't have to disturb Hugh's work-bench."

He sprang to aid her, and I saw the slight embarrassment of their meeting had worn off. They were again the good comrades of three years ago. It was pleasant to hear her joyous laugh and merry jest and Dick answering it with quick repartee, as they brought out the table, dishes, and chairs. I heard her sending him to the spring for a pail of water. It did me good to hear her order him about, and I knew it did him good. I nodded to Vanever.

"That's what she has needed — young life to brighten hers."

He looked at me gravely; his face had regained its normal color. "Dick is not much your junior, Hugh — only a year."

"I know; but I'm a century older in experience."

"True," he said abstractedly. I knew my friend, so let him alone. Dick came back with the water, and Twiddie was hither and thither and yon, intent upon her preparations, for she is a hospitable genius. When we drew up to the table — Philip had moved my cot close to the side of the Pen, and the table was on the grass just outside — I saw that Twiddie had done herself proud, and my house would not lack hospitable abundance through any shortcoming of hers.

She looked adorable, as she sat there at the head of the table, an unsuspected brush of flour on the side of her nose, her cheeks crimson with the quick baking of her flaky biscuits, her fingers stained rose-red with picking over the raspberries. A huge bib-apron enveloped her, but it could not hide a certain joyous grace in every movement. I was proud of her, and the supper as well. She had given us dozens of her tiny biscuit — she knows I can eat twice six and scarcely wink — a rasher of Uncle Shim's good bacon, with an omelette that melted on the tongue, and for top-off, the raspberries and Jersey cream, clear honey in the comb and some fresh sponge-cakes Aunt Lize had baked before she started for Scawsville. Our guests did justice to it all.

And when the inner man was satisfied, the outer took on a show of contentment, as is the way with men at such times, and Dick Malory said, pushing back his chair to look at the sunset reflection on Killington and Pico:

"I wish Madeline were here! She and I have spoken of this so often as an ideal to be realized some day."

"Your cousin is not in America, then?" I tried to speak naturally, but I felt a sudden let-down in spirits, for I had been hoping against hope that she had returned with him.

"No, she had made arrangements with friends to sail in September. I had engaged passage for us all, but was called home suddenly. My father needed help in some business matters, and my mother felt that the two years away from her one child had been twenty. I was glad to come; — Madeline looked dismal enough when she bade me good-by; I know she wanted to come. She sent all manner of loving greetings to Olympus." Suddenly he laughed, his hearty, good-fellowship laugh.

"Madeline told me to be sure and tell you about Trudel's wedding — I went up there for it." Just then Twiddie sprang up, for she heard Prince with the light farm-wagon coming down the Pent Road.

"Oh, do wait till I put on some more supper for

Aunt Lize and Uncle Shim, and get the dishes done up — then we can hear all about it. I don't want to miss a word."

"No more you shall, Twiddie," I assured her. "Just bring the tobacco-box and pipes before you go in."

Malory gave me a queer look. He sprang up. "Let me get it for you, Miss Twiddie; you have enough to do."

Perhaps he thought I did n't take, but I did; Twiddie showed herself a regular little brick in her answer: "Oh, no, indeed; I always fill and light Hugh's pipe for him — that is, hold the taper, you know."

"Now put *that* in your pipe and smoke it!" I thought, and, somehow, I began to feel as if, after all, because of the incomprehensible feeling of belligerent youth I suddenly experienced, there might not be a century's seniority on my part. But aloud I said:

"Twiddie's pipes have a knack of keeping lighted when they are neglected for a half hour's sober reflection."

"In that case, is your Cousin Hugh the only one to be favored with such a self-renewing flame, Miss Twiddie?" asked Malory, frankly enough, I must confess; and Twiddie answered just as frankly:

"No, indeed. I light Uncle Shim's, and Toughheel's too — "

We all laughed, and Malory said with mock pleading in his voice:

"Then won't you add my pipe to the list?"

" Why, of course I will — wait till I get the box, and I'll light them all."

Sure enough, when Aunt Lize and Uncle Shim had finished their supper, the table had been cleared and set away, and they had all gathered in and around the Pen, — for the night was warm, — Twiddie lighted the four pipes, " In the order of primogeniture," Dick said. At any rate, she lighted his last. Then, when the smoke curled upward from the Pen, our talk ranged from Olympus to Rome, from Scawsville to the Frohe Alp, and just before we separated for the night, Malory told us of Trudel's wedding.

I noticed Twiddie listened as if fascinated. She was within the Pen, near me, on a low stool of her own. In her absorption she had leaned forward with both elbows on the railing, her chin in her palms. It was late, about eleven ; the moon was rising to the east of Killington, and its level, white light touched the girl's face into a Madonna-like beauty. I saw that Dick was telling it all to her — telling it well too. At times I heard Aunt Lize sniff; at others, Uncle Shim chuckle softly to himself, particularly when Malory described the wedding-procession, and the advance guard of the musicians, followed by the six goats washed and scrubbed within an ace of losing their hair ; how they nipped along with wreaths of wild Alpine flowers about their horns, followed by the cow, likewise adorned with one around her neck, two bells on a leather collar at her throat, and long strands of red yarn braided into her tail. And all so decorous !

But when he told of the simple service in the

village church, of the robed priest, the village choir, the chamois-hunter in the roll-chair that Madeline had provided; of Trudel in her gay skirt, her embroidered blue bodice and the silver chain — another of Madeline's gifts — and how she knelt by the roll-chair to pray, and Hansl laid his hands upon her bowed head, — I heard a sob beside me, and Twiddie rose with a sudden, impetuous movement and flung herself forward across the threshold of my door. We did not see her again that night.

Those next two days passed all too quickly for Malory; I saw that plainly. But I was n't sorry to have him go; for I felt that Philip would not be quite himself until he should be alone with me. We had seen so much of each other from time to time during the last two years, he had been so much to me, that I had learned to know his ways. Since this last coming of his I knew there was something weighing upon his mind. I call myself his "silent" business partner; for he is a man of large affairs, carrying out his father's schemes, which, towards the last of his life, assumed colossal business proportions. So it has come about that he has run up for a day or two to get, as he terms it, a true perspective through my eyes. *My* eyes, that have n't seen a railroad for years! It amuses me, but I indulge him in his fancy that he is getting help from me. I see he thinks he is, and therein lies all of help there is. So we lay out new railroads, make combinations of others, discuss syndicates, brotherhoods, travelling libraries, employés' disabilities' insurance — anything, everything, along the trend of our Country's progress; and at all times, through him, I touch world interests, and am in the thick of the battle, where I love to be. He says he goes away rested and enlightened! I tell him he leaves me stimulated and refreshed; so it's an even exchange.

I saw he felt more at ease the very evening Dick left. We were smoking in the Pen late at night. All the rest were abed, and the silence had lasted fully half an hour before he spoke.

"Hugh, I suppose you've had your eyes opened as to Dick's coming up here?"

"Yes, but I hadn't thought of it before — she's so young."

"How old is she now?"

"Seventeen; eighteen next January."

"What would you think of it?"

"Think of what? — You mean marriage — for those two?"

"Yes; eventually that is what it will come to, if things go on as they have begun."

"But, Philip — " I hesitated without knowing why. I suppose I was feeling my way, for it had come upon me suddenly after all. "He's an only son, isn't he?"

"What if he is?" The question sounded sharp, unlike him.

"I know 'what if he is' is all right in theory, but when you come to put it into practice, there are a good many things you will have to reckon with — "

"For instance?" — I felt he was pressing me, and my impulse was to resent it. I pulled away at my pipe for five minutes; that always helps; then I said:

"I've never spoken of it before, but I take it for granted you know of her parentage?"

"Well?" The laconic inquiry irritated me.

"Well," I repeated, "it's just here; no one knows who her father was, or is, and the girl is handicapped when it comes to men of Malory's class — "

He interrupted me with a scornful: "Humph! Was it the girl's fault? And what is this talk about 'class'? Seems to me you are hedging a bit with your principles as set forth these last three years in the Pen."

Franz Waldort's wise words flashed into remembrance, and helped me to keep my temper, for I saw he was in an unusual mood, and that something was stirring in the dregs of his life. I spoke out as man to man.

"Philip, if you've got anything to say — say it; but don't keep me treading water this way any longer. Let me touch bottom just once, and perhaps I can answer you. Now, go ahead."

In reply, his hand felt for mine and gripped it hard; then we both pulled away in silence for ten minutes and got calmed down. When he next spoke, I thought he had switched us both off the track.

"Have you finished that last batch of Balzac I sent you?"

"Yes."

"Then you've read *The Village Priest?*"

"Yes, and re-read. It has been a spiritual eye-opener for me. That woman's case moved me profoundly; in fact, it was like looking at Twiddie's through the other end of the glass."

"How? I don't quite follow you."

"Why, that boy, her child, had reaped the benefit of a long repentance; and it was a woman who fought that awful spiritual battle in the thick of the world. But that man who begot Twiddie, left a girl, innocent of any wrong, who was to grow to womanhood and be obliged to fight her own battle without knowing where her enemy lay in ambush. It rouses me so when I see her, when I think of it, that I curse him for a poltroon; the gallows are too good for such. Don't you say so?"

"Yes, they are too good." I could scarcely catch the words, but I heard him groan, and, straining my eyes in the light of the waning moon, that was partly obscured by clouds, I saw him drop his head into his hands. His pipe fell to the floor, and, mechanically, he put his foot on the fire and stamped it out. Then he spoke:

"That book will always remain a marvel; the expression of a profound insight into the sinning as well as the redeeming soul. You recall the attitude of the woman to her confessor, don't you?"

"Yes; and in reading that scene, I think I understood for the first time the hold of the Roman Church upon all classes of its communicants. It has met in the provision of the confessional a great, unmet human need, perhaps the greatest — the necessity that a human being finds, once at least in his life, of disburdening his sin-laden soul upon another. All men can't find Christ in Humanity as you and I do,

Philip, but in the Human they may find Christ-like
consolation, and, after all, it may be only a confusion of terms."

"You are anticipating my words, Hugh. I, too,
have felt the need of confession, and now I have come
to you as to my spiritual Camaldoli — a sanctuary in
truth — " He interrupted himself: "Do you feel too
much of the night air, Hugh? I 'll move you in if
you do."

"Oh, no," I said, wondering what was the length of
his tether, and when he would come to the end of it,
"I often sleep out here in midsummer."

He went on: "You recall that woman's hair-shirt,
and the rôle it played in her life and the lives of
others?"

"Indeed, I do; it was a mortification of the flesh,
symbolic of the mortification of the soul; a veritable
scourge to her, but a clothing of hundreds of others
in the vestments of a charitable love and material
well-being."

"Hugh, *I wear the hair-shirt of philanthropy.*" I
heard him draw a long breath: "Thank God, I have
spoken at last! I am going to tell you all, even if
thereby I lose your friendship — " I interrupted him:

"Let me say right here, Philip, that nothing,
nothing — do you understand? — can lessen my friendship for you. Tell me all, without reserve, if you
can."

"I know by that note you 've struck you are young
yet, Hugh; but don't say what you 'll do or what you
won't do; you may swallow your own words yet, for
there is a woman in the case, and I should be a hypo-

crite to allow you to continue to idealize me as you
have the last three years."

I turned sick as I took in the sense of what he was
saying; I remember looking at the sickly, waning
moon, and thinking it looked as I felt so suddenly —
old, decrepit in spirit.   He went on calmly enough to
the finish.

"You know something of my father's ambition
through the work as I am carrying it on, Hugh, but
of his unbounded ambition for me, you could have no
idea no matter what I might tell you.   To understand
that would necessitate your having known him as I
knew him for twenty-nine years.   During my second
year in college — I went to Harvard, following the
tradition of five generations — our relation as father
and son very nearly suffered shipwreck.   I was not
eighteen when I entered.   Perhaps I was as poorly
equipped for the hand to hand scrimmage with college
life and its manifold temptations as a youth could be,
for I had known little of the influence of women.

"My mother died when I was born, and, after the
usual nursery governesses and tutors, I spent two
thirds of my boy's life in one of the great preparatory
schools.   Then I was pitched in with two or three
thousand men to find my bearings as best I could,
and take my one three-thousandth chance of coming out all right in the end.

"But just because I had not known the influence of
women in my home and my life, I idealized them to
such an extent that I failed to discern the clay feet of
the image.   I have knocked a man down for speaking

an ill word of a notorious actress in my presence, and thrashed a junior for swearing at the laundress who did up shirts for both of us. I constituted myself the special patron of the hall scrub-women, and at the same time offered my incense in the form of flowers and bonbons at the shrine of every pretty girl at the Harvard Assemblies.

"In my sophomore year, while I was at home for my usual Christmas vacation, I went into one of the large shops that sell a little of everything to buy some trifle for an old servant of ours. It was a bitter day, and a keen wind from the north was drawing down the Hudson. As I passed in with the crowd and an Arctic draught, I saw a girl at a near-by counter, which was unprotected by a screen, huddle her shivering shoulders, and heard her say to the girl next her: 'I'm frozen stiff; I'd get out of this if I could, you bet.'

"I saw her face, pretty, delicate — and weak, only I wasn't old enough to know that. It was blue and pinched with cold, and her small, shapely hands were half numb as she made up a parcel of articles I ordered immediately of her. I can't account for the suddenness of its coming, but then and there I revolted in spirit against all law, order, society; all so-called convention, pre-established principles of trade, and against a deadly commercialism that could show such a resultant of its forces.

"There was no obstacle. Within the two weeks of my vacation I had her away from there — clothed and fed to her satisfaction, after a regimen of no flannels, a continual draught of icy air, and starvation

diet on a salary of five dollars a week.   When I went
back to college, I established her in Boston in a small
well-furnished apartment, and for a few months I was
flattered and fooled to the top of my bent — and
thought I was happy!   Then the unexpected happened — and I promised to marry her to legitimatize
the child.

"That plunge into cold water realities brought me
to; but by that time my father had in some way
obtained an inkling of the affair and came on unan-
nounced to see me.   There was a scene — I don't
like to recall it; but he vowed that so long as I was
a minor he would move all the machinery of the law
to prevent my disgracing his name by marrying a
good-for-naught — so he termed her.   I swore I would
keep my word, that my honor was more to me than
my name.   You should have heard him laugh me to
scorn, Hugh.   'Honor!' he cried; 'you fledgling
fool!   You don't know the meaning of the word yet!'
and proceeded to try to break me on the wheel of his
wrath, his pity for my foolishness, his scorn of my
weakness.

"I could n't see why I had been born, when I flung
away from him at twelve o'clock that night, and, crossing the bridge over the Charles, walked aimlessly till
that June dawn.

"When I went next day to see her, she was gone,
bag and baggage — nor to this day have I ever found
a trace of her.   I put detectives at work; but whether
they were bribed by my father, or whether they
worked indifferently, I can't say; all is, she was
never found.   I accused my father of all things under

heaven and on earth in regard to it, but he preserved absolute silence and let my impotent rage wear itself out. She told me she had no relations, and, as matter of fact, no letters came to her during the five months I knew her. She gave me her name, but I have always believed it to have been a fictitious one. No answers to the advertisements were received.

"But, Hugh, when I knew she was gone — when I stood in the empty apartment, the key in my hand, and realized the bond had been but a rope of sand, I drew the first free breath for months, and felt as if a nether millstone had slipped from my neck.

"I went to Europe that season, for I had refused to go home; and when I came back I settled into the work of my junior year determined to make amends for wasted time.

"It was then I came under the influence of that Preacher of preachers, whose life may still be read written large in the lives of thousands of men who were privileged to know him, to hear him, to follow where he led. 'He shall drink of the brook in the way, therefore shall he lift up his head'; — that was the key-note to my life that he struck. There are no heights for me, Hugh; those are for other men. My work lies nearer the subsoil, at the source of the springs that fill the little runs, the 'brook in the way'; it is there I gather strength.

"I pleased my father in my last college years, and, to please him further, I studied two years in Berlin and took my Ph.D. degree; my work lay entirely along economic and sociological lines.

"'Now, what can I do for you, Phil?' he said to

me the morning after my return, as we sat in the library trying to get acquainted with each other. I was ready with my answer.

"'Let me work shoulder to shoulder with you, father, and further your interests,' — he nodded a pleased, and, as I thought, surprised approval, — 'and, meanwhile, let me work out my own salvation along my own lines — '

"'And those are?' He interrupted me sharply, with the peculiar lift of his left eyebrow I knew so well.

"'I think I won't tell you yet, father,' I said quietly enough, but my heart was pounding like a trip-hammer, for I had always dreaded his indignation — often, I must confess, justified. 'I'm twenty-four, my own master, and my mother's fortune at my disposal — No! please don't say anything, father; you may trust me to make no unworthy use of it.'

"'See to it that you do not,' was all he said; but I noticed his face went white. He had never mentioned my mother to me but once, and that was at the time I came into full possession of my inheritance. I see him now, as he sat before the library fire in his leather smoker, — a large, heavy man, unbowed, for he was only fifty-nine. Suddenly he bent forward and took the tongs to pick up a brand from the hearth.

"'Phil,' he said, and his voice sounded hoarse, 'I want to live long enough to see you with a good wife of your own, some woman worthy of you; and to hold a grandchild on my knee. Don't disappoint me in this, will you?' The question was only a veiled demand; I knew that.

"'Father,' I replied, 'why bring this up — why keep it in evidence in our lives? You, and you only, know how matters stand with me; so long as I do not know the fate of that other — the fate of the child that was to be — *my* child — I am bound. I feel that I should have no moral right to belong to another. There's no use saying anything more about it.'

"'Isn't, hey?' he snorted. I could see the working of his suppressed wrath; but he kept himself well in hand.

"'Don't mistake me, father,' I went on; 'I don't love her —'

"'Love her!' he thundered, 'I should think not. My son, the son of his mother, love *her* — God in Heaven, Phil! it makes me sick to think what you've got to live through yet before your eyes are opened. Love!' — He breathed heavily. 'Listen to me, Phil, I *will speak once* — and heed what I say. I had my fling like other men when I was young — then I loved, *loved* — you can't understand it even in its repetition — I say, your mother. I would have waited a lifetime for her — I had only to wait ten years. She was mine for two, then she left me. I have walked alone for twenty-four years; and to-day, if I could but see her shadow — her shadow, mark you — on the wall there, I would give the rest of my life, my entire fortune, yes, even you, — and *gladly*, if I might embrace it. Now you have heard what Love is.'

"He sat back again in the chair, and his hands hung limp, nerveless, over the arms. It was then I saw for the first time the shadow of what was to come — he died of paralysis — creep over his face and discolor his nails. I sprang to his side, and for the first time, in the presence of such a soul-rending revelation of a man's nature, my heart went out to him as a son's to a father. I got hold of his hands to chafe them.

"'Promise me you will marry *so*, sometime, Phil.' His breathing was still labored.

"'Father, father,' I groaned, 'I cannot—spare me; I dare not until— Oh, if I had that mother, she would know, would understand, would make you see.'

"'That'll do, Phil,' he said, but without withdrawing his hands; 'you need not bring your mother into the matter; still I understand. I'm not blaming you. It is only the ever new, the ever old case of *Fathers and Sons* — the book is on my shelf there; — I've needed a woman's hand on the helm all these years; I should have been a different man, and you — God help you! no mother, no wife — ' He broke off there, told me to ring for the carriage and come down to the office with him.

"After that I was with him constantly. He came in time even to take note of my special work, and I think in his heart he approved, although he never mentioned it. That work can be laid before you in a few words. I found wherever I went, into the by-ways, as well as along the highways, many an unfathered child, boy or girl. Of course I was looking for them; and with the thought of my own unfathered child ever with me, I stood sponsor to such children, that Life should not browbeat them, that the world's cold water should not quench all their young enthusiasms and aspirations.

"There are now over thirty who look to me for fatherly advice, for help, for love. But they know me only as their friend. They are scattered far and wide, even as the sins of man — sporadic. Coming up on the stage, Uncle Jo Cheatle let fall a word in his garrulous county gossip of Twiddie's birth; that is why I came up here the first time. But I found her protected by such a bulwark of love that I knew she had no need of me. On the contrary, I found I had need of all on Olympus. Still, I have hoped that, in time, I might be allowed to do something for her; but I have never dared ask. Now that Dick Malory must be reckoned with as an element in our life here, perhaps the way is opened to me. However, we'll talk that over when I come up in November — You're cold, Hugh; I felt you shiver —" He broke off abruptly; his hand had been on my cot. "I'm going to get you in at once." He struck a match to look at his watch.

"A quarter of one!" He exclaimed at his thought-lessness, and moved me in; then he made up a good fire, which soon warmed me through and through.

"How about the friendship now, Hugh?" He was laying a stick on the fire, softly, not to awaken the others, so I could not see his face, but his voice spoke for him.

"Come here, Philip," I said. He came and sat beside me on the cot, and, taking my right hand between his, chafed it, — gently, with almost a woman's touch, — for it was cold. It wasn't easy for me to acknowledge my sin even in the face of his.

"Philip," I said, "there are sins and sins; I, too,

have a confession. For nearly two years I cursed my Maker day and night, and I could not die. I not only cursed Him, but I cursed every living thing that had the power of locomotion — and man in His image. Yet, out of the depths, even my cursings were heard and interpreted as prayer; a man's hand was sent to grasp mine — even as it grasps mine now. No, no, Philip — first the beam out of our own eyes — "

I felt two hot tears plash on my hand, then his head was bowed upon it, and my left hand rested on his hair. "Tell me the rest, Philip," I said, half an hour afterwards.

"It's too late, Hugh; you'll be worn out."

"Oh, no; it will help to fill those night-watches of which I have written you. I have so many of them, even now." He drew up a chair to the cot.

"My father died, suddenly, when I was twenty-nine, but not before he had seen something of the truth of his words to me verified; for, two years before, I had met the woman without whose companionship my life will prove, in a measure, abortive. He knew and admired her — loved her in his direct, uncompromising way; and she understood him far better than I; she knew how to make him unbend, how to soften him. I saw then what my mother, had she lived, might have made of him.

"I can't tell you how I knew it, Hugh; I can only say I knew that she was my mate — not another's — in the highest interpretation of that word, and what it implies of that perfect spiritual and intellectual at-oneness which, together with that third factor — an

all-powerful physical attraction — in the trinity of
forces denominated Love, is the complement of what
we call 'I, myself.' It was the 'sense of the identity
of soul,' indestructible even if the body perished, even
if I were never to possess the body. These things
are of the mysteries, Hugh, and admit of no last
analysis. When I began to realize the strength of
my love, to know that every fibre of me, spiritual,
intellectual, physical, was vibrant to her every fibre,
I felt the weight of those fetters of that 'early indis-
cretion,' as we men term it, chafe until, figuratively
speaking, they performed the office of the regulation
hair-shirt.

"I have never told her my love, but I know I must
have shown it, despite the restraint I put upon myself;
for, Hugh, souls may kiss when the lips are uttering
commonplaces. What was the use of my speaking?
I should have had to tell her all. She would have
been repelled; I know her purity of thought. I
could not ask her to be my wife, bound as I con-
sidered myself to be. I think — God knows I am
humble enough in saying this — she began to realize
that she might come to love me. But she is a
woman who keeps herself under in a way, and only
once during the years that she knew me did she
speak to me through her eyes. Then I read her
soul through them.

"It was time to call a halt; I could at least spare
her. It seemed cruel; and sometimes I have felt that
I may have been thoughtless; perhaps just the avowal
of my love would have helped her, although I am
sure she knew it without words. But women are

women, and men are men; and whereas she might have welcomed the acknowledgment of my feeling towards her, and contented herself as women do in stress of circumstance with just that and its idealization, I knew that I, as a man, should break every barrier once I could hear from her lips that my love was returned. So I have safeguarded myself — possibly at her expense; but that is like us — the best of us are inherently selfish.

"She comes home in September. She put the ocean between us, I think to help me; and I have been thinking of late that it is best to tell her all, once and for all, and take the consequences. But I suffer at the thought of losing her respect, and I suffer more at the thought of losing her — help me, Hugh; what shall I do?" He bowed his head into his hands, and for a while there was no sound in the room but the snapping of the fire.

All the time he had been occupied with his confession I was aware of two distinct states of consciousness: the one concerned wholly with him and his relation to the events with which he had acquainted me; the other concerned wholly with my relation to those events, the knowledge of which must effect a radical change in my attitude towards myself and others.

In this conscious confusion of distinct but counter currents, I had but one compass, that was — a clearly recognizable duty. Out of my depths I had reached to find Philip Vanever's hand; out of his depths he was reaching to find mine, and it should not fail him; I realized also, without logical sequence of any sort, — and the realization came as a shock, laming me in

feeling, — that of the love with which Philip Vanever's
father had loved his wife, of the love which Philip
himself bore to Madeline Cope, of the love, even,
which Franz Waldort had given her, I knew as yet
only the initial letter; and, with an uprising of the
old-time bitterness, I accepted the fact that such as
I could never experience that bliss or that torture.
For me there was only renunciation.   When I spoke,
I weighed my words.

  " Philip, I believe the greatest wrong you have
done is in having kept silence so long — how many
years?" — " Seven, Hugh." — " towards the woman
you love. I believe that other of whom you have
told me, never could have suffered through your sin
the humiliation that this one whom you love has suffered through your silence. Go to her, Philip; tell
her all as you have told me; her love will stand the
test. I know whereof I speak."

  By the light of the fire I saw a change pass over
his face, which had been turned towards me as I spoke
with a strained expression wholly unlike his usual
controlled serenity.   It was like the lifting of a shadow
to show every feature illumined from within.

  He rose and stood by the cot silent for some
minutes; then, after ministering to me, he seized his
cap and went out of the east door, whence could be
dimly seen Killington and Pico showing black against
the coming dawn.   He did not return until long after
sunrise and the household had been astir for an hour.

  For weeks after he left us I was good for nothing
— lost in profitless speculation, to the neglect of my

work, Aunt Lize, and Twiddie. Finally I roused myself for the girl's sake. Where were our evenings
with the French readings? our delightful travels with
Réclus? our classifying of the minerals Franz Waldort
had forwarded to her? our German study? our game
of chess? our one hour a week with Carlyle's heroes,
or the regular Dickens Club at which Uncle Shim
and Aunt Lize were always present, an absorbed and
emotional audience?

Already Aunt Lize and Betsey Trotwood were
great cronies, and Twiddie had again and again to
read the "donkey scene" for her delight. Twiddie
was devoted to Little Nell and Little Em'ly, and
Uncle Shim had enshrined in his heart Mr. Peggotty
and Ham. In my waking hours I roared over Pickwick till the rafters rang, but in my dreams I kept
company with a little lame boy, my small brother in
misfortune, Tiny Tim.

I went to work with a vim one frosty morning in
November, and Aunt Lize, hearing the unwonted confusion, looked in after breakfast.

"I begun ter think 't wuz most time ter put up them
coffin-plates agin, Hughie," she remarked drily, wiping the suds from her arm with her apron. "It's ben
'bout ez solemn ez er fun'ral in here ever sence Mr.
Vanever left, 'n' I, fer one, much ez I like him, wished
he'd keep erway ef sech doin's is goin' ter be the
upshot of the visits." I laughed at the vision of
the "coffin-plates" on my mantel with its present
accessories.

"It's not Philip Vanever's fault, Aunt Lize, it's
mine; it's been my moulting-season, that's all."

"I'm glad ter know what 't wuz; I thought mebbe ye wuz bilious, ye hain't looked jest nat'ral lately. But ye seem all right this mornin', 'n' it gives me courage ter begin ter think er Thanksgivin'. Mr. Vanever hain't never seen er real old-fashioned, New England one, 'n' I promised ter go the hull figger, even ter hevin' the spinnin'-wheel down, 'n' the reel."

"He's looking forward to it, Aunt Lize; we couldn't celebrate very well without him this year, for we owe so much to him — all this work that has helped us pay off the mortgage. Just look at that for my bank account!" I drew out my bank-book from beneath the cot and showed her the balance of three hundred dollars. She gazed at it admiringly.

"And that isn't all. The California check is due for the last of the carvings — five hundred more. Isn't that a noble balance, and the mortgage paid off to the last cent?"

"Oh, Hughie! Seems ez if I couldn't sleep nights jest fer thinkin' how hard ye've worked fer it — 'n' he's so awful rich; Uncle Jo Cheatle says the folks down ter Alderbury know all 'bout his father, 'n' it seem ez ef — ez ef — "

"What, Aunt Lize?"

"Ez ef the Bible wuz truer 'n' truer the older it gits."

I began to laugh, for her startlingly illogical sequences never fail to produce — contrary to all reasoning — a distinctly common-sense conclusion. "That's a good sign for the noble book, Aunt Lize; come, say out what you have tucked away there under your sweeping-cap." She smiled tremulously.

"I ain't denyin' but he's jest splendid, Hughie, but ef he's so rich, 'n' yer friend, what's he let ye work yer fingers ter the bone fer when he could pay up the hull thing — not thet I don't b'lieve in bein' independent ez long ez ye can — 'n' be no poorer fer it? I never git stuck threadin' er needle 'thout thinkin' er thet rich man 'n' the needle's eye."

"Come here, Aunt Lize, please."

She came to the side of the cot and stood there with her thumbs and forefingers twirling the corners of her apron — a sign I knew so well.

"You don't know Philip Vanever; there's no 'needle's eye' for him, I can assure you. Three years ago he wanted to place at my disposal a sum that would see you and me and Uncle Shim, and even Twiddie, through in comfort and plenty. I refused it — and why? Because he had been the means of bringing to me here on this mountain-top something which no money could provide, something which money cannot buy, something wholly beyond price — the salvation of work, Aunt Lize, and through my work the heaven of my art; and to have owed my support to any man while my art was crying within me for life, would have been a moral, and, in the end, a speedy physical death." Aunt Lize drew back in a curious, awed way.

"Ye're jest like yer father, Hughie; ye'd oughter ben er preacher. I wished yer mother hed lived ter hear ye." She stooped and kissed me: an unwonted demonstration on her part.

"But he does want to do something now for Twiddie, Aunt Lize, what I want to do and can't; and who knows "— I struck a lighter note — " you may see her dressed in silks and ' satin shoon ' and driving behind her ' coach and six,' if we let him have his way."

Aunt Lize's eyes sparkled. " I 'll take it all back, Hughie. I had n't oughter spoke ez I did; but it 's grind, grind, grind, day in day out, 'n' sometimes I git mad at rich folks 'thout jest knowin' why nuther." Then she was off at a tangent. " I heerd Mr. Malory tell Twiddie he 'd never seen er real New England country Thanksgivin', 'n' I sorter thought he wuz fishin' fer 'n invitation. He seems ter be er likely 'nough young man, Hughie." She tried to hide it, but I read it all in her eyes, and in the way in which she smoothed down her apron with both hands. Woman-like, she was planning a match.

" You think he likes Twiddie, Aunt Lize? " I asked abruptly.

" My land! how ye scairt me, Hughie! Why, who said anything 'bout likin' thet child? " She parried adroitly.

" She 's no longer a child, you 've been telling me that these last four years, and anybody that has an eye can see why he comes up here." She took the bait.

" 'N' did ye see it too, Hughie, 'n' never let on? " she said eagerly, crossing the room to close the door into the kitchen.

Now perhaps another man can tell why I did just what I did. As Aunt Lize turned from me to close the door, I raised my right fist and shook it vigorously at her back! *My Aunt Lize!* Then I took up my tools and told her I had work to finish, but that I would ask Twiddie, as she seemed the one to be consulted, whether or not she would like Dick Malory as our guest over Thanksgiving.

"Where is Twiddie now?"

"Up in her room puttin' up them curtains; I can tell ye it's goin' ter look neat with all thet rose-bud cotton stuff Mis' Cope sent her."

"Tell her to come in here when she gets through, will you?"

"Yes. She told me she warn't goin' ter hev this room outshine hern, ef she could help it. It does beat all, Hughie, what er change ye've made, 'n' the Pen, 'n' everything. Thet's what ye call Art, I s'pose." She laughed in her pleasant, contented fashion: "I'll show ye *my* Art 'bout Thanksgivin' time."

"It's a noble one, Aunt Lize," and I meant what I said. I heard Twiddie in the kitchen.

"Twiddie!" I called; "come here a minute."

"I can't, Hugh; I'm busy."

"Just a minute."

"Are you *awfully* busy too?"

"No, any amount of time on my hands — do come."

"Well, in a minute." She came in, demure in her great bib-apron — she is always most provoking in that — a dish, a bundle, and a small knife in her hands.

"I'm so glad you aren't busy, Hugh," she said sweetly.

"Why?"

"Because I'm swamped with work, and here are

four pounds of raisins I want you to seed. Aunt Lize is going to begin on the pies to-morrow." She put everything down on the bench.

"But I hate to seed raisins, Twiddie, you know well enough."

"I know you do," she replied, still with dangerous sweetness, "and I propose to ameliorate your state of mind while you are thus occupied by sitting here and resting me a bit while I read 'Carlyle' to you."

"Oh, Carlyle go to grass!" I muttered.

"Why, but it's *Heroes and Hero Worship!*" she said in an aggrieved tone, "and you always —"

"No, I don't always," I interrupted her; "not in the middle of the forenoon with my fingers all stuck up with the moist, unpleasant things."

She laughed, softly, merrily. "Goodness, Hugh! I thought you were going to swear; 'moist unpleasant' sounds dreadfully profane."

"Now, look here, Twiddie, I'll have no nonsense —"

"Nor I," she interrupted, flouncing out of the room, and leaving me with the darned job on my hands. I went to work with a vengeance.

"Twiddie!" I called softly about ten minutes afterwards. There was no answer, but I knew she was somewhere within hearing.

"Twiddie!" I called again, "would you mind bringing me a bit of rag? I've cut my finger."

"Oh, Hugh!" there was a genuine, melting tenderness of anxiety in her voice that made me chuckle under my breath. I heard her scurrying about for string, rag, and arnica bottle; then in she flew.

" Here, let me bind it up for you — you poor dear. Which finger is it?"

"Am I a 'dear,' Twiddie, honor bright?" I said wheedlingly, but hiding my hand.

" Of course you are — at times. Now be good, and let me put on the rag."

I held out my third finger, on which an infinitesimal drop of blood was oozing from a tiny scratch I had given myself to excite her sympathy.

" Hugh!" She started back when she understood my feint, but not before I had caught and held her by her two hands.

" Let me go, Hugh." Her eyes flashed dangerously; I love to see her so.

" I can't, Twiddie; I want company."

" Hugh — " she stamped her foot and set her pretty teeth, " you — you are abominable!"

" Only at times; at others, you know, I am a — "

" Hugh Armstrong, let me go. I 've no time to waste on you."

" On one condition, Twiddie — easy there, don't pull away so; you can't go until I choose to have you."

" What 's that?"

" That you will sit here with me till I 've finished this job you 've foisted on me. I want to talk, Twiddie."

" About what?"

" Dick Malory."

" Oh!"

Such a radiant "Oh!" I was n't quite prepared for, I must say, accompanied as it was by a flashing smile.

" That 's something worth talking about; just let me get the citron to slice while I 'm sitting here, and you may talk on that subject as long as you like — the longer the better," she added, as I let her go.

" The deuce I may!" I muttered. She was back and seated with her work beside me in less time than it takes to tell.

" Now, let 's begin," she said with apparently joyous anticipation. I growled out something; this was not according to my program. She took the initiative, and I felt outflanked.

" He told me he had never seen an old-fashioned Thanksgiving; I know he would like a taste of Aunt Lize's mince-pies. — Look out, Hugh! You 're wasting the raisins, cutting so deep."

" M. Y. B.," I said, half laughing at my novel method of venting my irritation.

" What 's that?" she said brightly, " Dick?"

" So it 's come to that, has it?" I asked severely. " Seems to me your acquaintance has progressed rather rapidly."

" Why, no, Hugh." She looked up in innocent surprise. " I 've known him three years, besides, — " she manufactured a charming blush, — " you know we corresponded all the time he was in Europe."

" The deuce you did! Well, this is news to me. How often, may I ask?"

" Of course, Hugh, you know you really have no right to ask — only Uncle Shim has that; but I don't mind telling you if you want to know. Not quite so often as you have written Miss Cope, but I managed

to send off one to Dick almost every time I took one
of yours to her down to the mail."

"Humph!"

"Please interpret," she said with all seriousness.

"Now, look here, Twiddie; I am in dead earnest —"

"So am I," she hastened to say, puckering her
lips, while she busily sliced the citron.

"If you want him up here for Thanksgiving, just
say so.   Of course, it's my house, but any guest of
yours would be welcome."

She laughed a little before she spoke, and I
caught the mischief in the curving corners of her
mouth.

"Who said I wanted him up here for Thanksgiving?"

"Why, you said yourself you — "

"No, I didn't, Hugh."   She shook her head emphatically.   "I said *he* said he had never seen an old-
fashioned country Thanksgiving, and that's quite
another matter."

"But don't you want him to come up here?   I
insist upon your answering me, for if I've got to
write his invitation I want to know my ground."

Suddenly she looked up from her work.   "Do you
want me to want him to come, Hugh?   Because if
you do, I'll say so to oblige you."   I knew by her
look we had both reached the limits of persiflage.

"Twiddie, I don't want you to want him to come,
selfish as that may sound; but if you do want him,
whether I want you to or not, I'll write him as cordial
an invitation as I know how."

An expression showed for an instant in her eyes
that I failed to interpret.

" And I 'm selfish too, Hugh, and should love just this year to celebrate our Thanksgiving with only us four who belong here."

" No more? "

" ' Us four, no more,' " she quoted, smiling, but in all earnest.

" I should like to say ' Amen,' Twiddie, if it were n't for Philip Vanever; he is a lonely man, and my friend."

" But he seems like one of us, Hugh; he is different."

" How, Twiddie? "

" He has suffered more than Dick Malory."

I looked at her in surprise. " What do you know about suffering, Twiddie? — you who have been so sheltered in our love? " Just then Aunt Lize called to her from the kitchen. She sprang up. " I must go, Hugh. Here, give me the dish — you 've done them beautifully; I 'll do the rest. I 'll get a wet towel for your hands."

" Your praise is reward enough, Lady Theodora." She beamed on me.

That same day, at the close of one of our old-time delightful evenings with our French, our game of chess, and merry chat, as she bade me good-night, standing in the doorway with a lighted candle in her hand, I called her to me:

" Twiddie — "

" Well, Hugh? "

" Come nearer to me and give me your hand." She drew near, but did not offer me her hand.

" You say Uncle Shim alone has the right to ask

you such — such private questions about correspondence, but are you willing to tell me if you showed those letters to Uncle Shim?"

"No, Hugh, Uncle Shim knows nothing about them; but I read them all to Aunt Lize."

"Ah — I see." I felt relieved.

"What, Hugh?"

"Through a barn door when it is wide open," I made reply, smiling to myself.

"You're very provoking." I realized then that, without intention, I had seriously offended her, and, as I knew by experience, that was a risk it would not be wise to run.

"Twiddie, come back!" I cried. There was no answer, but I heard her go upstairs to her room. I called again. Then I took my shepherd's crook and rapped sharply on the wall; that is my signal when I am in urgent need of something.

Aunt Lize flew in in her nightcap and gown, her eyes wide with excitement.

"What d'ye want, Hugh? I wuz jest gittin' inter bed; I knew Shim would be in in er minute to put you ter rights; he's gone out ter the barn."

"I want to see Twiddie, Aunt Lize. She is angry with me, and you know what you taught us both about not letting the sun go down upon our wrath; anyway, I don't want it to rise on hers — you know, yourself, that is n't so pleasant."

"Thet's so," said Aunt Lize, emphatically; "what's she mad 'bout?"

"Oh, the way I said something to her."

"I don't blame her er mite. Ye hev er dretfully

masterful way with ye of sayin' er thing — it riles me clear through. I 'll call her, though."

She went to the foot of the stairs; I heard her speak and Twiddie answer her. Then I waited. At last I heard her coming through the kitchen. She stood again in the doorway — a white clinging woollen wrapper thrown about her, her hair hanging in long braids, the candle lighting her flushed, resentful face.

" Twiddie, tell me — I can't sleep unless I know; — did Dick Malory ever begin his letters 'Dearest Theodora' like that other chap?"

"No, Hugh." I saw her face soften.

"Does that other chap ever write you so now? I have n't thought to ask for — why, it 's nearly three years!"

"I know it is. No, he does not write me any more."

"Why, Twiddie?"

"He has forgotten me, Hugh."

"Are you sure?"

"Sure, Hugh."

"Will you say good-night to me, Twiddie?"

"Good-night, Hugh."

" Twiddie, give me your hand — I 'm not satisfied."

She crossed the threshold and came over to my cot. She gave me her hand, but passively. I held it a moment, nor did she withdraw it. " Twiddie, do you remember years ago when you smiled up into my face — sitting here beside me — and forgave me, just by smiling?"

I saw the flame leap upon her delicate neck — the cheeks — the temples; her eyes brimmed with tears.

She drew away her hand, but not before she had leaned suddenly above me and smiled down into my face. She caught away the loosened end of her braid that dropped upon my forehead, straightened herself, and, holding one hand before the flame of the candle, hurried from the room.

Those next three weeks were filled with good things. There were unwonted preparations, and Aunt Lize was in her glory. The weather was stinging cold, the skies lowery, with a daily spitting of snow; but this house of mine was filled with the sunshine of a girl's joyous presence, and the rooms echoed to her merry song and jest and laugh.

One afternoon Aunt Lize, Twiddie, and Uncle Shim filed into my room, each with a tin tray of pies — the whole tribe. They were set out in noble array on the bench that I might see, smell, admire, but not taste! Oh, no, not so much as a bite till *the* day, Twiddie said. And when that day came, we surveyed our work with satisfaction. I say "we" because I had been pressed into service and furnished my quota of muscle in beating, stirring, and chopping. At eleven o'clock the turkey, a noble bird of twenty pounds, outdid himself by bursting the trussing and disgorging the dressing. While Aunt Lize was kneeling with flushed face before the oven-shrine repairing the damage, and Twiddie with scarlet cheeks was burning her nose in the steam in her efforts to help, Philip Vanever drove up from Alderbury; he had come on the night train.

It was a glad day! and Philip Vanever's joy in it

all a thing to remember. The old kitchen was redolent of every kind of New England cheer, from turkey and turnovers to cider and celery, and, thanks to our guest's thoughtfulness, had blossomed into summer fragrance with the flowers he had brought up for Aunt Lize and Twiddie — roses, violets, carnations. Twiddie's face was a study when she opened the box and leaned to inhale their fragrance. And after the table had been cleared and the dishes washed, Twiddie changed her gown, and came down in the white serge Madeline Cope had sent her the year before, and the dark crimson velvet girdle that came with it. She took two roses of that same rich color — Jacqueminots, Philip called them — and fastened them in her girdle, and the stem of another she tucked into the waves of her bronze brown hair; and then, looking at us who were looking at her, she said happily : " Do I suit now? "

We three men were dumb, and could do naught but look and try to drink our fill of such beauty; but Aunt Lize, seeing our admiration, snapped suddenly :

" Harnsome is thet harnsome does; remember thet, Twiddie Lewis ! " At which we all laughed but Twiddie, who, slipping behind Aunt Lize's chair and leaning over the back, clasped her two arms about her neck, saying : " How dare you quote that, Aunt Lize, in the face of the pound-cake I made for to-night's tea? " And after that tea, which we had late, they all came into my room, and while we three men smoked, Aunt Lize, to please Vanever, sat in the chimney-corner and spun by the firelight, and Twiddie, on the rug, minded the chestnuts she was roasting, and her forehead into the bargain. Our talk ranged from the new inn at Farnsfield, which some New York men were financiering, and the late rumors of a prospective railroad in the Valley of the White Branch, to the wanton destruction of the forests to feed the pulp mills, and the new game laws. It was good to be together, — but I caught myself wondering if Philip Vanever had spoken. At bedtime Uncle Shim opened the east door to look out, and a dash of snow whirled into the room.

"Thet 'll give us good sleighin' by ter-morrer," he said. "Ye 'd better take Prince 'n' exercise him er leetle."

"I shall be glad to, Mr. Lewis, if one of you will go with me; I 'm poor company for myself."

Oh, that to-morrow! It broke clear and shining on a mountain-world mantled in white. After breakfast I heard Twiddie in the kitchen, teasing him to stay over one more night — just one; but he would not give his word.

"By the way, Twiddie, you promised to show me the made-over room; I want to contribute my mite towards it. What do you say to a rug, white ground and all rose-buds to match the curtains?"

Twiddie clapped her hands. "Oh, that will be lovely! The floor is the one thing that has distressed me. Come up and I 'll show you."

Perhaps ten minutes had passed, and I was wishing that I, too, might see the pretty room, when I heard Vanever's voice in the kitchen asking Uncle Shim, who had just come in, if it would be convenient for him to take Prince for a few hours. I heard Uncle

Shim assure him that he would hitch up at once; after that, Vanever came into my room, closing the door behind him.

"What is it, Philip?" I cried when I saw him, for over his face had crept that strange ash-gray wave leaving every feature rigid, drawn. He dropped into Aunt Lize's rocking-chair and leaned forward, his elbows on his knees, his head bowed into his hands.

"I've had a blow, Hugh, — I've had a blow — " he groaned rather than spoke. "Don't ask me now; I shall be back this afternoon."

I knew there was nothing to be said — I could not feel my way in such dark; so waited until I heard Uncle Shim drive round the house. Vanever reached for his overcoat on a peg by the east door, and went out, seeming half-dazed, as if the blow had stunned him.

It was five o'clock and dark before he drove into the yard. My eardrums had been strained to bursting for the last two hours, and I heard the " tankle " of the old cow-bell away down the road towards 'Lympus-Gilead. When he went, he drove up the other way through the clearing. He came in at the east door with a quick, firm tread, and, throwing off his coat, drew up a chair to the fireplace and spread his hands to the blaze. I saw that he had had time to pull himself together, that he was himself again. But I was n't prepared for the tone in which he spoke even the commonplaces. It sounded as if a suppressed joy, an exultant triumph, were the basal-note of every word.

"I shall have to go back, as I planned, on the

night train, and leave here a little earlier than I intended — about six."

"You will want Uncle Shim to drive you down, won't you? The team you ordered from Farnsfield will be too late."

"Oh, no; Prince must not be imposed upon to that extent. I'll just take my grip and walk down, even as far as Scawsville if necessary; but I know I shall meet it a good bit this side."

I began to protest, but he cut me short. "This has been in truth a 'Thanksgiving,' Hugh. I wish I might make some thank-offering other than a grateful heart. Supposing we ask Mr. Lewis in and talk over some little plan for Twiddie, for her pleasure, her improvement, if you will, although I see little chance to improve her. You may well be proud of your pupil, Hugh."

"I am; but how will you broach this to Uncle Shim?"

"Leave that to me; I know my ground now," he said with such a sure emphasis, such a flash of his dark eye upon me, that it staggered me for a minute. In a curious way I had a sudden vision of the truth, only in eclipse. Before I could answer, Uncle Shim came in at the east door.

"Ye'd better wait t'll arter supper, 'n' let me take ye down ez fur ez Scawsville," he said with his back to the fire.

"Thank you, Mr. Lewis, but I prefer to walk; besides, I am already under too many obligations to you for the use of Prince for so many hours."

"I take it ye druv quite er piece, seein' ye went

Farnsfield way 'n' come back 'Lympus-Gilead road."
I could see that Uncle Shim was over-full of curiosity.

"Yes, it was a long way around, but I wanted to head off Uncle Jo Cheatle ' over the Mountain.'"

"Did ye ketch him?" asked Uncle Shim, eagerly.

"Yes; but, Mr. Lewis, before I go I want to talk about something of great interest to me and, I think I may say, to Hugh. I've been the recipient of so many favors here from you all, that I must refuse to be under greater obligation, unless you will allow me in some way to make a return."

"Wal?" It was not an encouraging sound. Uncle Shim straightened himself in a curiously defiant fashion, and clasped his hands behind his back. He stood facing me and Vanever, his old felt hat set well off his forehead; his old overcoat of nondescript color, faded, bleached, sunburned, patched, hung loosely from his shoulders.

"Has it ever occurred to you, Mr. Lewis, as Twiddie's guardian —" I saw Uncle Shim start, and his light blue eyes suddenly open wide under his bushy brows — "that possibly it might be well for Twiddie to have an opportunity to see something more of life than she can on this mountain-top, beautiful as this is? She is gifted beyond most girls of her age, and — and —" Even Philip Vanever hesitated in the face of the uncompromising, wide-open stare with which Uncle Shim was regarding him.

"I guess I can git the gist of what yer tryin' ter say 'thout many more words," he said in his deliberate, drawling speech. "I s'pose ye mean ye want ter marry her, 'n' air axin' my leave —"

"God forbid!" exclaimed Vanever, interrupting him with such a look of horror that Uncle Shim's face turned white, then worked strangely.

"What ye ben comin' here fer, I'd like ter know, ef 't warn't fer her?" Vanever looked at me as if he had been caught in a trap.

"Uncle Shim," I said, and I was so mad my voice trembled, "this is my house, and you can't speak that way to any guest of mine. If you'll hear Mr. Vanever out, you'll be well ashamed of yourself for this."

"I will, will I?" He laughed with a strange shake in his throat; "I did n't know ez ye'd j'ined the majority. I know the house is yourn, 'n' the land is yourn, 'n' yer aunt is yourn, 'n' yer friend is yourn, but Twiddie's *mine* — mark thet, both on ye, 'n' yer Aunt Lize, too; 'n' ef wust comes ter wust, Twiddie 'n' me'll take the outside er the house, 'n' yer Aunt Lize 'n' yew can keep the in. I've seen the hull thing — " I saw he was working himself into a passion, and that the passion, because of the extreme rarity of its occurrence, was affecting him physically. I tried to stop him.

"Uncle Shim, you don't know what you're talking about; we won't say any more to-night; I can easily explain to you afterwards, when you are calmed down."

"Calmed down! Jest talk thet ter some other man; ye'll hear honest Injun from me, I can tell ye, calmed down or calmed up. I tell ye both now, I ain't er-goin' ter hev no city chaps hangin' round my leetle gal. She's good 'n' true 'n' sweet; 'n'

ruther 'n hev her go down inter thet hog-pen er rottin'
human — "

"Uncle Shim!" I thundered, "stop, or I'll — "

"Yew shet up, 'n' let me say my say, then I'll go;"
he took a step half-threateningly towards the cot.
"I say," — he raised his voice, but his words were
just as deliberately spoken, — "I'd ruther lay her
in her coffin 'n' screw down the lid, *tight*. Ye can't
tech her," — he faced Vanever, who had stood im-
movable since he last spoke, — " nor thet other feller
thet 's tryin' ter hang round her. I see her goin' fer
the mail, furrin stamps 'n' all, 'n' he eatin' 'n' drinkin'
'n' talkin' her the las' time he wuz here, *'n' I won't
hev it!* " He brought his fist down on the corner of
the mantel with such force it was a wonder it did not
break the bone. "She's my own flesh 'n' blood —
mine, d' ye hear? — 'n' her mother wuz my — "

Something passed between those two facing each
other with their nostrils white and jaws set. Vanever
told me afterwards he had not intended to speak,
knowing it was no time; but that suddenly an elemental surcharge of feeling mastered him, and he
lost control.

"More *my* flesh and blood than yours," he said in
measured tones, but with exulting conviction ringing
through them, "*for I am her father.*"

It was said, and my first thought was that he was
free for Madeline Cope; the next was for the two
men — I feared for both.

For a minute there was a dead silence in the room;
even the fire did not crackle. Outside in the kitchen,
Twiddie was singing while she was setting the table —

that old verse of Watts's.   I looked at Uncle Shim. His jaw had dropped, his face grown a sickly yellow. Then I heard an oath.   Such an oath I dare not blacken this page with writing it down.   He staggered to the door, and Vanever sprang to put his arm beneath his; but Uncle Shim threw it off, and went out into the night.

"My God!   What have I done, Hugh?   Shall I go after him?"   Vanever turned to me in such distress that I knew I must be calm for both.   I got hold of his hand.

"Philip," I said, "'the ways of God — the ways of God'; remember that; it will come right; believe me, and leave him to me.   Call Twiddie."

He opened the door into the kitchen; how her sweet voice rang out:

> "'Change me, O God! my flesh shall be
>   An instrument of song to thee,
>   And thou the notes inspire.'"

"Twiddie, Hugh wants you."

"I'll come, Hugh, — just a minute."

"Twiddie," I said, speaking quietly, "I don't think Uncle Shim is feeling very well — he went out of the east door just now; I think he has gone to the barn. Just put on a shawl over you and run after him and bring him in."   She had flung on my plaid and was off almost before I had finished.

"Hugh, I've done wrong — managed badly, and it is better for us all that I should go now, without delay. Tell Twiddie and Mrs. Lewis; I will write you all, — and give the letter to Mr. Lewis —"

"But, Philip, where are you going?"

"Home on the night train as I had planned, Hugh, and then"—he paused, drew a long breath—"to Madeline; for I am free, Hugh, FREE!"

I saw then that his first thought was not for his child.

"I will write to-morrow; be on the lookout for it and keep me informed of everything, will you?" He was putting on his overcoat.

"I will."

"God bless you, Hugh." He was gone.

VI

THE GIFT OF GOD

VI

THE GIFT OF GOD

ON that Saturday following Vanever's return, there was an unnatural calm within the house. It was as if a cyclone were sweeping the Mountain and we were in the storm centre. But on the Sabbath there was a change, a lessening of the tension, and the quiet of Nature and the peace of the Spirit brooded my soul like a great beneficent Hand.

About eight o'clock I saw a flock of snow-buntings whirl, like dark, driven leaves, in a snow-flurry before my window. Fifteen minutes afterwards came a marvellous sunburst. The sky suddenly freed itself from the gray and white clouds, rolling them back like a scroll to the south-east, and afterwards there was one clear blue, a dazzling sun, and the immaculate white of mountain-snows.

I re-read what, for want of a better name, I call my Mountain-Litany — jottings by the way: marks, by which I may keep in mind the trail I have followed through the wilderness of doubt into the sunny open of faith.

My Mountain-Litany.

— I spoiled a piece of work to-day, because I failed to see that to bring out a certain effect I must needs cut with the grain of the wood. Must not Life run so, — along the line of one's grain, if one is to work according to a natural law?

Twiddie brought me a mullein-leaf covered with hoar-frost. What a marvel of texture, bediamonded! Every tiny globule shows in the sunshine the chord of the seven colors.

What a pleasure it must be for Some One to create this! If I take such delight in creating, in materializing the idea, which is the essence of the tangible — what, primarily, must the creating of this mullein afford — and to Whom?

Some stalks of the bee-balm stand in my pitcher on the bench. What an imagination it must have required to originate the factors of this! — a composite of trumpet, chalice, cardinal's hat, that "scarlet thread" of the Bible, and blood-stained leaf; shape, color, symbolism, and fragrance, — frankincense and myrrh, — all there.

I used to like to see Orion wheel to his setting; about April, the belt, like a huge arrow, transfixed the western hills. "The firmament showeth his handiwork." That truth has been distilled into my soul-consciousness hour by hour during the night-watches in the Pen.

"His handiwork" — my handiwork; — and between the two, the vibration of some wonderful accord which unites the choiring of the spheres and the note of the song-sparrow in the lilac-hedge; some bond of intimate union in which is interwoven the elemental forces, whether of gravitation, or the power of the mounting sap that in the end gives me the fibre of the wood.

The forest is yielding me its secrets in this intimacy with the wood and the designs. And the secret of the forest lies deep, deep in the subsoil — deeper still in the elemental world of a mountain's heart.

That is a curious matter to ponder! — Elemental strength of all kinds at work for æons upon shifting sands and deposits of detritus; fire and water doing their utmost; hearts of mountains incandescent; quiescence of strata for untold ages, — then Upheaval, and our geologist on the mountain-top may ring his hammer on the earliest formation!

Such, I take it, is the process of Humanity stratified into Society. A great truth there.

Even the " dung-heap " has its secret. I heard the hens *churring* about it this morning while Uncle Shim was forking it over preparatory to drawing two loads up to the corn-patch. To-morrow he will plough it under, and in five months the corn will be ground and Aunt Lize's Johnny-cakes steam golden-brown on the breakfast-table. So are we all indissolubly linked with the earth-elements — the nourishing and the nourished; and the one returns to the other, and the other yields its return. What a harmony of provision! — and thereby the sustenance of the Spirit during its short earth-pilgrimage. Ay, ay — " see deep enough and we see musically."

The Soul of Man is a pilgrim with the scrip of the body filled for his sustenance during the earth-tarrying. On his long journeying, he entereth into the Temple of Human-Life-on-this-Earth through the portals of Human Birth, and tarrieth for a while in crypt or cloister, in nave or chapel, in choir or chancel — marvelling, praying, begging, sinning, repenting, loving, worshipping, praising, delving, investigating; then passeth onwards, out through the portals of Human Death, — still marvelling!

A flower in its perfection: the expression not only of the Divine Imagination, but of the utility of economics — grace springing from satisfied needs. Should it not be so with our lives?

There are so many avenues of approach to God for the wandering soul! Even a spiritual *cul-de-sac* may prove eventually a straight, if narrow, path.

My approaches have been through work, the friendship of a man, the love of a woman; yes, and the open fire, the stars in the night-watches, the ministrations of Aunt Lize, and Twiddie's sunny presence, have been lights unto my devious paths.

This, I believe, rounds to as much perfection of happiness as may fall to my lot as a man.

There has been a fearful tempest, — the thunder crashing ceaselessly, with a snarling, splitting sound; the lightning playing incessantly through the cloud that enshrouded the Mountain. There has been havoc in the forest.

It swooped down upon us with a great wind, blotting out the sun, sky, everything beyond the spruce-bush; and it cleared almost as suddenly. The sun broke through the huddling, scurrying cloud-masses; there was a glimpse of intense blue, a sudden clearing of a sapphire circle in the zenith, then the last reverberation of the thunder, and a sparkle and glitter and dazzle of flashing reds and greens among the myriad drops caught on grass-blade, bush, and tree.

The silence was broken by the thin bleat of a lamb; then a song-sparrow sang its *Te Deum*.

Again and again I have put off the carving of the Fate's head from the seasoned black birch. The desire has grown less and less to materialize my conception of it; — Life is showing me another face.

Uncle Shim got me out a plank last fall, and one day I went to work to carve, not the Fate's head, but a crucifix for Toughheel. I had Hansl's for a model; but something not in the face of his Christ got carved into mine, and made me loath to part with it, — " a man of sorrows and acquainted with grief." It was loving, worshipping work, and did me good.

When I gave it to Toughheel for Christmas, the fellow's face was a study.

I tried; — but I could not think it out, could not reason it out, could not discover it, search as I might; but, lying with open eyes, open heart, open mind, receptive soul — it was *revealed* to me that *God is,* and there is naught old, and there is naught new, and faith remains the compass for the Soul.

What a revelation! — here on my Mountain-Patmos. —

I was interrupted in my reading by Uncle Shim.

It was near sunset, and in the waning light his face looked old and haggard. He closed the door into the kitchen and sat down, brokenly, in Aunt Lize's rocker. I had been expecting him all day, and had the pipes ready filled.

"Draw up your chair to the fire, Uncle Shim, and we 'll light up," I said, hoping to cheer him. It cut me to see his dejection.

"No, Hughie, I don't want no pipe; I hain't slep' any fer two nights, 'n' Lize hez got scairt 'coz I hain't eat nothin', 'n' won't say grace."

"Oh, Uncle Shim, it is n't so bad as all that. Let 's talk the whole thing out, and you 'll feel better; I 'm sure I shall." He shook his head slowly.

"Ye ain't got it on yer conscience, Hughie; — I would n't Lize should know on 't fer my soul's eternal salvation. She 'd git er bill er divorce quicker 'n lightnin' ef she 'd heerd it."

"Heard what, Uncle Shim? I think I 'm not sure just what you mean — about the relationship between Twiddie and Mr. Vanever?"

"Lord, no, Hughie! 't ain't thet; she 'll be tickled ter death ter know thet. She 's hed her idees 'bout what Twiddie ought ter be — mighty up-in-the-world ones they be, tew — "

"Well, what is it then?" I began to feel impatient; like Aunt Lize, I feared "long-windedness."

"Hughie," he turned to me with such a stricken look in his sagging jaw that I felt troubled. "I 've damned er man! I 've damned him in this world and the next. I 've damned my feller-man, Hughie, 'n' how be I er-goin' ter make my peace with my God?"

Poor Uncle Shim! How he had suffered!

"Uncle Shim," I said, "you were in a tight place and hard put. It came too sudden; Vanever said that to me before he went — " He interrupted me.

"No, 't warn't so sudden ez ye think, Hughie. I've allus felt thet Twiddie warn't the common kind, 'n' thet she might turn out ter be er millionaire's child; she ain't er mite like her mother, but, Hughie, blood's thicker 'n water, even ef 't ain't only half 'n' half; 'n' ef she warn't only my half-sister — "

"Your half-sister! How is that, Uncle Shim? I never knew that before."

"I know ye hain't. I hain't said nothin' 'bout it. Shet mouth 'n' live it down, is my motto every time. Yes, she wuz half-sister ter me, 'n' fifteen year younger. I couldn't tell ye, nor nobody else, what got inter mother ter git bewitched, arter she 'd ben widdered fourteen year, with er low-down, rum-'n'-water land-shark thet come perspectin' up in the north part er the state. Anyhow, she married him, 'n' er year arterwards, Marier come erlong, 'n' the man dusted. Mother got her bill, 'n' kep' father's name, 'n' I worked out my freedom keerin' fer her 'n' the baby."

"What was her name?"

"Rasle; Marier Elviry Rasle; but mother wuz cut up so bad with the disgrace, thet she never called her nothin' but Marier Lewis, 'n' I don't know ez ther's more 'n two-three livin' souls thet know her real name. She went agin her mother, jest ez soon ez I 'd left 'n' come over here ter farm it with yer grandfather, 'n' when she wuz eighteen, she went off down country

ter earn her livin'. Thet's the last I heerd from her
t'll I got word ter come down ter Old Town Gilead;
'n' thar I found her with the child. She said she 'd
ben deserted, 'n' hed come up here ter die some-
whars near me; mother 'd died long before thet. It
teched me arter all in er tender spot, 'n' the leetle gal
come ter me, 'n' put her leetle arms round my neck,
'n' Lize 'n' I hed n't any — "

I heard a gulp, and looked out of the window not
to see his emotion and to hide mine.

" 'N' she seemed so kinder erlone in the world, 'n'
I knew the man thet hed fathered her hed left the
poor, innercent leetle soul ter shift fer herself, fer
Marier hed one foot in the grave when she sent fer
me; 'n' I took 'n awful grudge, Hughie, agin thet
man. It's ben ranklin' 'n' eatin' in, jest like gangrene,
inter my life, 'n' when he stood thar before me so
kinder sudden 'n' proud-like, knowin' nothin' 'bout
trials 'n' privations, 'n' Life sech ez *we* know it,
Hughie, the venom riz right up under my tongue,
'n' I spit it all out — all the gatherin' fer eighteen
year — onter him in thet one oath; 'n' I hain't hed
er minute's peace sence."

" Uncle Shim, I wish you would let me tell you all
I know about it, and by to-morrow there 'll be a letter
explaining what none of us can understand."

" Go ahead, Hughie; I guess I dew feel er leetle
mite eased fer speakin'."

" Yes, Uncle Shim, and I believe you are going to
feel eased for the rest of your life because you have
spit out all the venom that is in you in that one oath."

"D' ye think so, Hughie?" He looked up wistfully, but I could see his face had brightened a little.

"I 'm sure of it; but before I tell you what I know, I want to ask a question or two."

"All right, Hughie." He settled himself in the chair and stretched his legs. I saw in the movement an expression of the relief he was experiencing.

"You remember you did n't say grace for nearly two years — not so very long ago?"

"I 'member, Hughie."

"And that you did n't feel like saying it because you could hear me cursing and blaspheming in the little bedroom?"

"Ye 're tellin' it jest ez 't wuz; — it went agin me ter mix words er grace 'n' words er damnation in the same minute 'fore the Lord."

"Well, Uncle Shim, you cursed your fellow-man once, — a fearful curse, I must own, — but I not only cursed the creature, but the Creator, and that, not once, but a thousand times in the course of those nineteen months; and if I can say I know I am forgiven, don't you think you 'll find forgiveness too?"

He drew the back of his hand slowly across his eyes. "Ye 'd oughter ben er preacher, Hughie; I never thought nothin' 'bout yer doin' it. It only seemed kinder nat'ral fer anybody thet hed ben under sech discipline ez yourn — "

"And it seemed just as natural to me that you should utter that oath with the provocation you had. We 're both men, and pretty human ones, too, Uncle Shim — "

"Thet's so, Hughie," he broke in eagerly, coming over to the cot, "we're er durned selfish lot, the hull on us, 'n' I hain't no right ter fling stones. I've tried Lize most ter death, 'n' 'mounted to nothin'." He grasped the hand I held out to him, and the slow tears coursed down his furrowed, unshaven cheeks.

"Just get me a coal to light my pipe, will you, Uncle Shim? I want a smoke to ease me up a bit."

"Jest what I wuz wantin' myself. I can kinder think things out clearer when I'm drorrin' 'n' puffin' fer all I'm wuth, 'n' seein' things outside er me through er blue smudge." He lighted his pipe and took his seat in the rocker. We talked till late in the evening, and threshed family affairs to some purpose.

"Tell him," he said, when he rose to bid me good-night, "not ter lay it up agin me — I've forgiven, ez I hope ter be forgiven."

I told Aunt Lize the next day, and when the letter came I read it and handed it over to them both. When Aunt Lize gave the sheet back to me, I saw by her face that Philip Vanever had one stout ally for time and for eternity.

But — after all was said — there was Twiddie. I held the letter, when Aunt Lize had finished reading it to Uncle Shim, long in my hand, and pondered. Finally I asked Aunt Lize to tell her; but she put up her hands as if to ward off a blow. "I can't, Hughie; don't ask me *thet*," she said.

"Then, Uncle Shim, you must — you are her guardian."

"My God! Hughie, I can't; don't ask me — it's

like turnin' loose er whole stream er mud onter her
purty white life — "

"But, Uncle Shim, she must be told; she is of age
next month, and you would have no right to keep it
from her."

"'T ain't thet, Hughie; but I dassen't say sech
things ter the gal; let — let her father do it." I saw
how hard it was for him to speak the word and what
a victory he had gained over himself.

"It would n't be wise; she could n't bear it from
him — not now."

"Hughie," said Aunt Lize, speaking abruptly, "it's
borne in on me thet ye 're the one ter tell her; ye
know how ter put things better 'n we do, 'n' she 'll
take anything from yew. Ye 've allus known how ter
manage her, 'n' she sets er sight by what ye think on
her; — ye 've got ter be the one. Ef 't wuz on the
mother's side, I 'd do it fast 'nough, but it 's on t' other
side, 'n' it b'longs t' er man ter say it."

"I 'll do it, Aunt Lize, to help you and Uncle Shim
— you have been so good to your boy and girl."

"Don't, Hughie, don't!" cried Aunt Lize, and flung
out of the room.

But how to tell Twiddie! I thought and thought,
but could find no entering wedge, and the longer I
pondered the matter, the more the difficulties multi-
plied. I said to myself: "To-morrow, I will tell her
without fail;" but on the morrow she came back
from the butternut tree with a letter — and what a
letter! — from Madeline Cope, and the reading of
that gave me, as I thought, the end of the string
which should unravel the ball. To answer that letter

I felt to be my first duty.   It shall lie here between the leaves, for it has shown me the strength and purity of a true woman's first love.   I know she will let me keep this one, despite my promise.

HUGH, DEAR HUGH,

Philip has come from you to me, and something tells me you know why he has come, at last.

What are we women good for but just loving and forgiving, for comforting and supporting?   He has told me *all*.   Oh, Hugh, it has needed the discipline of all these years to show me how to be humble in accepting such love; and he thought during all this time that, because of that Past, because of his sin, I could not love him!   Oh, how little you men can know, even the best of you, of a true woman's heart! And I, too, have confessed all to him.   I have told him how I have felt all these years: as if I were married to him in soul — and that is the eternal part, say what we will.   It is that which holds and binds in this world — and hereafter, *however it may be*.   Even had he married, there could have been no divorce of my soul from his.

And now to know that such has been his feeling for me!   To know we may live our life, not our lives, together, not apart any more; that I may take his dear head between my hands and comfort and love as a wife loves — A rain of tears is blotting this page; but you will understand, — the long waiting is at an end.

And Twiddie — dear little Twiddie, *my* Twiddie, because *his*.   How strange all this is!   Make known to her in your own way, dear Hugh, what she is to me, how I feel to her — as a mother.   I had planned, before this surcharge of happiness, to have her with me during February and March; that is, if I could persuade her to leave you. I want to know her more intimately in my own home, and I know there is much young pleasure I can provide for her. Moreover, Dick is looking forward to her coming, and planning to run over often while she is here.

Can't this be made a surety, now that the tie is so close? Let me know after you tell her; let me know, too, how she looks upon all this from her girl's stand-point — I long to help her, for she will need some help sorely.

I am writing in the morning-room with the beautiful panels all about me — and here is a confession: it was not wholly, nor firstly, because I wanted a work of art with which to live, that I ordered these panels from you. No, Hugh, it was because Dick told me Philip had been so interested in your work and in you, that I — that I — oh, how despicable this must seem to you! — wanted to know you because *he* knew you, and I planned the trip which included Olympus, because He had been there before me. And, after-wards, Hugh, I loved you, not only for your own sake, but because I knew, through Dick, that Philip loved you and had made you his close friend. I felt nearer to him when I could chat, by means of letters, with you. When you, too, Hugh, shall find the scales fallen from your eyes, you will be able to forgive a woman this because she is a woman, and a loving one. You remember what I wrote you? — the time will come when you will experience the difference; till then, think as kindly of me as you can.

Philip told me of those words of yours to him — " The ways of God — the ways of God." Indeed, they

are " past finding out," and in witness thereof, I humbly and lovingly acknowledge myself

Your affectionate friend and *debtor*,

MADELINE COPE.

I had written the answer and asked Twiddie to
carry it down to meet the stage at noon.   She was
gone unusually long — three hours; and when she
came in, I noticed she went directly to her room,
instead of coming, as was her wont, to me.   Nor did
she show herself until it was time to set the table for
supper.   When she brought in my tray I asked her:

" What kept you so long to-day, Twiddie? "

" I 'll tell you when I come in after supper; I want
to talk with you, Hugh."   My heart gave a queer,
frightened thump — at nothing, so it seemed, for she
spoke as usual, but earnestly.

" Shall we have a bout at chess to-night? "

" Not to-night, Hugh; I 'll bring in my sewing;
I 'm a little tired."

" What a brute I have been," I thought, as I
watched her brighten the fire and light the lamp,
" to send her down so often in all weathers just to
carry my mail, or get a letter; — and what has it all
amounted to? " I felt down, without knowing why.
Madeline's letter had radiated such intimate, human
love, that I felt its warmth only to realize the more
the chill of my own isolation.   Now and then I heard
a dash of sleet against the south windows, and I
vowed it should be the last time I asked Twiddie to
do such an errand for me.

After the dishes were finished, she came in with

her sewing, and sat in Aunt Lize's rocking-chair by
the bench on which stood the lamp with its yellow
porcelain shade — a gift of Philip's. I felt strangely
oppressed.

"Well, Twiddie?"

Her head was bent low over her work, and I could
see only the pure profile. "Hugh, do you remember
the teacher that stayed with us over Sunday four years
ago? — the one with the eye-glasses?"

"Yes, to be sure I do; a nice girl she was too.
Where is she now?"

"In Boston; she has been there ever since she
left her position at the Academy two years ago."

"What is she doing — teaching?"

"Yes, she is a day-governess. I went down to
Farnsfield to-day to see her cousin, who has come as
housekeeper at the new inn. She is going to get
things in readiness during the winter for the opening
next May."

"How does it look there, — greatly changed?"

"You would n't know it, Hugh. It is like one of
those old English inns such as we have admired in
that book on Windermere that Mr. Vanever sent you.
They are going to make the most of everything when
spring comes; you remember the lilac and syringa
hedge opposite, and the great elm at the corner?
The signboard hangs from that, and to-day it
creaked in the wind just as I imagine all the sign-
boards creaked that advertised those wonderful
taverns in *Pickwick*."

"What an imagination you have, Twiddie! But
it helps lots, does n't it?"

"Indeed it does, Hugh," she answered earnestly, but without looking up. "Do you remember how I used to imagine the people in the stage — and the 'going off,' away as far as Rutland and New York?"

"Yes, I remember it all. You never do that now?"

"No, — because I'm going to make it come true; so there will be no need for 'making believe.'" I saw her head bend more closely over her work.

"What do you mean, Twiddie?" I spoke sharply, for there was a fear clutching at my heart.

"Don't speak *so* to me, Hugh; if you do, I won't tell you anything."

"But what do you mean about it's 'coming true' — tell me."

"Just that; I'm really and truly 'going off,' Hugh."

"Look here, Twiddie, be reasonable — what do you mean? Are you going to Miss Cope?"

Her eyes flashed and her work dropped. "I should like to know why you think I am going to Miss Cope, Hugh? *Your* imagination outstrips your common-sense many times."

This — from Twiddie! Suddenly the girl seemed to have vanished from my life, and left a woman sitting there in Aunt Lize's rocker, — a woman with whom in future I must reckon. And I, realizing this, found my task of telling her assuming the weight and proportions of an intolerable burden. "Best have it over with now — once and for all time," I thought, and braced myself mentally to the work. Perhaps Twiddie saw that; she spoke rapidly, shortly:

"I should really like to know, Hugh, why you intrude Miss Cope at every turn in the conversation?" I controlled myself and answered quietly:

"I will tell you, Twiddie; because she thinks so much of you that she has planned to have you come to her for February and March to enjoy everything the city can offer."

"Did she write you this?"

"Yes."

"Why did n't she address herself directly to me? And since when has she looked upon you as my guardian?" Was *this* Twiddie!

"She wrote me because she knows perfectly well the interest I take in everything touching your life, Twiddie —" She interrupted me with a short laugh, not a pleasant one.

"Really, Hugh, I can't see any reason in that why she should not give me the invitation herself."

"I am sure she will later on, when she knows —"

"Knows you are willing to let me go? — Thank you, I prefer to be consulted first."

"Well, all I can say is, it is n't every girl who can get such a chance. I should think you would like just for once the real balls and parties and dinners — you 've imagined enough about them the last four years. Dick Malory is looking forward to your coming, and —" She interrupted again:

"You really think I should like that, Hugh?"

"Why not? You 're young, and it belongs to you by right."

"By what right, I should like to know?" How she flashed out at me!

"By right of — of a good many things: your youth, for instance."

"Hugh, tell me truly; do you think I belong there — with them?" She looked at me earnestly, questioningly.

"Yes, I do," I answered stoutly, for now was my time. "You do belong there — of right too."

"Hugh," the blood rushed to her face, then as quickly receded, leaving it white; "do you remember once when you talked with me and comforted me, yet told me truly about — about *what that boy told me?* Do you suppose I have forgotten *that?*"

"No, Twiddie, but — "

"And do you think for one moment that I could place myself with such people as Miss Cope and Mr. Vanever and Mr. Malory, to be reminded every minute in the *heart* of me, Hugh, that I was not of them, or their friends? — Do you suppose, if — if Mr. Malory knew *that* — that — that I — O Hugh!" She buried her face in her hands.

I felt the sweat bead my upper lip; this was awful. I wet my lips, for they were as dry as chips.

"Twiddie, won't you come nearer to me? I have to tell you something."

But she shook her head and remained where she was; I was forced to go on. I told her as well as I knew how — which was poorly enough — and tried to prove to her that as Philip Vanever's daughter she belonged of right among them, although all the time my heart was crying out against the forswearing of my lips. I told her as gently as I knew how, soften-ing, smoothing, yet not daring to condone. She neither spoke nor moved; but sat motionless, with bowed head, as if all the waves and billows of Life's deluge of experience were breaking over her. "Twiddie," I pleaded, "say something to me — speak!"

"Read me the letter, Hugh," was all her response. Her voice came muffled through her hands. And I read:

"DEAR HUGH,

"You are in possession of all the facts up to the day after Thanksgiving, and those I know you have laid before Mr. Lewis before now. There remains but the account of the developments by which I was able to establish the identity of Twiddie's mother with the one I wronged eighteen years ago, and the consequent proof of her child's relation to me. The links in this chain of evidence are as follows:

"As I have told you, my father died of paralysis; there was an interval of but two days between the second and third shock, which proved instantly fatal. During those two days, although deprived of all speech and movement, he nevertheless made known to me that I was to put my hand beneath his pillow. I drew out a small velvet case containing a miniature on ivory of my mother. I had never seen this one before. I realized that he wished it near him, and placed it in his hand, raising both his arm and hand on two pillows to bring the case opposite his face. He died so — looking at it. It was one of the fairest faces I have ever seen: that of a girl of eighteen with bronze brown hair, dark violet blue eyes, and an exquisite complexion. She was in ball dress, and upon her hair there lay a wreath of ivy leaves.

"The miniature was buried with him. But that **day**

in July, when Malory and I went up to Olympus, and
Twiddie came singing around the corner of the house,
and suddenly stood before us with the rich color in
her cheeks and the grape-vine upon her hair, I saw
before me the living lineaments of that face in the
velvet case. It was a shock, and I think you must
have seen the physical effect it had upon me. The
two faces haunted me until I came up again the
other day.

"That morning after Thanksgiving, I went — you
will remember — up into Twiddie's room, and there
on her little table I saw a tintype likeness in a small
carved, wooden frame. The face was that of the
woman whom for seven years I had tried to find.
I was unable to speak, but Twiddie, seeing that
something was wrong, spoke quickly: 'That is my
mother; Uncle Shim gave it to me on my last birthday — and this, too.' She took out of her bureau
drawer a ring, gold, set with a small diamond. It
was the same.

"How I found my way downstairs I cannot say. I
took Prince and drove to find Uncle Jo Cheatle. He
told me all he knew, which was little enough, and
directed me to Old Town Gilead. There I found
that the physician who had attended her in her last
illness was dead; the minister, however, who had
read the burial service was living, but had removed
to Alderbury. I had inquired for Maria Lewis, the
name by which Uncle Jo Cheatle said she was known
after her death. In the town-registrar's office there
was no entrance of any death under that name. All
the man could tell me was that, up to the time of her
death, she was known as Mrs. Smith; he had that
from the minister who knew the former town-clerk.

"I drove then to Alderbury, and found the minister, who failed, after long thought, to recall her name. He is old, about eighty-two; and in such a case, where, until just before death the person was unknown to him, he said his memory was not to be trusted. However, he assured me he could go to the grave, and that would help us both out.

"I left Prince at the stables at Alderbury, and hired a trap to take us back to Old Town Gilead. On the way over there the old gentleman recalled from time to time little things in regard to the woman, and told me he remembered distinctly being called in just before her death to baptize her and christen her little child; but the child's name had likewise escaped his memory. In the graveyard, he sought among the graves, and, as often happens, by some powerful law of association the environment worked to the quickening of his memory. 'It was here,' he said suddenly, and, stooping, he read the name, 'Elvira Rasle.'

"'That's the one,' he said. 'Poor woman, it was strange I could not recall her name; but it all comes back to me now. Strange I should have forgotten it!'

"The name before me was not the one by which I had known her, but nevertheless I had seen the name. After my father's death, in settling the estate and looking over his private papers, I came upon a draft on a New York bank. It was for a sum of ten thousand dollars, made payable to Elvira Rasle. At that time I felt that it would furnish me some clue to what I had been seeking, and immediately advertised in papers East and West, placing the advertisement upon a 'claimant for property' basis. I had but two answers, and they proved to be spurious claims.   Of course, the looking up of the death-entry at the office proved without difficulty.

"On the drive back to Alderbury, the old gentleman suddenly struck his forefinger to his forehead with an exclamation of surprise.

"'Sir,' he said, 'you have not told me your name, but I take it for granted you have an interest either in that woman or her child?' I assured him I was looking up the mother's death, as there was property waiting to be claimed by her heir.

"'Then, surely I can help one of God's little ones, for it has come to me little by little that my friend, the good physician of this place, just before his death, intrusted to my care and keeping a little package containing the name of that poor erring woman, the name of her child and, if I mistake not, the name of the father of her child.   As you may be aware, Sir, it is the custom when a physician is called to aid a woman in such straits, to require her to reveal under oath to her physician the true name of the child's father, and this she did to my friend.   He gave me the package, with the request to keep it for reference in case any inquiry should be made for the child.   I recall, moreover, that he told me the child was born somewhere in the Adirondacks, where he was summering for a few weeks, and that the woman had told him she had settled in Old Town Gilead to be near him; but that afterwards, before she died, he had learned that she had relations who lived in another township not distant from here.

"'If you will stop in at the rectory for a few minutes, we will look over these papers together.'

"In that package I found all that was necessary

for proof. There was her full name, Maria Elvira Rasle; Mr. Lewis's name and address; Twiddie's baptismal certificate with her name, Theodora; and my own in her handwriting.

"On the back of that draft was an indorsement 'Elvira Rasle,' and the handwriting was identical with that on the slips of paper in the package. Presumably, she had received the check from my father, and, in her pride, returned it to him; but that is conjecture.

"This is all; but it is sufficient for me to claim my own, — to claim Twiddie legally for my own — "

"Never! — Never!" She sprang to her feet with a suppressed but heart-breaking cry; her hands were clinched, and a spot of burning scarlet on each cheek accented the pallor of her face; "I tell you, Hugh Armstrong, I will never be claimed as his — *His?* How dare he, when he has filched my very life; what right has he to take me from — Oh, Hugh, Hugh — " She sank on her knees by the cot and, bowing her head upon it, sobbed as if her heart would break. I tried to draw her up to me, for my own heart was bleeding for her; but she pulled away and rose quickly again, crying out under her breath:

"Oh, I will go — will go — "

Then in my extremity, seeing hers, I spoke — but it was the wrong word:

"Twiddie, hear me; heed me just this once. If you must go, promise me you will go to Madeline Cope; she will be as a mother to you — "

"Hugh — " She interrupted me; her voice caught in a sob on that word, but thereafter she spoke in almost a monotone and with a perfect control, which gave to the passionate words an emphasis wholly disproportionate to the manner of their utterance; "there are limits — and I can bear no more. For three years I have run and waited and tended and fetched and carried — for *her*, and I'm sick of it. It's been 'Twiddie this' and 'Twiddie that' day in, day out, and I am no longer a child. No — don't say a word; I know what I owe to you; but do you think for a moment that I, as a woman, can in the future be dependent for support upon you and your work as I have been as a child — when no tie of blood binds us? — No, don't say anything; it's too late; I shall go, the sooner the better — but not to Miss Cope; I can assure you of that. She would be the very last in this world to whom I would turn — "

"You do her great wrong, Twiddie;" I raised my voice; "I *will speak* — you have no better friend — "

"Hugh, stop!" She pressed both hands over her ears; "I tell you I will hear no more — "

"You *must*." I was terribly roused, and I almost thundered at her. Her hands dropped by her sides and every particle of color left her face. She stared at me as if I were about to pronounce some final judgment upon her. "You may go — to the ends of the earth, if your wilfulness lead you there, but one question you shall answer me before you go: Do you want to go? Are you fulfilling your own desire in this matter? Answer me."

I saw the corners of her mouth tremble, and a sudden contraction of the white throat. "Yes," she spoke slowly and as if weary, " I want to go — I can't wait to get away."

"Then go," I said, and turned my face to the windows, against the panes of which the sleet, driven by a strong southeast gale, that since sunset had been howling through the forest, was rattling like small-shot.

When I turned my head again she had left the room, but not before she had laid fresh fuel on the fire. Seeing that, I buried my face in my hands, and had it out with myself.

The next day, when Aunt Lize and Uncle Shim came to me in their distress and trouble, — for Twiddie had laid all her plan before them, but had not even asked permission of Uncle Shim to carry it out, — I assumed a cheerful manner that was but a mask for my outraged feelings — for had she not told me in so many words that she wanted to leave me? — and spoke encouraging words that belied the heaviness of my heart.

"The plan is a good one, Uncle Shim, and I believe she will make it work. There is no harm in her going down to Boston to board two or three weeks with her old teacher, and, meanwhile, advertising for a place as companion. Twiddie has a level head and can make her way in the world with the contents of her knowledge-box at her disposal. She reads French well, and her Latin has astonished me. She has even tackled the German. Oh, she'll do — you'll be proud of her some day."

He smiled, but uncertainly. " I dunno, Hughie, ez I 'd mind her *goin'* so much; she 's young, 'n' 't ain't nat'ral fer the fledglings not ter want ter try their wings, 'n' we air all gittin' erlong in years — 't ain't thet; but it 's the idee er her bein' in thet great hog's wash er city life — "

I laughed. " I should think you had been reading *Carlyle*, Uncle Shim."

" I don't know nothin' 'bout Carlyle, Hughie, 'n' I don't keer nuther; I hain't much on readin', but I 've heerd tell; 'n' only t' other week, I see in the *Granger* where er gal went down country 'n' got pickpocketed 'fore she left the depot, 'n' hed ter go ter the lockup fer er night's lodgin' 'fore she could git word hum ter send her some cash. — I dunno — I dunno — " He shook his head dubiously.

" I 'll tell you what I 'll do, Uncle Shim; I 'll write to Miss Cope and tell her all about it, and ask her to go on to Boston and see Twiddie and report just how things are; and then I 'll send a telegram to her father to-day, and you can take them both down un-beknown to Twiddie, and I 'm sure you and Aunt Lize need not to worry."

Aunt Lize put her hand on my hair and began to stroke it. I knew by that she was satisfied. Uncle Shim drew a long breath.

" Thet 'll take er load off 'n my mind, Hughie; kinder seems, arter all, ez ef things wuz goin' ter work round all right. But I feel sorter meechin' ter be feelin' thankful ter my God thet my leetle gal 's got er father ter look out fer her, arter what I 've said! — Yew git them despatches ready, 'n' I 'll hitch up, 'n' take 'em down ez fur ez Scawsville ter make sure."

In three days' time we had answers from both that they would be in the city by the time Twiddie should be there. Philip thought it would not be best to let her know of his presence, but he had planned to have an old friend of his mother's, who had lived in the city for years, answer all advertisements she might see in the papers for a position as companion, and so procure Twiddie's service, assure her a home, and afford her the protection and care that would put all our hearts at rest while she should be away from us.

Twiddie was apparently in the gayest of spirits, promising Aunt Lize this, that, and the other with the money she was to earn; teasing Uncle Shim, who never takes a pen in his hand, to write her regularly once a week, and threatening, when he begged off, to stay away from him five years; coming in a dozen times a day to show me the few new things she had bought for her journey; practising her French upon me and Toughheel, much to the latter's amazement, and singing, "Roky tummy me là, là, *là —*"

I entered into it all—but I could but wonder. Was this gay girl the woman who had knelt by my cot? I answered jest for jest, smile for smile—and she never knew, she never knew—I did n't mean she should; and I would n't ask her to stay—not I. But on that seventeenth day of December, when Uncle Shim drove the sleigh around the house that she might wave good-by again to me at the window, I knew that a part of my life was bidding me farewell. I strained my ears to catch the last "tankle" of

Prince's cow-bell; then I turned my face to the David
— and refused my dinner.

Oh, that winter! I tried to work, I tried to read, I
tried to study — but my hand had lost its cunning,
my eyes roamed from the page to the bleak mountain-world in the east, my brain refused to work in
the old grooves.

The cold was piercing, penetrating flesh and marrow, and numbing the soul. And the dreary, empty
house! My eardrums were strained to the aching
point in trying to hear a light footstep on the garret
stair, to catch some sound of the sweet voice and the
joyous laugh. The routine of the work went on, day
in, day out, without let or hindrance, unbroken by a
jest or a merry retort.

Aunt Lize's step seemed to have lost the elasticity
that had been peculiar to it for fifty years, and Uncle
Shim stooped more than ever. Day after day, in
snow and sleet and bitter cold, he went down for the
mail, and letters from Philip and Madeline came
often and regularly, filled with the cheer and love of
perfect friendship. Even a batch from Waldort made
its appearance just after Christmas, with a box for
Twiddie. We sent it to her at once.

I lived from Tuesday till Thursday, from Thursday till Saturday, and again till Tuesday, when her
tri-weekly letters came regularly to Aunt Lize —
bright, cheerful, full of hope and kindly messages;
but to me she never wrote. She was leading a
new life.

There came a day, the last of February, when I
laid aside my work. A strange weakness had come

upon me, almost a numbing of my faculties. I laid it at first to the excessive cold. But as the sun warmed in early March, and I felt no stronger, I laid it to my loss of appetite. Aunt Lize tried to tempt me with all my favorite dishes, but even to please her I could not eat a sufficient amount, or regularly. At last Aunt Lize's face took on the old worried look of five years before. I assured her I was all right, but I saw her watching me from the kitchen when I lay by the hour with my face turned to the David, seeing with unseeing eyes the play of the firelight upon it, and thinking over every little act of loving grace — and they were legion— towards me, selfish, unthankful, unwitting, unmindful of the treasure in my own chimney-corner.

Every look, every word, every gesture came back to me; — the willing feet, oh, how willing! the helpful hands that brought in my three meals daily and never tired; the loving smile when I was weary; the hours she had read to me while I toiled; and, in the night-watches, there came to me the touch of her long braid upon my forehead, and the clinging of her child's hands about my neck when she whispered that it was all " coming true."

It was then that Madeline Cope sent me those letters Twiddie had written her during the three years. I read them also in the night-watches, and again by daylight, that I might not be deceived. No, — the loving girl's heart was all there. It was "Hugh," "Hugh," and again "Hugh," that filled page after page. But I said to myself that was the child — *she* was mine; but the woman had awakened, and she was not for me; — for me! How dared I? — helpless, useless almost, or so it seemed to me; my life mortgaged already for two-thirds — and ten years her senior.

One night I lay watching the fire, for I was sleepless, and often in following the flare and flicker of a burning stick I could lose myself.

But that night, as I continued to stare steadfastly, there was outlined on the rug a little figure, her elbows on her knees, her chin in the palms, and I knew, as we know between sleeping and waking, that it was Twiddie; and slowly the flame and shadow in the fireplace grew into a branching tree with the wind swaying its top, and a white, burnt streak in the soot at the back was a road with no turning; and far, far down it, I could see a yellow speck that drew nearer and nearer until I recognized it as the old Hornet; and lo! — it drew up beneath the spreading tree, and a boy — I started, when I made that discovery — was on the trunk-rack, swinging his legs; and the boy was myself, Hugh Armstrong. He jumped down from the rack, and said to the little figure on the rug, which seemed to be beneath the tree: " Miss Twiddie Lewis, here's your mail," and put it into a hollow of the tree; and the little figure on the rug, which seemed beneath the tree, rose quickly and took out the letters and read them in a low voice to herself: — " Dear Twiddie " — " Dear Miss Twiddie " — last, " Dearest Theodora." She laughed softly, as if fearing to wake me, and murmured: " H. A." — " H. A.," and kissed that letter again and again. But the boy, that was I, had not gone off with the stage, which had somehow disappeared without my seeing it.   He had hidden behind the trunk of the tree, and when she kissed that letter the third time, he sprang out from behind the tree —

I must have fallen asleep then or fully awakened, I don't know which.   But I awoke in the morning, refreshed, and took pen and ink and wrote to Twiddie; and I began that letter, "Dearest Theodora," and signed myself, "H. A." — and what was written between that beginning and that ending, let any man who has loved with all his heart and soul and body, his mind and strength, one woman, and her only, supply. — Thereof the deponent saith no more.

But of one thing I may tell, how on Thursday of that week — I had sent the letter on Monday — just before sunset, as I was hoping, praying that there might be some answer to ease my aching heart, I heard the "tankle" of the cow-bell, the squeaking of the runners as Uncle Shim drove the sleigh into the barn, and Aunt Lize go out into the shed.   It seemed a week before she came in again, and I could call to her.

"Aunt Lize, is there any mail?"

"No, Hughie, not ter-night."   I noticed that her voice had something of the old ring in it.   "I 'll hev yer supper ready in er few minutes."

"I don't want any, Aunt Lize; just a sup of milk and a piece of bread," I said, then turned to the reflection of the sunset fires in the east — disheartened, sick, weary of the game.

I heard Aunt Lize about the kitchen, and soon the

door was pushed open, and the clatter of dishes told me she was coming.

"I told you I did n't want any, Aunt Lize — " I spoke irritably, and turned to the door — lo! there *she* stood in the level soft light of the flushing east with the tray in her two hands that trembled so the dishes kept up a subdued, unsteady *clirring*.

"Aunt Lize thought you might eat some supper if I brought it in — "

Still I could not speak. I saw the color leave her sweet face and the hands shake until she was obliged to set the tray on the bench.

"Aunt Lize wrote me you were n't well, Hugh, so I 've come — home."

Then I found my voice. "Theodora!" — and held out my arms.

She came swiftly to the cot, and leaned over me with great unshed tears in her eyes. I drew her down beside me; and then, as of old, she nestled in the hollow of my arm, and, throwing back her head upon my shoulder, smiled up at me with such depths of promise shining through her tears, that I —

June, 189–.

Three months since then, and I am at work in the Pen — the days all too short even at this first summer solstice that ever has been since the world was made, to accomplish what I wish. I 've whistled till I 'm fairly faint, for she made me promise "to keep my spirits up" while she should be away. I have had need of it. She has gone up into the Old Pasture with Uncle Shim, and is to bring me a branch of the sweet-brier for a design. She has been gone already an hour; she is rarely absent from my side now for that length of time, either by day or night — there she comes! I hear her calling Tag —

I began to whistle for all I was worth, but as she neared the corner of the house I had to call just to hear the sweet voice answer.

"Theodora!"

"Yes, Hugh, I'm coming."

Oh, my Gift of God — my Gift of God!

VII

THE PASSING OF THE HORNET

VII

THE PASSING OF THE HORNET

TWO years ago the scream of the locomotive awoke new echoes in the Valley of the White Branch, and sounded forever the doom of the Hornet's post-horn.

Until the completion of the road, the yellow-bodied, black-banded stage-coach could still be seen daily lunging along the old Post-road from Alderbury "over the Mountain." On its last tenth of September, when the Hornet left that town, it had but two passengers: a man and a woman, who had kept the inside seats all the way up the Valley. Not until the driver, a stranger, — for Uncle Jo Cheatle had passed with the passing of the last century and the iron invasion of the new, — had left Scawsville two miles behind him, did the sound of pick and axe, of dynamite blast and hurtling rocks, of crashing trees, the ring of riveted iron and the creak of derrick wholly cease, and the unsightly scars of gravel-pit, cleared and blackened mountain-sides, rock-hewn roadbed, and meadows disfigured by the garish, yellow-white of new-timbered trestle-work, entirely disappear.

As the stage approached the slope behind the Bend, the late afternoon sun, that had been obscured by heavy cloud-masses, shone forth brilliantly beneath their rolled, dark edges, and lighted the walls and headstones of the Old Church Settlement.

The man put his head out of the window: "You may leave us here," he said to the driver who drew rein at the foot of the grassy hillside below the church to let the two out. Then he drove on; but at the next water-bar he reined up again, and, turning to look backwards and downwards, he saw the two, hand in hand, slowly climbing the steep path that led directly to the churchyard. He stared for full a minute; then, gathering up the reins, he scratched the back of his head with the butt of his whipstock, and chirruped encouragingly to his horses that strained to the steep rise before them.

Time has genially mellowed the marbles and embossed with lichens the other headstones of the Old Church Settlement, and its every grave is covered and graced with the glossy leaves of the myrtle. Year after year the grace of this green mantle is renewed, nor biting frost nor frozen ground endangers its vigorous life.

The man and woman made their way at once across the tangle of vines that obliterates the paths, and often a forgotten grave, to a corner overhung by a tall larch, where, at the end of a row of headstones, both marble and slate, stands a wooden cross of oak, some five feet in height.

The woman, the tears raining down her cheeks, knelt by the myrtle-covered mound before raising her eyes to read the inscription on the cross:

> "HUGH ARMSTRONG,
> WOOD-CARVER.
> AGED 30."

"Philip, O Philip!"—her voice was broken with sobs,—"it is more beautiful even than you said; and what do we not owe to him!"

Woman-like, she began to busy herself with picking off a withered leaf or two, and disentangling an obstinate vine that spoiled the symmetry of the otherwise perfect oval of the mound.

"He bridged an abyss for me with his friendship, Madeline; and when I knelt by this open grave four years ago, I consecrated myself anew to 'walking humbly with God'—but with you by my side."

"But, Philip, there was something more, something of which I have never told you—"

"I know it, Madeline."

"Did Hugh tell you?"

"No—never."

"Then how could you know, Philip?"

He smiled down upon her and caught away her hand from the vine she was lifting.

"Because my love for one woman had given me second sight where another man's love for her was concerned." An answering smile broke through her tears.

"See, Philip," she said, "what Hansl has sent us from the Frohe Alp for this very hour. It was his request; he knew they would keep, and that I was coming up this fall. I did n't want you to know of it before." She untied the pasteboard box she had with her, and taking out a large bunch of Alpine Edelweiss laid it among the myrtle just over the stilled heart beneath.

It was the man's turn to fight with his emotion.

"Come, dearest, we must be going. It is near sunset and the chill will fall with the dew; you must not risk too great a strain or exposure as you are. I see the carriage coming that I ordered from Farnsfield."

He put his arm about her and aided her to rise, tenderly, as is the way of a man towards a woman who carries another life beneath her heart. She leaned heavily upon him as they went down the steep path.

"Twiddie wrote she would be down with Aunt Lize to-morrow morning at the inn," she said, as he helped her into the carriage.

Her husband was silent, pondering many things.

As he neared the butternut tree he found himself hoping against hope that he might find his child awaiting him there. Yet he knew from the experience of the last four years that the hope would be in vain. He had been unable, aided and abetted as he had been by his wife, to change the old relationship which had obtained between them from the time of his first coming to the Mountain — now nearly ten years ago. She welcomed him ever as a friend — her friend and Hugh's; but, after her husband's death, whenever he had attempted to establish his natural claim — and he had tried in many ways, in all ways that his heart could prompt his brain to devise, in ways that could offend neither her pride nor her self-respect — he had been met with a stubborn, but gentle, resistance.

He had come to acknowledge, unwillingly, without reserve, in humiliation, that he would be allowed to be naught to her but a friend. The logic of the moral law was irrefutable; *that* never forgave. He recognized the justice; he bowed to the decree, — there was naught else left for him to do, — but he knew, as he passed the butternut tree and found no one waiting for him there, that he must long unto the End for that which would never be wholly his: his *first* child's filial love. And his heart was sore.

It was his wife who spoke as the carriage climbed the steep rise beyond the tree:

"Twiddie wrote me a few weeks ago that Franz Waldort was coming on in the spring. I wonder —" She did not finish that sentence, but her husband heard her murmur:

"Poor Dick! —"

Falling leaf, drifting snows, springing green had marked two-thirds of the cycle of another year. It was the Hornet's last trip, and it carried the mail and but one passenger as it left Scawsville.

Along the route not only the farmhouses but entire hamlets were deserted, for on that day the grand opening excursion of the Valley Railroad had gathered its hundreds from far and near to celebrate with brass band, colors, and speeches the Progress of the Inevitable.

All along the River Valley the construction of the road had had its interest for the passenger. He had, however, asked no questions concerning it, nor had the driver volunteered any information; but when they left the valley for the heights, the latter, hitherto uncommunicative, pointing with the butt of his whip-stock to a shoring of piles and stone, broke the silence:

"They've ben tryin' to fence in the Branch; but jest let it come ter 'n ice-jam j'ining hands with er spring freshet, 'n' I can tell 'em ther'll be music ter beat the band down thar," he jerked his whipstock backwards towards Alderbury; "the River'll do some waltzin' right over *thet* to er purty lively tune tew, — yer can bet yer life on thet."

"I noticed a few miles back that a heavy roadbed had been laid on an embankment of clay," said the stranger. "There will be a landslide into the river some day, just at that point. Why did n't they leave the heavy timber on the bank to protect it?"

"They say the Comp'ny cut it to run the engines on the spot, so's ter save coal — kinder worked their way along up thet way."

He relapsed into silence, for the stranger had merely smiled as if incredulous of such folly in enlightened times.

He was thinking what an anomaly it was — this small out-of-the-way corner of America, this North Country of the *New* England. The trained vision of the geologist was noting the dip of the strata, the outcrops, the old river-beds and terraces, the tracks of glaciers, the work of water; and the trained mind was intent upon certain problems, psycho-physical, that were presenting themselves to him in rapid succession as the Hornet slowly pulled up the overlapping foothills. The keen eye took note of the configuration of the ever-widening expanse of country.

It was old, this *New* England; there was no doubt about that. He could tell the signs of its age as he could tell them in a horse: by the wearing down of the grinders. The great primeval mountains had been ground down to their granite roots, and overlaid with new deposit.

He smiled at his fancy; yet it was a fact that this New England had come within an ace of being an island like the mother-country. Just a deeper furrow drawn here and there by the glacier's plough, an extra lengthening and deepening of the Hudson's gorge, a touch in the extreme east, — and the noble North River, Champlain, the St. Lawrence, the St. John, the Atlantic would have rendered it insular, impregnable.

Indeed, like the Old England, its characteristics were many of them insular. And how old the New was getting to be both politically and sociologically! Like the Old England, it had bred — already now for these three hundred years — *men;* was still breeding them: men who had been the pioneers in an Eastern wilderness; men who had been the pioneers in a Western one, who had made their way across a mountain-bastioned continent, who had rounded that mighty outpost of the two Americas, — the sentinel of two great oceans — the Headland of the Horn, and made for statehood in the early anarchic conditions and genetic throes of the newest and farthest West on the shores of the Pacific; made for Law, made for Order, made for Stability. — And from this poor soil!

He gazed around him; — it was so poor, so needy, yielding but grudgingly sustenance; the climate for a time rigorously arctic; the waters bound as with adamant for many months; its summers short and almost tropical, yet in a few weeks working a natural revelation even to his Western eyes — as witness that old apple tree ! — A mere roadside distortion, gnarled, warped, wind-riven, twisted of branch, hoar with moss and lichen, graced meagrely with half abortive foliage !

Yet — towards the road it stretched forth one straight, sturdy, ten-inch bough tufted with bushels of luxuriant pink-and-white blooms that, as they passed, charged the air with a delicately elusive fragrance.

That he felt was symbolic of New England : warp, gnarl, moss-growth, deep taproot, a holding-on-like-grim-Death to what of sustenance there might be in the barren subsoil ; wind-bent, bowed, bereft of various members, but never uprooted ; and so long as there should be life there would be somewhere delicate, entrancing, unexpected blossoming and, despite untoward conditions, promise of fruition.

Waldort drew a long breath and smiled again to himself at his pleasing conceit : he, too, was about to take from the impoverished New England soil a delicate branch to engraft upon his own life in the West — with promise of rich fruition.

He had seen her but once in all these years, in the summer preceding his friend's death ; but he had continued his letters to Olympus after the inspiration of its deity had been withdrawn.

He had known from the first that he must be wise for both, and give her time to attempt the readjustment of her life in her own way. He felt sure the attempt would prove abortive. She was not made for that isolated mountain-life. She was young, and — although she did not know it, could not realize it, would have resented any suggestion on his part in regard to it — he knew she would soon crave that which

is for the young: Life in its fulness, its richness, its
entirety, which, being interpreted for a woman, means
home, husband, children.

So he had waited patiently until this last year, his
" heart of oak " gathering the grace of a great tenderness; the " volcano," after Madeline Cope's marriage,
at last extinct; and the gentle growths of a protect-
ing love and anticipated domestic joys were clothing
the excoriated sides, the lava-filled crevices. He
rejoiced in his own deep feeling for this legacy of his
friend. When once it should have actually come into
his possession — ah, *then!*

A bluebird broke into sudden song by the roadside,
and the man's eyes filled.

He recalled that day in the early spring when that
letter came telling him of her inability to live *so*
longer; of the impossibility of readjusting her life in
the changed conditions of the Mountain — the Mountain that was no more to any of them without the Man;
telling him how Aunt Lize had said, " It was Hughie
that made the life for us all," and how they had determined to break up the old place, sell it, if possible, and
find a small home in Alderbury where she had obtained
the position of principal's assistant at the Academy
for the next fall term. The Mountain-life had become intolerable for them all.

And how he had rejoiced when she told him in her
next that she had been reading for the first time his
letters to Hugh. She had waited, at her husband's
request, the four years and a half before reading
them; and now what a revelation they had been to
her! How her heart went out to him in that un-

fathered boyhood of his — for had not she also been unfathered, unmothered?

It was then he exulted, knowing they had found each other on a common basis. It was then he had written her by return mail — and told her *all*.

And how he had gloated over the touch of bitterness in her answer which recognized his claim upon her: "It is strange that in my *two* diverging paths of life Madeline Cope should have been before me gathering the first roses."

How he cherished her in thought for that one bitter touch! It was so natural; it belonged to her youth. And how soon it would be changed to sweetness in different conditions, in a new environment: in a land prodigal in its sunshine, prodigal in its blossoms, prodigal in its serrated peaks of shining snow, in its spaciousness of sea and sky — Oh, thank God for California! — in a home of her own, in the protection of his cherishing love, in the clasp of a child's little arms about her neck. — He lost himself in reverie, and smiled to himself as he thought of Uncle Shim and Aunt Lize opening their New England eyes upon the wonders of that other land; he almost laughed aloud as he recalled the description in his last letter of the latter's enthusiasm for the prospective migration and a farm of their own run entirely upon the irrigation plan.

As the Hornet emerged from the forest-belt, the silvery flute notes of a hermit thrush deep within the green gloom aroused Waldort to a consciousness of his surroundings.

Just before him shone the white walls of the deserted House of God.   He bared his head as he passed the slope of the Old Church Settlement whereon the trees were rife with bird notes.   But he would not stop. — *That* was for another time.   To-day was for the living, and his face was set, not to the rising sun towards which one goes only the sooner to meet the night, but Westwards, anticipating the day.

Yes, this New England bred men ; — had bred even upon this Mountain one man who, with his battlefield narrowed to the space of a seven-by-four-foot cot, handicapped, armorless, beset behind and before by the horror of a bedridden despair, in the face of poverty and a blank future had fought valiantly, disputing the ground inch by inch until it had narrowed — ever so slightly — to the dimensions of a victorious grave. And he had died — still fighting.

A hero? — Yes, but only *one* of the forgotten millions.

On the heights above the Bend, just before he reached the butternut tree, the driver drew rein.

" It 's 'bout time fer it ter be leavin' Scawsville. Les' listen 'n' mebbe we 'll hear it whoop," he said to the passenger beside him.

They waited — five, ten, fifteen minutes.   A hen-hawk circled high in the soft June sky ; a chipmunk *chittered* along the stone wall.   For a moment there was no other sound but the champing of the bits as the leader grew impatient at the delay.

Suddenly from the depths of the Valley came a prolonged, piercing shriek — two of them — three of them.   The heights echoed stridently.   The driver turned to the man beside him.

"What'd I tell ye?" he said with a slow, triumphant smile; then, suddenly seizing the post-horn from its leathern socket, he tooted blast on blast in feeble mockery. The passenger caught him by the arm.

"What's the use of making such a racket as that? — there's no one to hear." The driver shook off the hand, and blew with the full strength of his lungs one more blast.

"Ef I've got ter celebrate my own fun'ral, I'm goin' ter toot while I can set on the coffin-lid. I thought I'd got er life-job jest like Uncle Jo Cheatle, 'n' then come the durned railway perspecters, 'n' 't wuz all up with me. — Besides she told me to," he added irrelevantly.

"Who?" asked the stranger, simulating indifference; but his heart leaped.

The driver pointed with his whipstock up to the Pent Road, which they were approaching.

"Mis' Armstrong; she's allus on hand fer the mail, 'n' she told me ef ther wuz anybody thet stopped off fer their place ter the butternut tree, ter blow on the horn, 'n' ye said ye wuz goin' ter git down here." He drew rein beneath the tree.

"Oh, that alters the case," said the passenger, swinging himself down; "I beg your pardon."

"I take it ye're er stranger in these parts," the driver said as he handed him down his bag.

"Not wholly," the other answered with a suspicion of a smile; "but I haven't seen it for five years."

"Guess ye're some used ter stagin', the way ye swung off thar jest now."

"I ought to be; I'm an old Californian," replied the man.

"Thet so?" said the driver without any show of surprise. "Jest tell Mis' Armstrong — thar she comes now! — ther ain't no mail ter-day ter celebrate the Hornet's fun'ral; she'll hev ter git it from Farnsfield ter-morrer."

The passenger watched the stage climb the rise beyond and disappear over the brow of the hill. Then he turned, and with outstretched hands went to meet the figure that was coming lightly down the pasture slope from the last bars.

"There's no mail, Twiddie," he said; and the two went back together up the Pent Road.

October, 1902–February, 1903.

By the Author of " The Wood Carver of 'Lympus"

A DAUGHTER OF
THE RICH

By M. E. WALLER

New Edition, Illustrated by Ellen Bernard Thompson

12mo, $1.50

A cheery helpful story. — *Newark Advertiser*.

The atmosphere of the book is sweet and wholesome. — *Chicago Tribune*.

Not since those charming stories of Miss Alcott's has any one written just such sweet and homely idyls of plain, unaffected family life. The book is cordially recommended to all those who have loved and enjoyed "Little Women" or "The Old-Fashioned Girl." — *Kansas City Star*.

The characters are drawn, not described, opening before the reader in their words and actions; every one is a study, and the plot is simple and well developed. — *New Orleans Picayune*.

The author has gotten away from many stereotyped themes, and has introduced as her heroine a little girl — the child of a rich father — who has to leave New York on account of ill health. The family physician finds a delightful corner of the world for her, where there are other young people. The unfolding of the story is highly interesting. — *St. Louis Globe-Democrat*.

LITTLE, BROWN, & CO., PUBLISHERS

254 WASHINGTON STREET, BOSTON

The Most Lovable Heroine in Modern Fiction

TRUTH DEXTER

By SIDNEY McCALL

Author of " The Breath of the Gods "

New Illustrated Edition, with 8 full-page pictures by Alice
Barber Stephens and title-page vignette by
Jessie Willcox Smith

12mo.   Decorated cloth, $1.50

A novel of united North and South of rare power and
absorbing interest.   It is but fair to say that not one of
the novels which appeared last year on either side of the
Atlantic (including those from the pen of the most gifted
writers) was superior to this in artistic quality, dramatic
power, and human interest combined.   We do not hope to
see it surpassed, even if equalled.—*Philadelphia Telegraph.*

Exceptionally clever and brilliant, it has what are rarely
found with these dazzling qualities,— delicacy and genuine
sentiment.—*Brooklyn Times.*

A fine, sweet and strong American romance.—*New York
World.*

I don't know how to praise it enough.   I can't recall any
novel which has interested me so absorbingly for years.
It is a matchless book ! — *Louise Chandler Moulton.*

The author at once takes place among the foremost
novelists of the day. — *Boston Transcript.*

LITTLE, BROWN, & CO., PUBLISHERS
254 WASHINGTON STREET, BOSTON